YOUNG CLAUDIA

by

ROSE FRANKEN

In YOUNG CLAUDIA we present a new chapter in the Claudia Saga. Rose Franken has carried forward her searching study of a modern marriage with the skill, the penetrating acumen and the high, rich comedy of modern manners in which she is so well known in the world of the theatre as well as in the world of letters.

This is the fourth book to make its contribution to the full portrait of a character who has commanded the attention and the growing following of more than five million readers. Rarely has an author embarked upon such a portrayal of an individual, with the disciplined literary style of never for even one line deviating from a single point of view.

Young Claudia

BY ROSE FRANKEN

rinehart and company, inc.
new york · toronto

Printed in the United States of America
By J. J. Little and Ives Company, New York

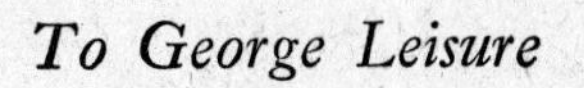
To George Leisure

Young Claudia

One

Half-way through the job, Claudia knew she was a fool to have begun with the hedge in the first place. As plainly as if he were standing beside her, she could hear David add hedge-cutting to the list of things women shouldn't be allowed to do. True, the war had put quite a dent into that list, but according to her knowledge of David, he was not going to change his mind about the fundamental laws of nature, war or no war. That thoroughly reactionary quality in him was what made him the ideal male, though not the ideal husband for a career woman. A career woman, however, didn't need a husband on the same terms that a wife and mother needed one, so as far as Claudia was concerned, David was perfect in spite of his pigheaded ideas.

Nevertheless, she couldn't resist getting in a dig now and again, by mentioning in her letters how well she had learned to handle the tractor and the milking machine; and once, not long after he had gone overseas, she wrote him that she had driven a truckload of lambs to the market and had got a better price for them than Edward had ever got. Possibly the price of lamb had gone up, which might have had something to do with it, but Edward had been too much of a gentleman to say so.

Edward was wonderful, with nothing wrong with him except a finger of his right hand that had been cut off by a saw when he was young. He was so wonderful, in fact, that Claudia heard in a round-about way that Nancy Riddle —although she wore the air of being very close to God in some new cult that was a combination of athletics and religion —had offered him twice the salary he was getting. Claudia boiled at Nancy's perfidy, but she went to Edward immediately and told him that neither she nor David would ever stand in the way of his advancement.

With his customary New England directness, Edward hadn't denied that Nancy had been talking to him, he'd simply mentioned that it would drive him crazy to work for a woman like Mrs. Riddle—which was gratifying to Claudia, since it apparently didn't drive him crazy to work for a woman like herself. Even this morning, when she had gone to the tool shed for the big shears, he had sharpened them without a word, except to remind her that, strictly speaking, it wasn't necessary to cut a hedge in the fall of the year.

"Aesthetically speaking, it is," she'd insisted. She hadn't explained that it was an excuse to wait for the mail lady out front.

It was over a month since she had had either a cable or a letter from David, but this morning she had wakened with a feeling that she was going to hear from him. She was as bad as Nancy, in a different kind of way, for her feelings had become a psychic warehouse, filled with faith and agony combined. She'd learned to count on what she felt, as surely as if it had been written down for her in black and white. There was the time, for example, when David's plane had run into trouble when he was being flown to an advanced base on one of the Islands. She hadn't found out about it until later, but she had known that things were not right with him by the indescribable heaviness of her heart.

Today she had been conscious of a lightness of heart the instant she'd opened her eyes. Although the clock had barely struck six, she could hear the children clumping about in the next room, with their slippers half off. She remembered the time when everybody in the house had slept until eight o'clock. The war had changed that. The war, and Jane.

She lay, for a few moments, thinking about Jane. Jane, the same as Bertha, had never seemed like a servant, but more like one of the family, and the loss of her had been a blasting shock. It had been so quick and short. With all the violence and bloodshed in the world, Death had sought her out one sweet quiet evening while she was doing the dishes with Edward. It was all over before Dr. Barry came. He'd called it heart failure for want of a better name.

Claudia had never seen a corpse. She had been in the hospital having Matthew when her mother died, and the routine of ushering life out of the world instead of into the world, was new and terrifying. At first she'd even been afraid to look at Jane, but afterwards she was glad she had. "She's so peaceful, I wouldn't want to call her back," she whispered to Edward, as they stood together at Jane's side. It was hard for Edward to acquiesce to Jane's supreme remoteness. Jane had promised to marry him some day.

Together, he and Claudia went through a catalogue of caskets. "I think she would like a nice grey one," said Edward.

"I have three grey ones in the shop," the undertaker said. "The most satisfactory thing is to go and see them, so that you can pick out the one you like."

One of the cows was having a bad time calving, so Edward couldn't leave the place. Claudia went alone. Mr. Ely met her at the door of his pleasant foursquare cottage at the end of the village green. "Come right this way," he said, and led her to an upper bedroom which held a colorful assortment of really quite attractive coffins, if only they had been couches. One of them even went so far as to be maroon. "It's for a man," Mr. Ely explained. "Men favor red."

Claudia shuddered, because she remembered how true this was of David particularly–David loved the faded old red of a chair that he'd used in his office and that now sat in the bay window of the farm, overlooking the terrace. Not for anything would he have it recovered. She hadn't realized that coffins, too, could have a personal touch.

"Don't you *mind* having those things up there?" she asked Mr. Ely's wife on the way out.

"No," Mrs. Ely said cheerfully. "I've got so used to them, it's the same as anything else."

Mrs. Ely had placid eyes and a comfortable body. It was enviable to be on such familiar terms with death. "I suppose if you know how to die, it's easier to live," Claudia concluded. It was something to learn, and probably the earlier one started, the simpler the lesson. In knowing death, it was a little like getting the hang of living.

"We all have to die," she told Bobby, almost as cheerfully as Mrs. Ely had spoken. "Jane's lucky, she doesn't have to worry about anything, not even about the war, it's like being off on a lovely vacation." She had been rewarded by seeing childhood return to his eyes, and a little later she heard him laughing at something foolish the dogs were doing.

It was such a small while afterwards–less than a week from the day Jane was buried in the cemetery down the road–that one of the Danes died of pneumonia. Claudia's philosophy deserted her; Bluff and Bluster, no less than Jane, had become a part of their lives; she could not face the new bewilderment in Bobby's eyes. She locked herself in the bathroom to sob, and every harsh word she had ever said to Bluff came back to break her heart.

Looking back on it, those first long months that David had gone overseas had not been easy ones. "Everything's fine," she kept on writing. She would have liked to describe, for his amusement, the incredible succession of maids that came and more often didn't come, but she didn't want him to know about Jane. Aside from being fond of Jane, it would have worried him if he thought there was no one to help with the house and children.

Edward was more fortunate in the labor shortage. He managed to find a fourteen-year-old boy, short of mind but tall of body, who was willing to work by the day at sixty cents an hour. But only when he felt like it. "Wait," Edward kept saying with grim relish, "it will be a different story when the war is over."

"When the war is over," Claudia promised herself with equal relish, "I'm going to take time off and finish that nervous breakdown I started out to have." At the moment, however, she was too busy to bother about either her mind or her body, and to her secret enlightenment, both of them seemed to be getting along very nicely. There were whole days indeed, when she had more energy than she could use, days when she all but forgot there was a war in the world, and in these spaces of release, her soul filled up with strength and hope.

Today was one of those days. "My lad, how would you like to rake the leaves from the lawn," she suggested to Bobby after breakfast.

Bobby considered the proposition. "My lad wouldn't," he decided at length. "Let Matthew do it," he said. "Edward wants me to candle the eggs."

Edward really didn't, and the eggs were better off with-

out him. Claudia used diplomacy. "Matthew," she scoffed. "How can a four-year-old rake a lawn, I'd like to know."

"He was five last month," Bobby reminded her.

"Oh well, he's still four to me," she said. "Anyway, Edward had better attend to it, raking is pretty much a man's chore."

Bobby's vanity pushed him headlong in the trap. "I'll do it," he told her shortly, and strode across the lawn to the tool house for the rake.

Guiltily, Claudia picked up the shears that Edward had sharpened for her, and went out the front gate to the farther end of the hedge, thinking how nice it was to have a job that was more fun than work for a change. She glanced at her watch with satisfaction. It was only ten o'clock, the beds were made and lunch was ready, except for frying the bacon. It seemed that the more one used of a day, the more of a day there was to use.

She waved to Edward as he went up the road in the tractor, with Matthew on the seat beside him. It was midsummer for October, and Matthew wore no shirt beneath his overalls. Whenever she looked at him, she realized anew how long David had been gone. When he left, Matthew had been pink and white and round. Now he was brown and gold, and the baby fat of his arms had turned into pipestems, and his shoulder blades stuck out like small pointed wings. He still talked like a baby, though. As he rolled past, he laughed inordinately and shouted back at her, "AyegoncuchwoodwidEdwer!"

She understood what he said because she knew that he was going to cut wood with Edward. She had her suspicions that Matthew's perpetually engaging laughter and his atrocious pronunciation added up to his stock in trade. Some day there would have to be a reckoning between them; perhaps, she reflected soberly, the thing to do was to send him to kindergarten this fall. She put the thought away from her. With Bobby in school all day, the house would be a tomb.

Loneliness lingered for an instant, and then vanished like raindrops in the sun. It was funny how she couldn't be unhappy this morning. The war and Jane and Bluff were but a gentle, somber backdrop to the high color of the day.

The hedge was part of the day. She remembered when she and David had started it—nothing but a line of scrawny evergreen shrubs. Year after year they remained, stubbornly frugal and awkward, intruders on the landscape, until all at once they began to put out shoots in wild abandon until now they were crowding together, looking remarkably as if they had always been a hedge. Claudia stood with the long shears poised against the higher branches. Woosh! Woosh! What a thoroughly pleasant sensation, like a glorified cutting of Matthew's bangs. "Where have these shears been all my life," she exulted. She tried them sideways, and cut a tidy corner—

All at once it was unbearably hot. She slipped off her blouse, manipulating her overall straps with caution, and emerged like a larger edition of Matthew. It was nice to have the kind of a shape that didn't need to be bandaged up. The absence of the shears from her hand was a pleasant sensation, too. She took her time, flexing her fingers and stretching her arm. A car sounded up the road. She hurried out to see beyond the bend. It wasn't the mail.

She dragged herself back to the hedge and squinted down the top of it. The last half seemed much longer in distance than the first half. Moreover, the last half started off by being a little lower than the first half. She debated whether or not to begin over again, and level it all off. "Nonsense," she decided. "I only imagine the last half is a little lower." To be on the safe side, though it might be a good idea to start to cut uphill just a trifle. She picked up the shears again. They probably needed resharpening, for they seemed to have lost that virgin snap which had flooded her with such a satisfying glow of accomplishment. It was like the time she had painted Matthew's crib. The first swish of the glistening white enamel on the dull yellowing bars had had a tonic effect upon her spirit, but it was surprising how fast the novelty had worn off, especially when she lay under the crib and looked at it from the bottom and discovered all the places she hadn't caught with the brush. By the same token, there were suddenly a lot of small hedge branches that she hadn't caught with the shears.

"Girls can't cut a hedge."

She jumped. It was as if David had spoken out of her thoughts. Moments like this made her realize how he stayed with her even when she didn't know that she was thinking about him. She turned to see Bobby standing beside her, eying her in glowering rebuke. "You didn't tell me you were going to cut the hedge," he accused her.

There was no use denying that she had reserved the more interesting chore for herself. She brazened it out. "Are you my guardian?" she inquired coldly.

He didn't know what the word meant, and therefore ignored it. "You cut crooked," he continued in stark contempt. "It's not straight. It goes downhill."

His relentless repetition of her incompetence nettled her. "Button your shirt," she retaliated. "And tie your shoelace," she added swiftly. "And close your fly!" she threw in for good measure.

He reeled a little from the well-aimed blows, but stood his ground nevertheless. "It is," he replied in a blanket refute.

"It is not," she said.

Their eyes locked in challenge. He fumbled a button of his shirt into a gaping button hole. "It came open," he explained haughtily.

"Everything comes open on you," she jeered. "Heaven

only knows how you're going to grow up," she went on in elaborate despair. "For myself, you couldn't pay me to marry a man who didn't button things."

He couldn't tell whether she was frivolous or serious, so he steered a middle course of compromise. "I'll finish the hedge for you," he offered magnanimously.

"So nice of you, but how would you like to mind your own little business and finish raking the lawn?"

"It's all going to be full of leaves again tomorrow," he objected.

"That's life," she said.

"What's life?"

"Nothing."

"You said it was," he insisted vaguely.

She had no desire to enter into a philosophic discussion at that hour of the morning. "I take it back. Now good-bye."

She returned to the hedge. He watched her with hungry eyes. Pride groveled before his desire. "Just let me try it once," he begged.

She let him try it. The shears were nearly as big as he was, and heavy. The blades wobbled against his straining grasp. "It's not all beer and skittles, is it?" she purred.

"Look what Shakespeare's doing," he said.

"Conveniently deaf, aren't you?"

"I bet it's a snake," he continued with pleasure, as the cat kept stalking an invisible something in the near by grass.

"You think of such sweet things," said Claudia. "Anyway, snakes are out of season." She broke off to listen. "The mail's coming!"

Bobby threw down the shears, and rushed with her to the road. The road was empty. "It is not coming," he scowled, but no sooner had he finished saying it than the car appeared around the bend. He favored her with a smirk of commendation.

The mail lady was a sparse woman, stingy of speech. She used "ayah" for yes, and "Couldn't say" for no, which did her well enough for all practical purposes of conversation. Claudia suspected that she had gotten too many handkerchiefs for too many Christmases, and last year she had tried the experiment of sending her a case of beer. Thereon after, the mail lady often smiled.

This morning she was even talkative. "Got plenty here for a certain party," she offered affably. "Mostly bills though. Seems as though, my Lord, bills is all we get these days, bills an' nothin' for it, my Lord. Ayah, that's what's happenin' these days."

Claudia felt Bobby pull impatiently at her arm as she accepted a goodly stack of feed catalogues sandwiched untidily with letters. "Anything from Dad?"

"I haven't looked yet."

"Why don't you?"

"I am," she said.

They sat down together on the steps. Her hand was unsteady as she riffled through the pile. The mail lady was right. Bills. More bills. A note from Julia, with a Washington postmark. An air mail border suddenly sticking out from somewhere underneath that set her heart to pounding—(Please, dear God, let it be from David)—but it was only from Roger Killian from California—and a post card from Bertha, in the spidery handwriting so indelibly foreign. "Nothing from Dad," she said, over the disappointment that crowded her throat. She thought, "My feelings don't work any more." It was as if some secret source of strength had deserted her.

Bobby must have sensed her bereavement. "Don't worry," he said, with the look of David in his eyes.

Claudia put her arm around him. "I'm not," she lied. "No news is good news. Who finishes the hedge?"

"I'll rake," he said meekly.

She would have gladly traded jobs with him. It was an effort to go back to the roadway, where she gloomily appraised the sum total of her handiwork. It would have been the better for a piece of cord strung up as a guide. "Oh no, you have such a wonderful naked eye," she muttered. "You're much too good for cord."

She had to use all her character, both good and bad, to make herself go on with the clipping. Edward went by in the tractor again, and if he noticed the ravished condition of the hedge, his face told nothing. "Weecushalottawood!" Matthew shouted from the seat beside him. Anybody could see that they had cut a lot of wood, for the wagon behind the tractor was stacked with logs.

At lunch, Matthew was full of his morning's activities. "You talk gibberish," Bobby disapproved. "Do we have to have applesauce for dessert?"

"Not if you don't want to," said Claudia, too pleasantly. "There's prunes."

Bobby winced, and stuck to applesauce. Claudia found it a little hard going herself, and embellished the unstimulating virtue of the meal by producing some cupcakes from a top shelf. Bobby eyed them indignantly. "I was looking all over for those," he said.

"That's what I figured," said Claudia.

"Can I have some ginger ale with it?"

"No," said Claudia. "Learn to chew instead of washing everything down."

"But I love ginger ale."

"Then take another glass of milk," said Claudia.

She piled the dishes and started Edward's lunch with a concentrated attack upon all the doodabs in the icebox. She emerged with a cup of ancient split pea soup, a dish of spaghetti, some cottage cheese, a half of a tomato, a bowl of pickled beets, two hard-boiled eggs and a slightly wrinkled peach. Edward was a joy to feed because he actually liked leftovers, and this particular lunch really made a clean sweep of the whole week. Tomorrow was Sunday, and she could start fresh with chops and baked potatoes.

While she was trying to combine the motley assortment into some kind of unity, the telephone rang. "Answer that, will you Bobby?" she called out to the terrace.

With reluctance, Bobby unwound himself from the chair on which he was reading the morning paper upside down. Answering the telephone had long since ceased to be a privilege; it had also ceased to hold, for Claudia, the fascination of the unknown. The unknown terrified her now, and the less the telephone rang, the happier she remained, for bad news came with telegrams, and telegrams, in Eastbrook, were read over the wire.

For once, however, there was no dread in her heart as the peal of the bell broke into the air. It was probably the insurance agent who had said he would check with her at noon about an increased barn coverage. There were five more cows and a hay loader since David had left, and although she wasn't crazy about throwing money away on insurance, especially since they had already had a fire, she knew that David preferred to be penny foolish and pound wise.

She had managed to achieve a marriage between the pickled beets and the hard-boiled eggs when Bobby came back. "The insurance man?" she asked, without looking around. "Edward! Are you in? Lunch!"

"I'm here," Edward answered, emerging from behind a towel in the pantry.

She was tardily aware that Bobby had not told her who was on the telephone. She turned toward him. He couldn't talk, he just stood there staring at her, his face wide open. Her thoughts leapt into the abyss of terror that dogged her day and night. "It's Daddy—"

He nodded mutely. She got to the telephone, somehow, with the floor weaving under her feet, and her tongue cleaving thick and swollen to the roof of her mouth. When she was a little girl someone had told her that if you held a seashell against your ear, you could hear the ocean roar. Oceans beat in on her now, drowning her so that she to reach for breath to push her voice out into speech.

"Hello–"

An eternity passed. She waited numb with agony for destiny to strike at her across the screaming silence of the ether. She knew that her lips had moved, but apparently no sound had come. She commanded all the strength that lay within her. Her voice rose above the invisible roar of oceans, and this time it shattered her eardrums with a thousand echoes. "Hello–"

"Darling!"

It was unthinkable that anyone else in the world could say that word as David always said it, and yet she could not believe that it was he. Bobby, standing beside her, must have known that her sanity was exploding into chaos. He must have seen that her poor brain was reduced to jibbering idiocy. He was her son and her father in one. He put his small, cold hand on hers. "It's really Daddy," he whispered. "He spoke to me."

Often, afterwards, she tried to relive what happened between the time she got back to the kitchen and driving into the station square twenty minutes later. All she could remember was Edward's eyes when she told him, and the way she'd found Matthew scrambling guiltily into his crib when she rushed upstairs. She'd swooped him up again. "Hurry up, put your shoes back on, we're going to meet Daddy."

He didn't catch the name, but he obeyed with alacrity just the same. No matter whom they were going to meet, anything was preferable to taking a nap. Exuberantly he started to eat up the side of a chair.

"Stop being crazy," Bobby commanded hoarsely. He couldn't find his belt. "You took it!" he shouted in a blaze of fury. "Give it back!"

Matthew laughed uproariously. He didn't say he took the belt and he didn't say he didn't take it. Bobby couldn't bear it. "I'm going to kill you!" he threatened.

Claudia sensed his excruciating tension. "Never mind the belt," she interceded swiftly. "Go without it, it doesn't matter."

She had no feeling in her mind. It was not to be believed, but she couldn't feel a thing. David was home. Home from the war. War. War was something she must have dreamed, fabricated out of the monstrous legends of history books. Battles lost, battles won, convoys sunk, convoys saved. No mail, then three letters at once. No cables, then suddenly a blessed life line thrown out from space to save her faltering reason. "Am safe and well. Don't worry. Love, David Naughton." It had always come as a little shock, this formal signing of his name. "David Naughton." The war had no regard for love. The war was a furnace of abnegation, a blistering hell designed for the purification of mankind. David was coming out of that hell for a brief moment. She must feel it, she must know it, she must throw out her arms and embrace the heavens.

Edward brought the station wagon to the front door. "Drive careful," he warned. His face was pale. "I'll do up the dishes," he said. "Don't worry. But drive careful."

"I will," said Claudia.

She had never driven so carefully in all her life. Her thoughts were concentrated on the road. Bobby breathed down her neck from the rear seat. He wanted to talk, she could hear him swallow. It was hard to talk. She knew how he felt. Matthew kept licking the window, pretending to be Bluster. "Don't either of you tell Daddy about the dog," she said. "Or about Jane."

"Won't he ever know?" Bobby asked.

"Not at first."

They drove on. A trim grey roadster shot past, then slowed. Claudia recognized the car, had already caught a glimpse of Elizabeth Van Doren, a trim grey figure in the driver's seat. As always, Elizabeth had the quality of being at one with her possessions. The house on the cove that David had designed for her was inescapably her own. It was clear and fragrant, filled with choice antiques, so beautifully kept and polished that Claudia felt they might just as well have been reproductions. She remembered how once she had been jealous of Elizabeth. She blushed to think of it. If David had been overkind and gentle, it was the gentleness of pity for a woman newly widowed. Now, suddenly, Claudia felt again that vicarious tasting of Elizabeth's vast aloneness. She could not bring herself to stop the car and ask Elizabeth to share the joy of David's home-coming. She kept her eyes on the road, and drove ahead.

Bobby jostled her shoulder in excitement. "That was Aunt Elizabeth!" he cried.

"Don't push me while I'm driving," Claudia told him.

"But it was Aunt Elizabeth!" he insisted. "She's not my real aunt, like Aunt Julia, is she?" he digressed.

"No," said Claudia.

"Then why do I call her aunt?"

"It's an old silly custom. Halfway between calling her by her last name, which would be too formal, and her first name, which would be precocious."

"What's precocious?"

"Fresh."

"Why didn't you wave 'Hello' to her?"

"I didn't know she was back from taking Candy up to college," Claudia evaded.

"Is Candy's real name Candy?"

"No, Candace."

"How old is she?"

"Seventeen, about."

"That's old," said Bobby. "How old were you when you met Dad?"

"Around Candy's age."

"Did you get married right away?"

"Almost right away."

"I have to go," Matthew remarked.

"You don't," Claudia contradicted brusquely.

"You went before you left," said Bobby, "you're a dope."

"I do," Matthew insisted, without fervor.

"Only babies have to go," Bobby taunted. "You're a baby!"

"I'm not!"

"Shhh—" Claudia stopped them. "Aren't you ashamed to fight, with something so wonderful happening as your father coming home?"

"Why are they letting Dad come back?" Bobby asked.

"I don't know," said Claudia. Her thoughts had tried to go that far, but had turned back in cowardice. Was he to be sent away again—this time to still another part of the world? Was she to school herself to see an empty sleeve, a crippled leg? She was grateful for the small interruptions of Elizabeth and Matthew. It was easier not to think.

She saw him standing on the platform as they turned into the station square. Her heart gave up a prayer of thanks that he was straight and whole. Except for his uniform, it might have been any one of a thousand days that she had called for him on the evening train from town. Only it wasn't. This was something that happened once in a lifetime—a husband and a father coming home from war. She was glad that Bobby was old enough to meet and hold this moment. She felt sorry for Matthew, who was not old enough to hold anything but the pleasure of a sunny day with the scent of burning leaves in the air. Years later perhaps, he would smell that autumn smell of burning leaves, and a small wooden station dappled with the reflection of tall trees would come into his mind, and fill him with some nameless yearning.

"There he is!" Bobby cried out suddenly. "Can you see him!"

"Yes, I see him," she said. It was strange that Bobby's eyes had only just found him. She supposed that different kinds of love were tuned to different kinds of sentiency. Bobby hadn't heard the mail lady either, until after her car had rounded the bend.

Time stopped until she felt herself in his arms. Even then, her emotions remained locked in the secret crevices of her bones. A button on his uniform pressed against her when he crushed her to him, and the pain of it stood outside her being and took up all her thoughts. She wanted to weep because she could not encompass the divine beneficence of this homecoming. She tightened her arms around him in the effort to hold him close until she came to life. She was conscious that he, too, was holding close, and that neither of them spoke a word. Perhaps Nature was working one of her merciful protections, for if they were to feel all they felt, it might be more than they could bear. Grief had worked that way too, when he had gone away.

The button kept pressing into her. She pulled away at last, and pushed Bobby toward him. Bobby hung back, self-conscious and inarticulate. They shook hands, like men, and then Bobby mumbled something about his shoelace. He bent down and knelt with his back to them, so that they couldn't see

that the shoelace wasn't untied. Claudia felt sorry for him; she knew the feeling of a bursting heart.

It was only Matthew who found welcome easy on his lips. He lifted his face for a kiss. "Comomwidmeseefashline," he said beguilingly.

"You're to come with him and see his flashlight," Claudia interpreted. "It'll take time for you to understand his conversational shorthand."

"I guess it will," said David.

"The car's over there," Bobby took up with loud importance. "I'll carry your bag."

He staggered off with it, finding it more than he had bargained for. "Hey, there, that's too heavy for you!" David called after him.

"It is not!" Bobby shouted back. "It's as light as anything!"

"He's grown tremendously," said David. "They both have."

"Matthew's skinny though, isn't he?"

"That's the way a boy should be," said David.

"We're talking like strangers," Claudia thought.

"Same old station wagon," David went on, as he opened the car door for her.

Later, as they came in sight of the little salt-box house cradled in the curve of the road, he said, "Same old place." He wasn't given to clichés. It was a key to the way his heart was bursting too.

Edward was standing at the gate to meet them. Their hands met in a long grip that whitened their knuckles. Bluster came up sniffing, and then started to bark. It was good barking. "Old feller," David said huskily. "Old feller." He looked around. "Where's Bluff?"

Claudia cleared her throat, and tried for nonchalance. "It's a shame, but we had to let him go."

"Come along, Bobby," Edward said. "Help me carry your father's things upstairs."

"Matthew too," said Bobby with a knowing look.

"You gave Bluff away?" David reverted, with a stunned look. "Claudia, why?"

"We had to. Two big dogs were quite a lot to feed and take care of. But don't worry about him," she hastened to assure him. "He's perfectly happy where he is."

"So Bluff is gone," David repeated, as if he couldn't believe it. He didn't say any more, but there was something in his voice that made her realize that it was the right of soldiers to come home and find the wholeness of a life that they had fought to preserve. "I'm sorry," she faltered. "I wish we could have kept him for you."

"That's all right," David acknowledged awkwardly. "They must have been a handful for you to manage alone."

They were inside the front door. "Don't let him say, 'same old living room'," Claudia prayed. She felt as if she could not bear the naked pain behind the words. He didn't say it. He said, instead, "Where's Jane? Isn't she going to say 'hello' to me?"

Claudia cleared her throat again. "Jane isn't here any more."

"Jane isn't here?"

Claudia nodded. "We'll go straight upstairs," she swept on. "You can see the barns later. Majesty has a great-great-granddaughter, the prettiest little dish-face of a heifer you ever saw."

"Where did Jane go to?" he persisted.

"Another place. A different kind of work. It was a case of bettering herself, so I couldn't very well hold her back."

"I suppose not," said David slowly. "But I thought she was like one of the family. I thought she and Edward were going to get married some day."

"Oh well," said Claudia, "maybe they'll get together again sometime. I really couldn't understand it either. I was almost sick about it at first, but we've managed very nicely without her."

"Look," said David. "Tell me everything at once. What else happened while I was away?"

"Not a thing," said Claudia, brightly. "Julia's in Washington being important, and Hartley still has his gallbladder even though it's out. Since he's your one blood relation, I suppose you ought to phone him right away, but not now, let's go on up." She wanted to be alone with him. Perhaps, when they were alone together, they could shut out the past and begin over again, as if the war had never been.

The first thing he saw were the flowers in front of his picture—the last of the zinnias from the garden. He pulled her to him and buried his head against her. "So you really missed me," he whispered, as if he'd been afraid to ask.

She thought of the long, widowed nights, the hurt of a sunset that he could not share with her, the crying need for him when they were afraid that Bobby's stiff neck last winter might have been a forerunner of infantile paralysis. But if she told him how much she missed him and he had to go away again, her loneliness would only burden him.

"Don't let's talk about it. You're back now." She wanted to ask him for how long, but her courage deserted her. She said instead, "Why didn't you let me know you were coming? I'm glad you didn't, though, I'd have been frantic till you got here. But I mean, when you landed at San Francisco?"

"Because I found I could make plane connections right away. And when I got into New York, I was so close—what I really wanted was to ride up to the house in a taxi, but there weren't any taxis at the station."

"I knew you were coming, anyway," she said. Some day

she would tell him how deeply she had known, but not now. It was something that belonged to a part of her life she could not yet share with him. There was a part of his life, too, that he could not share. On the way home in the car, Bobby had wanted to know if he had killed any Japs, and an invisible curtain had dropped between them. "I'll tell you about everything one of these days," David had answered jerkily, and Claudia had thought, "He doesn't want to talk about it." It seemed sad that they should be restored to each other, and that so much lay between them to make them strangers. It was the last bitter, niggling price that war demanded of lovers, this starting over again. It was like reweaving cobwebs.

A man coming back into a household made a difference. Supper was suddenly a problem, no easy short-cut of French toast or sandwiches, for David looked thin beneath his heavy tan. She had better use the chops, and ask Edward to cull a chicken for Sunday dinner. "I'll be back in a minute, darling," she said.

"Where are you going?"

"Just to see Edward a minute, want to come along?" It was as if he were a guest.

They stopped in the kitchen for a glass of water. Claudia poured a glass of milk instead, not stirring the can, so that it was more like cream. He drank it, surprisingly, without demur. "I wish we could get some of this stuff over to the boys on the Islands," he said.

"I wish so too," said Claudia. She looked at him, and knew that he was still over there. He felt her looking at him, and came back to her. "Tell me some more news," he said.

"There isn't much," she said a little lamely. It seemed wrong for them to be standing in the kitchen, with no one to celebrate his home-coming. "Nancy Riddle would be ter-

ribly excited if she knew you were back," she suggested. "Shall we phone her?"

He made a face. He'd always thought Nancy was a fool. "What's she doing up here so late?" he demanded, as if it were an intrusion for Nancy to be in Eastbrook beyond the summer.

"She's not going back to New York at all this winter. She wants to farm—and Elizabeth's still up here, too, we really ought to let her know you're home, she'd come right over."

He shook his head. "I'd rather not see anyone," he said. "Not now, anyway. No one but you." He put his arm around her.

"David. How long will you be able to stay?" There. The question was out. She had sneaked it in while her heart wasn't looking.

"I don't know yet."

"A week?"

"Longer than that."

"Ten days—two weeks—a month?" She caught his hand, not daring to hope. "For good, David?"

"Not so fast," he said.

She thought, "He knows, but he doesn't want to tell me." She did not press him. Time no longer meant what it had meant before. She had learned that in war a day must be stretched into a month, a month into a lifetime. "No matter how long or short," she said quietly, aloud, "you're here. That's all that matters."

Afterwards, he sat on the terrace making friends with Matthew and Bobby, while she fixed supper. She could hear the drone of their voices through the screen door. In a little while, he strolled in, and bent to kiss the back of her neck as she knelt before the broiler, turning the chops.

She looked up. "I'm letting them get crisp the way you like

them. I hope you're hungry, I have apple fritters, too. Remember Bertha's apple fritters? Mine aren't as good."

"Now I know where Matthew gets his nonsense." He was serious suddenly. "Claudia, shouldn't a boy of five talk more plainly?"

She was glad that he had noticed. He was coming out of those dim islands in the sea, he was beginning to be a father again. After a time, she could share with him the worries and the responsibilities that had lain so heavy upon her. But he must not know, yet, how much she needed him. It was his right to become whole, before she called upon his strength.

She blew a strand of hair out of her eyes and considered his question about Matthew. "Oh, nobody begins to talk plainly till they're three," she said. "He's only a couple of years behind."

"Matthew's a damn fool!" Bobby announced furiously from the doorway. "Matthew's a big damn fool!"

Matthew sidled in beneath his brother's elbow. "Janedidsogowayinabigbox," he said complacently.

"Shut up!" Bobby shouted, with his face getting red. "Mother, make him shut up!"

It was Bobby's agitation that made David know that something was wrong. He lifted Matthew in his arms. "Be still, Bobby. Now say it over again, Matthew. Slowly and plainly."

Matthew repeated himself, achieving excessive clarity.

"He calls everything a box," Claudia injected hastily.

"You mean," David corrected Matthew, "that Jane went away in a *car*."

"Box," Matthew reiterated, with his eyes riveted on the middle button of David's shirt. He began to twist the button. David held his hand quiet within his own: "What kind of a box, Matthew?"

"A big long box," said Matthew. "I want to get down."

David put him down. "Run on out on the terrace," he said.

"Go on with him, Bobby, we'll call you when supper's ready."

Bobby needed no urging. He grabbed his brother's arm with a pinch behind his fingers. The screen door banged behind them. Claudia said, "My chops," and peered again into the oven.

David turned her around to him. "Never mind the chops," he said. "Jane died, didn't she? That's what Matthew meant by a big long box."

Claudia nodded. She couldn't speak.

"Bluff too?"

Claudia tried to swallow the lump that jammed her throat. "I'm sorry, darling. I wish I could have kept everything just the way you left it."

"You poor little devil," said David huskily.

Supper was as gay as they could make it for the children's sake, but it wasn't very gay. A hundred times Claudia had planned this reunion. There was an old bottle of champagne in the cellar—one of Hartley's best. "For when David comes home," Hartley had said. Now David was home, this was their first dinner together, but champagne was the farthest thing from their thoughts. A heaviness hung between them. They couldn't seem to push through it. They had been closer with thousands of miles between them than they were at this moment, with their hands touching as they cleared the table of dishes.

"I'm going to stack them and forget them," Claudia decided. "Let's take a little walk up to the knoll and see the sunset."

"Let's," said David.

No sooner had they stepped onto the terrace, than Bobby and Matthew went into a huddle. "They're going to surprise us and do the dishes while we're gone," Claudia said. "It's been awfully good for them—taking responsibility and all that sort of thing."

"It's made men of all of you," said David.

There was a great sweetness, a great humility in his voice, but behind the words Claudia glimpsed the struggle in his heart. All over the world, men would be coming home to families who had learned to live without them. "If women don't go back to being women," she thought, "it will turn the whole world topsy-turvy."

They went through the garden to the bridge across the brook. David hadn't seen the garden yet. It wasn't much to see, except that it was as orderly as an empty house. "Edward was a little early in digging up the bulbs," he commented.

"That was me," Claudia took the blame.

"I bet you didn't remember to separate the tulips?"

"Yes I did, and I put the dahlias in the root cellar, so don't worry."

"Did you hill the roses, too?"

"Yes," she admitted without pride.

He stood there, not saying anything, just looking at her. "What a smart girl you turned out to be," he brought out at last.

"I was right," she thought unhappily. "If only I knew how to turn his kingdom back to him—"

They walked on, in silence, and at last they reached the knoll. The farm lay at their feet, with its white fence running around it, making it a giant toy.

"It hasn't changed," said Claudia. "It's the same as always. And if you have to go away again, it will be here when you come back."

It was then that he told her that he might not have to go away again. It was hard for him to tell her; she could see pain and defeat in the tightness of his lips. Apparently it had to do with that crash in the jungle. He'd had malaria after it, and

the nerves in one arm hadn't come back to normal. He was probably going to be let out—"retired" they called it, to make it sound prettier.

For an instant, she knew only fear that he was ill, and then the touch of him beside her was reassurance, and joy rose up in her. "Oh, David," she breathed, "why didn't you tell me before—" She turned her shining eyes upon him, and at once she was ashamed. She put her hand on his. "If it's hard for you to be out of it, darling, I'll try not to be glad."

"It's all right," he said. "Later on, I'll be glad, too. It's just that it's not easy to be useless."

Her spirit swooned. She might know how to run a tractor and manage accounts, but was she going to be equal to the greater task of helping a man live with his soul again? Once or twice in her marriage she had prayed for wisdom and maturity. She prayed now, as they walked back toward the house.

The grass was soaked with dew, so they took the road instead. They could see lights on the upper floor of the house. "The children are putting themselves to bed," said Claudia. "They're angels tonight, but tomorrow they'll be normal again. Which is what I'd rather." He did not answer her, and suddenly she was conscious that his steps no longer kept pace with hers. He had stopped. He was staring at something, and there was a funny look on his face.

"What's wrong?" she asked, apprehensively.

"Nothing," he said. "Who cut the hedge?"

The hedge. What a fool she was to have deliberately walked him past it and spoiled her record. There was no chance, either, of passing it off as a slight error in judgment, for in the falling darkness it looked even worse than it really was. It zigzagged along the pink horizon like a drunken sailor.

"Who cut the hedge?" David repeated on a rising note.

"I did," she confessed.

For the first time since he had come home, she heard him laugh, and there was jubilance, at last, in the way he caught her in his arms. She felt her heart thumping against his heart. They were close enough for that.

"You know what?" said David.

"What?" said Claudia.

"We forgot all about that old bottle of champagne from Hartley."

"So we did," said Claudia, as if she had.

It was reasonably chilled from having been in the cellar. They gave Edward a mammoth tumblerful of it, and brought some to the children in glass eggcups, which looked a lot but held hardly anything. The nursery lights were out. They pretended to be asleep, but when they heard the clink of something to eat, they bounced up.

"What's that?" Bobby demanded, eying the eggcup with distrust.

"Taste it and see," said Claudia.

He took a chary sip, while Matthew, who did not believe in looking a gift horse in the mouth, tossed off the contents in a single gulp. "More," said he, agreeably surprised.

"You can have mine," said Bobby, with a shiver of disgust. "I don't like this ginger ale, it has a funny taste."

David smiled, and kissed him. "That's for being your mother's son," he said.

Two

It seemed only yesterday that she had put the garden to bed, and now the crocuses were trying to push up through the straw and manure. One of them overshot itself, and exploded limply in a wisp of yellow blossom. Claudia picked it on her way back to the barn with some eggs for breakfast.

"It thinks it's spring," she said.

David didn't so much as grunt in answer. "I can't fix this," he said, slamming the electric iron down on the kitchen table. "It needs a new cord."

"But I have to press a shirt for Bobby," she protested in dismay. "He hasn't a clean shirt to wear to school."

"Bobby's shirt notwithstanding, it will need a new cord," David repeated in a tone which implied that she had jumped rope with the cord, or similarly abused it.

Her impluse was to tell him to shut up, even though he hadn't said anything she could put her finger on. There was no getting away from it, they were getting edgy with each other. She had the good sense to realize that it would have been different if he had had his office to go back to. Unfortunately there was little place for civilian architecture in a nation at war, and besides, after David went overseas, Roger had given in to his ulcers, and had retired to the California desert to write a book, so that now the firm of Killian an Naughton was a thing of the past. It wasn't easy to get starte again, especially for David, who was the sort of architect wh wanted to build cathedrals. "The day will come," Claudia told him with less faith than hope, "when the world will want cathedrals again."

In the meantime they were practically existing on Nancy Riddle's new barn unit. It was ironic. Claudia recalled how, when they'd first come to Eastbrook to live, David had flatly refused to have anything to do with Nancy's elaborately terraced house—no, thank you very much, he'd said. Now, when she asked him to design an up-to-date dairy barn he said thank you, without the No. Not that he had any respect for the enterprise, or for Nancy's ability to carry through. "She's going into it as an income tax reduction," he relayed to Claudia with as much contempt for himself as Nancy. "She doesn't know the first thing about cows, and neither does her herdsman, he's nothing but a drunken bum."

"He's the best she could get," Claudia pointed out, "which is why she's had her eye on Edward. I'd rather lose us than Edward, though, so why don't we apply for the position ourselves?"

She meant to be funny of course, but she could have bitten her tongue out, because it was one of the things that hit David in the wrong way. "Not a bad idea," he agreed with a short laugh. "I could make a better living for you than I'm doing now—two hundred a month and all expenses paid."

It was difficult to know how to handle him these days, he was so jumpy and sensitive. Suppose they were turning out to be one of those mental casualties of the war, unable to save their marriage from the hazards of readjustment? She was afraid to think what would have happened if they didn't have the farm, and yet with labor and grain soaring

s'y-high, the milk-and-egg check from the local market ırcely covered feed alone. "My compensation check cer-nly saves our necks," David often mentioned without pleas-e in the thought. He wore his retirement from the army like a bruise on his conscience. He wouldn't admit that he was physically less than perfect in spite of the malaria that caught him in unexpected gusts and the arm that refused to function every now and again. Edward had a hard time deciding whether or not to save him from the heavy chores of lifting and shoveling. "I think maybe it's better to let him do what he wants to do," he concluded eventually. "We should be glad. Many men come out of the war thinking they are sick. With Mr. David, it's the opposite."

Edward was right. No one could go through a war without paying for it in one way or another. Pride, Claudia reflected, had always been David's weakness, and the war had aggravated it into a disease. Even his irritability when he tried to fix the iron stemmed from sensitivity. It was a reminder of his inadequacy as a wage earner, a protest against the fact that she had to launder Bobby's shirt. "It's going to be worse after the war is over," he prophesied darkly. "Thousands of us, with no jobs."

"You've got a job," said Claudia. "Running the farm, and milking ten cows and a couple of thousand chickens is a job."

"Quite a job," David conceded dryly.

"And there'll be new building after the war—"

"Suburban houses," said David.

"Cathedrals," she countered stubbornly.

This morning, he was in a hurry to get over to Nancy Riddle's to check the color of the barn trim before the painters got started. "Please, no eggs," he stopped Claudia peremptorily.

"No eggs is a fine breakfast to start a day's work on."

"I'm not hungry."

"Edward eats everything I give him, including oatmeal–if I give it to him."

"Edward does a day's work, he needs it."

There was no use in reminding him that he did a day's work too, it would only irritate him. She closed her lips, and put the eggs back in the icebox.

Bobby came downstairs as his father was gulping down a second cup of black coffee. It was one of Bobby's less attractive days. He was bare from the waist up, with the bagginess of his trousers accentuating the adolescent scrawniness of his torso.

"You look pretty," David mentioned sourly.

"I'm waiting for my shirt."

"It's not your shirt, it's your hair," David enlightened him. "Don't you ever comb it?"

Bobby's face dropped. Claudia's heart went out to him. He was devoted to his hair. Every night he plastered it against his scalp with an oily pomade, but in spite of his efforts to train it, the morning would find little spikes standing up like children in a schoolroom wanting to be excused. Claudia knew that he had combed it until his arm ached, and still he looked like a porcupine. She sought to ease one grief with another. "I haven't any clean shirt for you," she said.

He looked stricken. "Why not?"

"Iron's busted," she explained briefly. "You'll have to wear the one you wore yesterday."

"I can't, it's got jelly on it," he protested on a rising note of tragedy.

"It serves you right," David put in. "Next time be careful not to spill."

"I wore that shirt twice already," Bobby stuck up for himself.

"Thanks," said David. "That was big of you."

Claudia saw a glimmer of hostility start smouldering between them. "Wear your nice brown shirt," she suggested with swift tact. "It always looks clean, no matter if it isn't."

"But it's wool," he expostulated, "I'll smother!"

"You and your smothering," she said. "Anybody would think you were a middle-aged woman with hot flashes."

"It itches me," he held out doggedly.

"Let it itch," said David. "Now march, and do as your Mother tells you."

Bobby seethed beneath the injustice of it all. "Why did the iron have to go and break!" he demanded of the universe at large.

"That's what I'd like to know," said David.

Claudia felt her nerves crack under the lash of innuendo. "Where's Matthew?" she asked quietly, feeling like a saint.

"Putting on his shoes, the dope," said Bobby.

"He was putting them on an hour ago," said David. "Run up and tell him to get a move on or he'll go without breakfast."

It was lucky that David had already departed for Nancy's by the time Matthew ambled downstairs, with his shoes on the wrong feet. Claudia pretended not to notice. "Sit down and eat," she said, "before everything gets cold."

Matthew looked crestfallen, having expected his inverted extremities to cause at least a minor sensation. Bobby, however signalled him to bide his time. They buried themselves in oatmeal, controlling convulsions of mirth against the moment of discovery.

Claudia continued to remain obdurately blind. "Stop dawdling, Bobby, the bus is due any minute," she remarked over her shoulder as she buttered some toast.

"I'm not going in the bus," said Bobby. "Dad can let me off at school on his way to Mrs. Riddle's."

"He's already left for Mrs. Riddle's."

Bobby was freshly aggrieved. "Why didn't he wait for me? He should have waited for me."

"He said to tell you he couldn't. He has to be back by ten to help Edward with something."

"Oh boy, they're going to cut the lambs' tails," Bobby remembered with relish. "I wish I was here, boy."

Claudia regarded him coldly. "It doesn't hurt them," he inserted.

"Who said so?"

"I know it doesn't."

"Don't be so cocksure. How would you like somebody to do that to you?"

"I haven't got a tail."

"Eat your crusts. Children are starving."

"I save them for the birds," he said virtuously.

"Charity begins at home. Kindly eat them."

"I itch," he complained.

"That's good," said Claudia.

"My feet hurt!" Matthew announced abruptly.

"That's fine," said Claudia. "Next time put your shoes on right."

His eyes found Bobby's in baffled accusation. Bobby shrugged. There was nothing he could do about it, it was just one of those days that started out with no good to anyone, including the lambs. "The bus is here," he exclaimed with relief. "Good-bye." He dropped a kiss short of his mother's ear. "Are you going to be home when I get home?"

"Am I not usually home when you get home?" Claudia inquired, a trifle raucously.

A faint grin tugged at Bobby's lips. It was where he liked her to be, it was the way he liked to leave things when he went off to school.

Funnily enough, she wasn't there when he came home that afternoon. The toothache began a little while after he'd left the house. She was wiping up the bathroom floor with a paper napkin, when the pain, with no warning, assaulted her senses like a violent slap on the cheek. Guiltily she dropped the draggled wad of tissue, and cradled her jaw in the palm of her hand. "I'll use a mop hereafter," she offered up to an unseen vengeance. "I'll use a scrubbing brush," she amended, as the pain streaked through her ears and whipped about her head in a scarf of agony. She got to her feet and leaned against the basin, tingling from the sheer excruciation of it. She hadn't had a toothache in years, she'd never even known that she had teeth, and now, all at once, she knew that she had forty-eight of them (or was that states). Dimly, through a haze of mounting torture, she was aware that a car swept into the driveway. David was back. She went downstairs to meet him.

"What's the matter?" he asked at once.

"Toothache," she said thickly.

He studied her in concern. "Does it hurt that much?"

She nodded mutely. "You wouldn't think a simple tooth could make you want to die."

"It can," he said. "I had to have a molar yanked in Buna one night. Worst damn pain I ever had."

"Thanks," she said gratefully.

"Were you eating anything? Cold, hot?"

She shook her head. "I was wiping up the bathroom floor. With a paper napkin."

"That shouldn't do it," he said. "Open."

She didn't know what he expected to see, but just the same she appreciated his interest, and pointed, with a wet gulp, to the region of her lower jaw. "Better go in and let Dr. Martin have a look at it," he prescribed. "You can catch the eleven-ten if you hurry."

"I can't go to New York. Who's going to fix lunch for you and Matthew?"

"Matthew and I will manage very nicely, Mrs. Jehovah."

She had an idea if she could find enough excuses not to have the tooth attended to, it would stop aching. "You'll be too busy with the lambs' tails to keep an eye on him."

"The tails can come off tomorrow."

In the midst of her agony, she reflected that she had done the lambs a good turn, anyway.

"Unless you want to let me drive you to a dentist in Bridgeport," he offered as a countersuggestion.

She resisted the idea because Dr. Martin knew her mouth from years back, and it was a nuisance to begin with somebody who didn't. "Besides," she added, "As long as I go to Dr. Rowland for babies and Dr. Martin for teeth, I can still count myself a native New Yorker."

"I know what you mean," said David. "Mother's going to New York," he broke the news to Matthew. "You can drive down to the station with me. Go wash your face."

The alacrity with which Matthew obeyed, sprang largely from the satisfaction of stealing a march on Bobby, and his flattery of David as they drove off was a subtle and beautiful thing to behold. "Daddy can't steer if you glue your head against his elbow," Claudia remarked.

"Yes, he can," Matthew maintained, in a tone that implied that his father was a superior being who could accomplish all things under all conditions.

"Hypocrite," David muttered, pretending not be pleased.

They passed Elizabeth Van Doren's house, and in spite of her toothache, Claudia automatically craned her neck. It was impossible to pass a house one knew, without seeing if it was alive. "Elizabeth must be here again," she said. "There's Candy—"

Candy caught sight of the car at the same moment. She waved and ran across the lawn to them. "What getups those college youngsters wear," Claudia commented. The trousers of Candy's blue denims were rolled up to her knees, and she wore her hair in two stiff little braids that sprouted out from behind either ear, and left the back of her scalp unashamedly naked. "Hello!" she shouted. "I'm home for Easter!"

David slowed down. She clambered up on the running board. "Uncle David! I can't believe it! Isn't it awful, really, that this is the first time I've seen you since you've come back from overseas! You look *marvelous!* Simply marvelous! So brown and everything!"

"You look pretty good yourself," said David. "About ten years old."

"I'm eighteen, if you don't mind."

David cocked his eyebrow. "Well, anyway, next month," she insisted. "Matthew you angel, give Candy a hug this minute—what's the matter, Aunt Claudia, what's your face all screwed-up for?"

"Toothache," Claudia mumbled. "I'm on the way to New York."

"Isn't that foul," Candy sympathized. "Can I ride down with you?"

"Hop in back," said David. "Where's your mother?"

"She went to Bridgeport to meet a cousin that used to belong to Dad. She's an old lady with habits, and nobody in the family likes her, so mother takes her in for a week every summer. It's from the dark ages, a sense of duty like that. She says it's for Dad, though, not for duty. I tell her Dad probably doesn't give a hoot any longer about anybody but us. Not that I believe there's anything after you die. I wish Mother would play bridge and things, and be suburban instead of civilized."

"You make as much sense as Matthew," David observed mildly.

"Matthew looks *marvellous!*" Candy digressed. "Simply marvellous. But he doesn't remember me—"

In answer, Matthew flirted his eyes until his lashes swept his cheeks. "My God, I used to be in heaven," Candy rambled on, "when I could come over when you lived in New York and wheel his carriage. Remember?"

Claudia remembered, but she didn't feel like talking. Candy's chatter was a running obbligato to her misery. How wonderful to be as young as Candy, without a toothache. How wonderful to be able to wear a part up the center of your scalp and not care how it looked. . . .

"Hey, don't breathe down my neck," said David.

"Oh dear, was I breathing down your neck?" Candy apologized. "It drives mother crazy, too. Isn't it deadly up here with no men around?"

"Much obliged," said David.

"I mean there aren't any young men left," Candy qualified. "They're all in the war."

"That's true," said David.

Claudia could see the look she dreaded come into his eyes. She changed the subject. "Candy, would you mind marketing this list? Uncle David can pick you up on the way back from the station. He loathes hanging around a store being waited on."

"I'd adore to do it," said Candy, accepting the slip of paper. "I can't read your writing though. What's this? Onions?"

Claudia took the list back and studied it. "Ammonia," she decided.

Dr. Martin's office was full of patients when she arrived. The war was certainly doing him a good turn. On Claudia's last visit, his appointment book had been so empty that he had had to keep it closed on his desk; he hadn't even bothered to get a new nurse when his old one got married. Now he had three nurses, and treated patients in two rooms at the same time.

Claudia was taken into the second office immediately. It was purely a propitiatory measure because a considerable time elapsed before Dr. Martin appeared. He hurried in, whistling boyishly in spite of his grey hair. He pumped her up in the chair, and bent over her. He smelled cleanly of antiseptic, and his fingers were so cool and fresh that Claudia tried to forget that they had just come out of somebody else's mouth. "How's the country," he asked, with an air of still whistling.

Claudia didn't care how the country was. "It hurts," she whispered. "Awfully."

"Same old molar," he concluded, after poking around a little. "The last time you were in, I warned you it was going to give trouble."

"But it didn't hurt then." She forbore to add that she hadn't wanted to spend money on teeth that didn't ache.

A nurse rolled the X-ray machine into place. Dr. Martin bent a film into Claudia's mouth, which she held with her thumb and no grace. After a moment he took it out, and gave it to the nurse, and then went back into the other office to see another patient. In a little while he returned, wearing a pleased air and a white mask. "All right, nurse," he said brusquely. "Let's get going."

He got going with several jabs of novocaine that eventually took away the pain along with Claudia's jaw, and most of her lip. She felt enormous and silly on one side of her face. Dr. Martin, who had now turned into a pair of remote and impersonal eyes, kept digging a sharp instrument into her gums, and she was affronted because she could feel nothing. "Relax," he said. She caught a glimpse of gleaming steel, felt a hideous crushing sound like a nutcracker tackling a stubborn nut. "This is silly," she thought, in no great panic.

Dr. Martin said, "Spit out."

She spit out. "That's a lot of blood," she remarked, with a degree of pride. He showed her the tooth, and her pride inflated. "It's gigantic, it looks like a Shakespearean production I once saw."

"You might feel like a Shakespearean production," he told her, "when the novocaine wears off. Let me see you at ten tomorrow morning."

"That's pretty early to get in from Eastbrook, I mean getting Bobby off to school first, and everything. Couldn't I make it in the afternoon?"

"I'm at the clinic all afternoon." He riffled the pages of his appointment book. "Ten is the only time I can squeeze you in."

She stopped in at a drugstore on Madison Avenue. It was one of those old-fashioned drugstores that sold only medicines and exuded an air of being twice as expensive as it should have been. The telephone calls, however, cost the same as anywhere else, and she had a sense that she was getting a bargain as she dropped a nickel in the box.

Eventually, Bobby's voice floated back to her, clear and sexless and stripped of human intelligence. "Hello, Hello. Who? Hello, who is it, who do you want to speak to?"

"Bobby," she exhorted him frantically. "It's Mother!"

"Who?"

"*Mother!* Call Daddy!"

Indignation quickened him. "Where are you, you weren't home, aren't you coming home?"

"I said to call Daddy! This is a long-distance call!"

"He's out someplace– Where are you?"

"Never mind that. Go find Daddy and tell him to hurry! Run quick, before I get out of dimes and nickels."

"All right," he gave in, but she could tell he wasn't running.

She held the wire, on pins and needles, kicking herself. She should have put in a person-to-person call instead of taking the gamble on David's answering, but he had said he'd be waiting for her to call. What was he doing, not being there?"

"I was in the barn, a man came to buy a heifer," he explained, when he finally got to the phone.

She was partially mollified. "That's good. Did he?"

"He's going to think about it– What was wrong with your tooth?"

"A big bouncing abscess. It's out."

"He yanked it already? How do you feel?"

"Fine. But I have to go back early in the morning."

"Then you'd be smart to stay overnight," he said.

"Except I happen to have a family."

"Your family can get along without you for once."

"There are shoulder chops for supper and you don't know how to fix them."

"I can fix them, Mrs. Jehovah."

"Stop calling me that! Bobby needs his hair washed."

"He's old enough to wash his own hair."

"He don't get the soap out. Also, I have to iron his shirt."

"He'll wear the same shirt he wore this morning."

"I haven't enough money with me for a hotel room," she climaxed her objections. "What's more, I don't want to run around looking for one."

"You shouldn't. Go to Julia and Hartley's."

"It would save the fare back and forth," she weakened.

"Never mind the fare," he said impatiently. "The important thing is to save yourself a trip. Doesn't your face feel sore?"

"It's beginning to. Like a snake in the grass."

"The novocaine's wearing off, it'll get worse if you don't stay quiet."

He was right. The idea of a soft bed instead of a jostling train ride was beginning to appeal to her.

"Are you sure you can manage without me?"

"We'll appreciate you when you get back," he said.

She hung up the receiver, hating the thought of being away from him all night, and liking the fact that she hated it. A certain flame that had seemed to be flickering out the last few months was suddenly rekindled. She emerged from the booth feeling lonely and alone, and something in the way he'd said good-bye told her that he was feeling the same way. The thing to do was to go home anyway, and telephone him to meet her from the station. It would be fun; exciting rather, like a reunion after a long absence.

She stepped out into the light of the store to read her timetable. She had no flair for timetables, but at last she found the perfect train—an express to Eastbrook, leaving in twenty minutes, with a star beside it that probably meant a dining car. Unfortunately, though, it turned out to be the kind of star that said, "Runs on Sundays only," at the bottom of the page. She gave vent to one of David's highly personal expressions under her breath, but it couldn't have been as much under her breath as she thought it was, for a voice at her shoulder said, "What a jolly suggestion."

Her cheeks burned up. She wheeled sharply, ready to give whoever it was a piece of her mind.

"Hello," he forestalled her pleasantly, "remember me?"

She remembered him at once, even though she hadn't seen him in years, but she was struck speechless by his smiling impudence. "Jerry Seymour," he went on. "I rented the little brown cottage down the road from you one summer."

"I remember," she acknowledged tersely. "You ought to talk to people before you talk to them."

"I'll do that next time," he agreed. He regarded her with

interest. "Look here, didn't you have a brace of Great Danes and a cat?"

"Also a brace of children and a husband."

He grinned engagingly. "Those are things I always like to forget," he said. "But since you've brought them up, how are they?"

She felt herself warming to him. "Fine. David was in the Solomons. Construction engineer. He was wounded. Now he's home for good."

Jerry's interest seemed to cool proportionately. "Really?" he murmured.

"What's been happening to you?" Claudia continued curiously.

He seemed surprised. "Haven't you read the papers? I've written a play. We go into rehearsal as soon as we finish casting. Sam Goldheart's producing it."

"I meant the war," Claudia elucidated shortly.

"Oh," he said. "I was too old."

She regarded him with disfavor. He didn't have a grey hair, and he was still good-looking in a purely handsome way. "You don't look at all overage," she remarked, with no desire to be complimentary.

The implication slid off his slim back like water. "You don't look overage either," he assured her. "In fact, when I saw you just now, I said to myself, 'She's exactly the type for Cornelia.' And then I realized who you were."

"Who's Cornelia?"

"The girl in my play. She's supposed to be twenty."

"I'm twenty-seven," she informed him.

"That's what I mean," he said.

The druggist approached, and unobtrusively slipped a small oblong package into Jerry's hand. "I hope they prove efficacious," he murmured with a discreet clearing of his throat.

"I hope so too," said Jerry.

The package looked as if it could hold almost anything. "What are they?" Claudia asked curiously.

The druggist cleared his throat again and took himself off. Jerry said gloomily, "I wish to God you could act. I swear you're the living counterpart of the way I see Cornelia. Elemental. Simple. . . . What I mean to say," he amended tactfully, "an audience isn't going to believe the suicide scene with that brassy-haired little tart Sam Goldheart's trying to sell me." His voice cracked. "Sally Evans has no more emotional content than a stuffed canary. She can't give the character any dimension. She'll ruin it!"

Claudia couldn't understand the sort of man who could get so passionate about a play with a war going on. She thought he was a fool. "I have to be going," she said. "Good-bye."

"Good-bye," he said.

At the door, she called back over her shoulder, "And anyway, don't be silly, I can act. I was acting the summer you met me. In a play called 'Ticket to Heaven.' With Victoria Manners. At the Eastbrook summer theatre."

He gaped at her. "I seem to remember something of the sort!" he said slowly.

"I was very good," she helped him along. "So good that a producer offered me the part on Broadway."

He was at her side in one long stride. "Is that true?" he demanded. "Or are you pulling my leg?"

"Certainly it's true. But I didn't take it."

He flung open the door for her and steered her across the sidewalk to the curb. She hung back. "You're hurting my shoulder, what are you doing?"

He relaxed his hold without releasing her. "Sorry." He hailed a taxi. "You're going with me to see Sam Goldheart."

"I don't want to see Sam Goldheart," she asserted brusquely. "I'm taking a train."

"Nonsense. Hop in."

"I won't hop in. I have to go home."

He shook her impatiently. "This might be the turning point of your life and you stand there quibbling. What's so important about rushing home?"

She thought of Bobby's shirt that needed ironing, and a frying pan she'd left to soak, and David's eyes that weren't happy; but Jerry Seymour would only pooh-pooh the urgencies that commanded her being. "I've got a lot of things to do," she said.

"Very well," he conceded. "I'll take you to the station. Now be a good girl and hop in, will you?"

"Thanks," said Claudia, and hopped.

He leaned forward in his seat. "Forty-seventh Street Theatre, driver, and make it as fast as you can."

She sputtered with rage. "Calm down," he said. "I meant I'd take you to the station afterwards. How tall are you?"

"You're completely unscrupulous. Crazy, too."

"Both indispensable assets in the theatre. . . . About five four?"

"Tall?"

"Yes."

"I don't know in inches. I'm a head shorter than David. He's about six foot."

"That's all right," said Jerry, "that's fine. . . . How do you project?"

"David says I do it beautifully," said Claudia.

He gave her a swift glance. They rode the rest of the way in silence.

Mr. Goldheart's office nestled inconspicuously between two theatres. The lobby was small and uninviting; a typewritten sign on the yellow plaster wall said, "No casting. Sam Goldheart." Jerry rang a bell, and after a long wait, an elevator came creaking up from the bowels of the building.

"Mr. Goldheart hasn't gone yet, has he?" Jerry asked the old man who was running it.

The old man said, "Couldn't say. Reckon I did see him go out a little while ago."

"Good. That means he's in," Jerry whispered to Claudia.

"Oh," said Claudia.

The elevator gulped its ropes and came to a halt. They stepped out into an uncarpeted entry lined with wooden benches. The benches were filled with people—girls, men, women, children. They looked as if they had been there for a long time and would be there for a long time to come. "They know we're casting a play," said Jerry, steering Claudia through a swinging gate.

"I thought it said 'No casting' on the sign," said Claudia.

"It did," said Jerry.

"But isn't anybody going to see them?"

"No," said Jerry.

"There might be somebody good, though."

"That isn't the way plays are cast," said Jerry. "Come along."

He pulled her into a cubbyhole wreathed in smoke. Two oak desks filled the room, and sprawled across each was a pair of legs. She followed them up, and found faces finishing them off—a fat, sleepy face with a piece of dough for a nose, and a narrow, dark face with a piece of granite for a nose.

"Hello, boys!" Jerry greeted them exuberantly, "I've discovered Cornelia!"

It was as if they had not heard him. He said it over again, and was rewarded with a hostile stare. After a long moment, the putty-nosed man shifted his legs to the floor. "What's she done?" he asked in a way that managed to seem insulting.

"Summer theatre," said Jerry.

The granite nose also moved its legs to the floor, and

leaned across the desk to chuck Jerry under the chin. "Look sweetheart, I'm directing this show, and we're not running an amateur-night."

"But I must have a particular quality for Cornelia," Jerry insisted with his voice cracking up on him again. "You might be directing the play, but I wrote it, and I tell you that quality is a hell of a lot more important than experience."

"Says who," drawled the putty nose." What authors don't know about the theatre would fill a book."

Jerry ignored him. "Be a good fellow, Jim, and let her read for you," he implored the granite nose.

"I don't want to read," said Claudia. "I don't even want to come. I'm going home."

Jim reached out a long bony arm. "Not so fast, sister, I like your spirit."

"Kindly don't call me sister," said Claudia, shaking herself free.

Jim hoisted himself to his feet. "All right. What have you done on the stage, brother?" She was fool enough to laugh. "She's got a good set of teeth on her," the putty-nose remarked. "You can see 'em from the balcony."

She wondered whether she ought to tell them that one of her teeth was newly missing, but what they didn't know wouldn't hurt them.

"I want Sam to see you," Jerry said. He whisked out of the room.

Claudia turned to the door. "I'm catching a train."

Jim put his arm out again to stop her. "You're a smart baby," he approved. "Where'd you get the technique? Okay. I'm hooked. Read a few lines." He thrust a script into her hand. "Where it says 'Cornelia.' "

The touch of the manuscript did something to her. Her eyes skimmed over the page before her; it spoke a language that she had forgotten was alive within her. "CORNELIA–

Palpitant"—(How could you be palpitant out of a clear sky? She needed some hint. There were a lot of ways of being palpitant.) "Is this where she commits suicide?" she asked.

"She doesn't commit suicide."

"Mr. Seymour said she did."

"Pay no attention to him," said Jim largely. "The script stinks enough without suicide."

She was affronted for Jerry. "Then why do you do it?"

"Look at the hits this year," the putty-face said. "Why in hell not?"

"Go on, read," said Jim impatiently. "Never mind the stage directions, just read where it says 'Give me my gloves'—with a chip on your shoulder. I'll read Timothy. That's the mother's lover. Timothy. I'm the mother's lover. All right. Start. Timothy says, 'Why are you in such a hurry—?"

"Give me my gloves," said Claudia, with a chip on her shoulder.

"I think she's got something," said the putty-face, "But don't think you're Duse," he added hastily to Claudia. "The part pays minimum. You heard that, didn't you, honey chile?"

"I never heard of minimum," said Claudia.

Jerry came to the door, triumphant, "Sam wants to see her," he announced.

"I don't think I'd better," said Claudia.

"All you have to do is read the way you did for me," Jim said. "Don't be nervous."

"I'm not nervous," she protested, "I just want to go home."

"Come along," they all said together, and propelled her toward Mr. Goldheart's private office.

She didn't expect to see what she saw. Hidden around the end of a narrow, dingy corridor, Mr. Goldheart's office opened up in a sumptuous splurge of satinwood and velvet draperies. "Hello, hello, hello, hello," a voice bellowed forth across a vast expanse of oriental rug. "Come in, come in, I won't eat you!"

Sam Goldheart surveyed her from beneath disorderly white brows. He seemed to be a massive man, but when he rose from behind his monumental desk, the bottom of him dwindled into thinness, and he wore pointed shoes on feet that were a little small. He came over to her and put his arm around her. Her impulse was to push him away, but his stomach being so large and he being so elderly, made the whole thing add up to a mere fatherly gesture, so she resigned herself to remaining quietly in his embrace until he had finished with his inch-by-inch appraisal of her physical assets.

"Not what I'd call pretty," he decided at length. "Walk over to the mantel, darling, and let me see if you're knock-kneed."

"I'm not," said Claudia.

"You wouldn't know," said Mr. Goldheart. "By God, you're not at that, you've got a very pretty pair of legs. . . . What experience have you had?"

"Seymour says she was at the Eastbrook summer theatre," said Jim.

"Let her talk for herself!"

"I was in a play called 'Ticket to Heaven,' " Claudia anlarged. "The producer wanted me for New York."

"The damn thing was a hit. Why didn't you do it?"

"I wasn't interested. I mean I didn't want a job."

He regarded her shrewdly. "You want a job now, though, don't you?"

"No."

His face got ready to yell. "Then what the hell are you here wasting my time for!" he shouted.

"I don't know," she said.

He stalked back to his desk. "What are you fellows doing, what in blazes do I want with an actress who's married to a rich playboy with a farm in Connecticut and a couple of hundred pedigreed cows. I want 'em hungry!" He broke off to shake his finger in front of the putty-face. "But make no mistake, a couple of hundred pedigreed cows is damn good publicity! If I only had a press agent instead of a bump on a log . . . Get the hell out of here, the whole lot of you! Send a couple of secretaries in—dammit, why don't I get a little service, where's my barber, send him up here, I want a shave, I'm donating ten thousand dollars to some goddam fund or other at some goddam dinner tonight . . . "

"Yes sir, I have the photographers all lined up," the putty-face injected deftly.

Mr. Goldheart grunted approval. "High time you earned your salt. Now leave me alone, why the hell can't I have some privacy! Go on, get out and close the door, the whole lot of you!"

"Yes sir," said Jim.

The whole blooming lot of them drifted meekly from the room, but once outside, their meekness vanished. "That's the baby!" Jim whispered hoarsely, and slapped Jerry on the back. The putty-face whooped softly, and slapped Jerry on the back too, at which Jerry pushed the putty-face in the stomach, rather awkwardly, but very happily.

"Good-bye," said Claudia.

Nobody paid any attention to her. They swung down the hall, back to the smoke-filled cubbyhole, and Claudia kept on walking. She couldn't find her way out. She opened the wrong door, and found herself in another cubbyhole. She said "Excuse me," and closed the door quickly. Two very thin young men with pale moustaches rushed past her. "How do I get out," she called after them.

One of them waved his hand vaguely, but he didn't answer. "They're the secretaries," she concluded.

Eventually, she made her way to the elevator, past the

crowds of people who were still waiting. They eyed her with avid curiosity. A girl with a mink coat and gold hair said maliciously, "Did you get the job?"

Claudia shook her head. She didn't want to explain that she already had a job, that she was married to a playboy with a couple of hundred pedigreed cows. It would sound like bragging.

It was dark when she reached the street. A little man, rushing busily along, bumped into her. White flapped around his legs underneath his overcoat. "Pardonna me," he gasped.

"And that," she decided, "is undoubtedly the barber." A feeling of unreality invaded her, as if she'd taken ether instead of novocaine. She herded her thoughts into a straight line, and took up from where she'd left off. Six o'clock. There was no point in going back to Eastbrook at this late hour, she might as well sleep at Julia and Hartley's and call it a day.

The upstairs maid admitted her. She was a new one, with eyeglasses and puffy lips—Julia wasn't proud since the war.

"I'm sorry, but Mrs. Naughton is away," she said with finality, and started to close the door in Claudia's face. Fortunately. Hartley came downstairs at that moment. "Who is it, Lucy?"

"It's a young lady," Lucy informed him coldly.

"A young lady?" Hartley's middle-aged voice sharpened with eagerness. "Let her in!"

"It's me," said Claudia, emerging from the dimness of the hall.

"Well, well, well," Hartley exclaimed, making every effort to seem pleased to see her. "What a nice surprise!" He put his arm around her; his stomach felt as uninteresting as Mr. Goldheart's. "Come on in," he said, and led the way to the library at the rear of the house. "Julia's not home, she's in Wisconsin. Or Oregon. Anyway, she's on some war drive.

Come on in . . ." He seemed to have forgotten that they were already in. "Where'd you drop from?"

"The dentist. I had a tooth out."

"Dear me," said Hartley. "Are you going back to the country tonight?"

"I wasn't," said Claudia.

Hartley got the point belatedly. "Then stay here," he said. "There's plenty of room. Too much room. You and David ought to come in oftener. The house is empty, four servants with nothing to do. Sorry I have a dinner engagement, but Lucy'll take good care of you, won't you, Lucy?"

Lucy hovered in the doorway. "When the young lady wishes to go upstairs," she said stiffly, "It's the third floor front."

"I know where," Claudia assured her, which made matters worse as far as Lucy was concerned. With an emanation of immense disapproval, she turned on her heel and left them alone.

"Well," said Hartley, sitting down with his mind elsewhere, "what's been happening?"

"Not a thing," said Claudia. "David's a little discouraged."

"He'll get over that," said Hartley. "Reaction. Readjustment. He ought to be glad he got out of the mess, with all his arms and legs."

"He is," said Claudia. "We both are."

"You're lucky to have that splendid couple," Hartley went on, in a dogged determination to keep the conversation alive. "Help is very scarce."

"What splendid couple?"

Hartley wrinkled his brow. "That nice fat German woman and her husband . . ."

"Austrian," Claudia corrected. "Bertha and Fritz."

"That's right, that's right," said Hartley. He looked very pleased with himself for remembering.

"But we haven't had them for years," Claudia disillusioned him. "Bertha had to leave to take care of her grandchildren. We have their son-in-law, Edward. And Jane. Only Jane died. Now we have no one. Except still Edward."

"That's not so good," said Hartley.

"It isn't," Claudia agreed. "David works like a horse."

"What about you?"

"I work like a horse too."

"You both ought to get in town oftener," said Hartley which made a circle back to where he started. "A little variety changes your point of view, does you good." He patted her shoulder. "The place is yours, come in for a week of concerts and shows. I'll get you tickets whenever you say."

"That would be wonderful," said Claudia wistfully. "We haven't seen a play in ages.—But I've just been offered a job in one," she added.

To her astonishment, Hartley knew quite a lot about the theatre, he even knew about Jerry's play. His approach was quite professional, in fact. "How much does the part pay?" he asked directly.

"They said minimum. But I don't know how much minimum is."

"Fifty-seven fifty," said Hartley.

"A week? Really? How do you happen to know?"

Hartley gave a sheepish smile, and something about him reminded her of David, even though they were so different. "Oh, I've backed a couple of shows this year," he said.

She was increasingly amazed. She couldn't imagine Hartley backing a show. She wondered if Julia knew about it.

"A little protege of mine," Hartley went on, with mingled pride and reticence, "is playing in 'Music Behind the Moon.' A little dancer."

"Oh," said Claudia. She couldn't imagine Hartley being interested in little dancers, either. The theatre was a peculiar disease; apparently a person was never too young or too old to catch it.

She moved thoughtfully up the handsome, curved stairway, and paused for an instant at Julia's luxurious bedroom, with its white, virginal bed, and pale blue draperies. Hartley's heavy walnut room lay beyond it, separated by double dressing rooms and baths. She hoped that she and David would never have enough money to live so privately.

On the floor above, Lucy was turning down one of the satin spreads in the guest room. "Will you be having a tray of supper up here, Miss, or would you care to eat in the dining room?" she inquired aloofly.

"Up here," said Claudia. "Is there a new toothbrush anywhere around?"

"You'll find everything including a fresh nightgown in the dressing room," Lucy replied, with her lips a rosette of righteousness.

Claudia stood looking after her as she marched from the room. "I'll bet twenty cents Lucy thinks I'm another little dancer," she concluded.

She took a bath, and climbed into bed. It was the sort of bed that constrained one to company manners, with its delicate quilt and monogrammed linen. She lay quietly, absorbing its perfection, until Lucy appeared with a supper tray. Dr. Martin had told her to take only soup, but it would have been ridiculous to forego fresh shad roe and asparagus. She wondered who would have eaten all that expensive food if she hadn't come. Julia's household seemed to keep on functioning whether anyone was there or not—like sound waves in the air.

As she dipped her fingers in the crystal finger bowl, she thought compassionately of David, frying shoulder chops. A shoulder chop had to be catered to, like a pot-roast being cajoled into posing as an oven roast, and even then it was in the lap of the gods as to how it turned out. Shoulder chops were messy to clean up after, too. She winced away from the image that crowded untidily into her mind. David wasn't the comic strip type of man who could wear an apron with equanimity while his wife went forth to earn a living. How funny that such an image should have come into her head—David in an apron, indeed. Spending the night in luxury was filling her head with ideas. She should have gone home, where she wouldn't have had the time to imagine herself a great star with a bloated salary.

It was Julia's bath towels that had started her off. They were as big as sheets and as thick as the fleece lining of Bobby's windbreaker. It had been sheer heaven to wrap herself up in one of them, without thinking about the laundry bill. The long panelled mirrors that lined the walls of the bathroom gave her ideas, too. In a New England farmhouse, you went as far as your shoulders, and took the rest on faith, so it had been a novelty to make her full acquaintance. Jerry was right. She could easily play a twenty-year-old. From the looks of her no one would have guessed she'd been married nine years and had two children. Why had she been so quick to turn her back on the chance to read the part of Cornelia? Fifty-seven fifty a week was a lot of money—enough to pay for a maid, and the insurance, and many of the small expenses that were worrying David half to death. Moreover, there was no telling what would follow if she made a success of Cornelia. A bigger part in another play perhaps, or a contract in Hollywood. Such things happened these days, oftener in real life than in novels, and in her case, it wouldn't be in the least farfetched, since she'd studied at dramatic school before she was married, and had always wanted to be an actress.

Lucy came in for the tray. "Is there anything else, Miss?"

"Nothing, thank you," said Claudia. "Except a little sanity," she amended inwardly.

She reached for the telephone to call David. It didn't occur to her not to tell him about what had happened that afternoon, but when she heard his voice, she changed her mind. There was no use in telling him. Nothing would ever come of it now, and it would only hurt him to sense her disappointment. She hadn't expected to have this reaction. Up to half an hour ago she hadn't felt the least twinge of self-sacrifice, but all at once it was creeping over her like the dull throb of the tooth that wasn't there. All at once, she couldn't bear the thought of housework and cooking, day after day. That was why David must never know anything about Cornelia, even though it was the first thing she had ever kept from him. But this was different, it was a declaration of her love, as well as an admission of her weakness.

He sounded lonely. The children were in bed, he said, and the dishes were washed, except for the frying pan from the chops.

"Leave it," said Claudia. "There's another one you can use for breakfast–or you can boil instead of fry. Anyway, I'll be home before you know it."

"What train are you making in the morning?"

"Noon. I'll have a sandwich in the dining car," said Claudia, who always loved to eat on trains.

"I'll meet you," said David.

"Are you missing me?"

"None of your business," he replied.

"That's that," said Claudia aloud, as she hung up the receiver. She pulled Julia's fleecy blankets up to her chin, and resolutely thought of nothing.

He was standing, when the train rolled in the next day, exactly where he had waved good-bye the day before, and Matthew was clinging to his hand, just as if they had never moved from the spot, but had stood waiting for her to come back.

She kept her cheek against his face for an extra instant. "Your skin feels so fresh," she murmured, "and you smell like the barn."

"Thanks," he said.

"It's a compliment. Nobody I met in New York smelled of manure, the dopes. How *is* Bobby, by the way?"

"He's got shell shock from wearing his brown shirt to school again."

"I should have bought him another one. I forgot all about it," she said remorsefully.

"It's good for his character," said David. He held her at arm's length. "You look tired."

He had eyes like an eagle. She could never hide things from him.

"I thought I looked unusually well without my tooth," she evaded. She turned her attention to Matthew, who stood staring at her with his cap too far down over his forehead, and generally in need of a mother's care. "No kiss?" she said, prettying him up.

Acute embarrassment overcame him. "Come, come, I haven't been away as long as that." She hugged him while he squirmed. "I bet the tulips will be up before we know it."

"What kind of a non sequitur is that?" said David. "I brought the truck down. I had to pick up some crates at the freight station."

"The truck is my favorite limousine," she said.

They met Shakespeare half a mile from the house. David climbed down to catch him, but he scurried under some bushes, and, amazingly, was home before them. "He really is a remarkable cat," said Claudia. "Did we sell the calf?"

"No, but we cut the lambs' tails," said David.

"Ouch." Her tongue explored the tender cavern where her tooth had so recently resided. "I know how they feel."

"They don't," said David. "Does it still ache?"

"Just sore. What did you have for lunch?"

"I don't remember."

"You do."

"Scrambled eggs."

The first thing she did was to tackle both frying pans, and after that the living room rug and the beds which would have looked tidier if he had left them unmade. Then she started a split pea soup for supper. The school bus lumbered up to the door at four o'clock. The dog barked. A door slammed. Something fell over in the living room. Bobby was home.

He was so glad to see her that all he could say was, "Why don't we have tangerines any more?"

She thought about it. "I don't really know," she said.

He sniffed the air, scowling. "It's split pea soup. Why do we have to have split pea soup all the time?"

"Because it's a hell of a lot of nourishment," she said, "in one fell swoop."

"Where's Dad?"

"In the chicken house."

He gave her a belated kiss of welcome. "I have to do the chores," he said. "Good-bye."

"Good-bye," she said. She opened his lunch box and rinsed out the thermos bottle, and offered the crusts of bread to Shakespeare, who put up his nose and walked away. Bluster emerged from under the table, and put up his nose too, but he ate them.

The telephone bell rang. It was long-distance. She didn't care, because everybody was home. She wouldn't even have cared if it were a telegram or a cable. It was like having all your possessions in a single suitcase, close beside you.

David appeared with some freshly-killed broilers while

she was waiting for the call to come through. "Who is it?" he asked.

"I don't know. For you, probably. Better get on the extension and listen."

It took a little time for the connection to be made, so they talked to each other, feeling that they were getting something for nothing. "You don't think something could go haywire and we'd be charged?" Claudia asked in sudden apprehension.

"It's possible," said David. "Listen, how much would those broilers cost if you bought them?"

"Less than if I got them for nothing off the farm," she said, cruelly. "Are they all cleaned up inside?"

"No," said David, "but their heads are off."

"Always grateful for small favours," she said.

"I want to speak to Mrs. Naughton," a voice intruded from nowhere. "Mrs. Claudia Naughton."

She recognized the voice immediately. He had no right to make her sound like widow. "This is Mrs. *David* Naughton," she elucidated.

He ignored the distinction. "Look here, this is Jerry Seymour. Where'd you disappear to yesterday?"

She could literally see David's ears go up on the other wire, but there was nothing to do except give Jerry a forthright answer. "I slept at my sister-in-law's, and then I came back to the country."

"I wish you would have stuck around. Sam wants to see you again tomorrow at eleven."

"But I don't want to see Sam again," said Claudia. "It's awfully nice of you and everything, but really."

She tried to be elliptical, but he came straight to the point. "Don't be a fool. He'll pay you a hundred and fifty a week."

She was taken off her feet. "I thought it was minimum," she exclaimed.

"It would be," said Jerry, "if that old skinflint thought you had wrinkles in your belly."

She heard David's receiver go up with a bang. Apparently he didn't like anyone talking about her belly, and she didn't either. She gave Jerry to understand as much.

"Oh for God's sake," he said, "It's just a theatrical expression for not having any money. Hungry, in other words. Which you're not. Can you be in the office tomorrow at eleven?"

She was conscious of David, glowering at her side. "No, I can't," she said. "Thanks just the same. I have to ring off now. My split pea soup is burning. Good-bye."

"Wait a minute!" Jerry protested, but she put the receiver back in its cradle. "It loves to burn on the bottom the minute your back's turned," she explained to David. "Quick, I have to stir it, get out of my way!"

David did not get out of her way, he deliberately blocked her. "Who," he inquired, "is Sam?"

"Goldheart," she answered faintly.

"And what possible interest can Mr. Goldheart have in your anatomy?" David continued.

"Oh," said Claudia indifferently, "that's just an expression. The theatre has a lot of expressions. They always say a play stinks, too, which means it's probably a hit."

"Attractive language."

His lofty attitude was slightly out of order, considering the four letter words which larded his general conversation, although Claudia approved his disdain of less than the consummate. "I can't stand the word 'stinks' either," she agreed companiably. "Now will you let me pass?"

He let her pass, and she went back to the kitchen and stirred the soup. She expected him to follow her, but he didn't, so she had to go and find him. He was putting logs in the fireplace in the bedroom. He did not turn when she came in.

"Don't be a silly ass," she said.

He got to his feet, and brushed off his dungarees. "You don't have to tell me anything you don't want to tell me," he said, quite gently. "That's all right."

"No, and I never would have told you," she admitted. "But now I might as well. Sit down. And take that look out of your eyes, I don't care for it."

"I'll take my eyes out, if they bother you," he returned politely.

It came out funny enough to make them laugh, and after that it was easier. She recounted the whole story, embellishing it here and there when she saw that he was enjoying it. But at the end of it, he turned serious again. "You didn't want to tell me because you thought I couldn't take it, is that it?"

He caught her unawares. All she could think to say was, "Don't be silly."

They didn't talk about it again until after supper, when Bobby laid down the law on the issue of his brown shirt. "I smothered in it, I can't wear it again tomorrow," he announced.

"Oh darling, I'm afraid you'll have to smother one more day," said Claudia. "The iron's busted, don't you remember?"

"Don't bother your mother about a shirt," David reproved him. "Your mother's going on the stage. She's going to be a great actress."

Claudia threw him a look, and saw nothing but sweetness in his face. "And your father," she added softly, "has just built a beautiful cathedral."

Bobby got lost at that point. He veered back toward the familiar. "Can I take a piece of cake up to bed with me?" he demanded.

"Definitely not," said Claudia. "You just had supper."

"I'm still hungry."

"Next time finish your soup. Clear the rest of the table for me like a good boy."

He cleared the rest of the table, a dish at a time. Claudia turned to David, who was looking for his pipe.

"It's over there on the window sill exactly where you left it.—What did you mean, 'your mother's going to be a great actress'?" she reverted brusquely.

"Just that," said David, shining the bowl of the pipe against his nose. "You're going to play 'Cornelia'."

"How nice. And will you tell me who's going to take care of you and the children while I commit suicide every night?"

"Look, you little idiot," he said, "I want you to be happy."

"I'm happy. And I'm not being noble about it either," she added hastily.

"Also, you're not being practical," he said. "We could use two hundred dollars a week."

"A hundred and fifty. Don't exaggerate just because you're in the theatre."

"Two hundred," he insisted. "You'll have a call from Sam Goldheart tomorrow, offering you two hundred."

"You're crazy," she said, but she could feel her heart lurch up into her throat at the very thought of it. She, like Bobby, sought the haven of the commonplace. "I wonder," she said, "if I could possibly use the cord of my old iron."

"No," said David, "you can't." He disappeared for a moment and came back with a small package. "It's the last one in the hardware store, so see that you take care of it."

"Bobby!" she called. "Your dear, delightful papa bought us a new cord, I can iron your white shirt for tomorrow!"

Bobby hovered over her, grinning sheepishly while she dampened the shirt in blobs, and ironed it, quite badly, especially around the collar. "I love to iron," she said, as she pulled the plug out of the socket.

"That's because you do it so well," said David. He rescued the cord to fold it properly, giving her a dirty look while he did so.

"Oh shut up," she said.

They went to bed early. Claudia was horrified because she couldn't keep her mind from wandering. David got it immediately. "Come out of the theatre," he said.

"You had no right to tell me Sam Goldheart was going to phone again tomorrow," she blamed him. "Not that I put any stock in it, but it's distracting . . . What do you want to bet he doesn't?"

"Shall we talk?" David asked.

"No," said Claudia, "let's dance."

Before they fell asleep, he leaned over to kiss her. "I bet you twenty cents," he whispered.

For all he was so certain, there wasn't a peep out of the telephone the next day, except a mistake. Claudia was in the cellar when it rang, tidying up a stack of old shutters and screens that David refused to throw away. She dashed up the wooden stairs, and stumbled over Matthew, who was on his hands and knees, pushing a cracker box across the floor.

"Don't kick my train," he reproved her grievedly.

"Excuse me," she said. "And if you don't mind, stop that unearthly noise."

"I'm the engine."

She registered, out of a remote corner of her brain, that he was talking quite plainly of late. Perhaps she ought not to keep thinking of him as a baby, perhaps it would be good for both the children if she went away for a little while. She wouldn't consider it, of course, but the idea had its constructive side.

She tried to be nonchalant as she lifted the receiver, but it was like a blow in the solar plexus to hear a woman's scrawny voice demand two pounds of fresh mackerel. "I am not the fish store," said Claudia through gritted teeth, and hung up.

Through the living room windows, she could see David hotfooting it across the lawn from the barn. She had to smile, because he was the image of Bobby the way he slowed down to an indifferent stroll as he reached the terrace; he was like Bobby, too, the way he said "What time will supper be ready?" instead of asking what he wanted to know.

"Supper will be ready at the usual time," Claudia informed him. As she spoke, she was conscious of an irrational sense of letdown that he had been wrong. She was used to relying on his being right. "It was the wrong number. And I hope," she said ungraciously, "that you feel like a fool."

"Not yet I don't," he brazened it out.

She never ceased to marvel how completely they understood each other. At times their marriage almost boiled down to pantomime. David could do more with his left eyebrow than most men could accomplish by an immense amount of talk.

His eyebrow was particularly expressive as he passed her the newspaper across the breakfast table the next morning. Even Bobby recognized something momentous in the air. He was about to go upstairs before the school bus came, but he drifted back to peer over her shoulder. Ever since his mother's name had been in the newspaper the time she had been hit by a truck, he lived in hopes that lightning would strike twice in the same place.

Claudia glanced down at the neatly folded sheet—the neatest thing about David was his newspaper—and saw Sam Goldheart's picture at the top of the theatrical page. Underneath the picture was the caption: *Producer Starts Rehearsals of Seymour Opus Today.*

"Stop breathing down my neck," said Claudia. "You're as bad as Candy."

"But I don't see what it says," Bobby protested.

"It says your father is a fool," David told him.

"Where?" he queried eagerly.

"It doesn't," said Claudia. "It says your mother never was, and never will be an actress."

Bobby's lower lip jutted forth distrustfully. "I don't see your name and I don't see Daddy's name," he said.

"And anyway," Claudia continued over the lump of disappointment in her throat, "I wouldn't go to New York for anything and miss all this beautiful spring weather up here."

Bobby dropped the newspaper and hurried to the window to reobserve the condition of the freakish April day. "It's snowing," he reported, with increasing belligerence. "The pond has ice on it."

"You're seeing things," said David.

Bobby's eyes narrowed shrewdly. "Then can I go without my coat?"

"*May* I go without my coat?" Claudia corrected.

He started to rephrase his question, only to recall from past experience that it would avail him nothing. It was hard not to laugh, and as he didn't want to laugh, he wrapped himself in dignity and stomped upstairs.

"His wife should be grateful to us," Claudia remarked.

"Provided," David qualified, "she's a madwoman like her mother-in-law."

Three

They didn't either of them, allude to the play again, but each morning, after David went to the barn, Claudia scanned the theatrical page. On Sunday, there was another picture of Sam Goldheart in the magazine section of one of the papers, accompanied by a long article. It called him the Grand Old Man of the Theatre, and told how many great stars he had discovered in his forty-odd years of producing. In his current production of *Sad Ecstasy*, it went on to say, he had wooed Sally Evans from the musical comedy stage to essay her first straight dramatic role. Sally Evans, Claudia remembered, was the girl Jerry Seymour hadn't wanted for Cornelia—but evidently an author had very little to say about anything. "Which is all there is to it," Claudia decided. It was the nearest she came to admitting that until that moment she hadn't actually given up hope.

"Now that the cellar's behind me," she said to David, as she tossed the paper into the wastebasket, "I'm going to tackle the attic tomorrow. It's been hanging over my head for weeks."

"You poor old slob," said David.

The quality of his understanding made her want to cry.

She was glad when he said in the next breath, "Don't touch any of my stuff up there or I'll break your neck."

He didn't trust her, and took time off in the middle of the afternoon to check on the extent of her cleaning-up. She lifted her head from the musty insides of an old trunk and drew a red herring. "What'd you do with Matthew?"

"I threw him in the lake." He rescued a box of ancient hardware from a pile of trash, and she could literally see the architect in him spring up like a jack-in-the-box. "What are you doing with these?" he demanded.

"Pitching them out, they're no good—I mean it, where's Matthew?"

"Riding on the tractor with Edward—You uncivilized nincompoop, these latches were on the doors when we bought the house, they're a hundred and fifty years old!"

"Exactly. That's why they're no good," said Claudia.

The distant ring of the telephone broke into their argument. "It's the freight station about our carload of grain," said David, back to farming. "Let Bobby answer, he just came home from school."

He went to the top of the stairs. "Bobby!" he called down, "answer the phone, and take the message!"

"I can't!" Bobby called up.

"Why can't you!"

"I'm drinking my milk!"

"Well stop drinking your milk!" David commanded raucously. He turned to Claudia with an air of depositing the whole of Bobby in her lap, as if he'd had no hand whatsoever in conceiving the child. "The young gentleman's drinking his milk," he relayed with an outraged snort, "can you tie that?"—He blocked her way to the trash heap. "What are you doing with that cane?"

"Throwing it away, it's full of bumps."

He lost his voice with fury. "It's a shillelah," he bleated. "Put it back where you found it!"

Bobby's face appeared above the attic ladder. "Are you fighting?" he asked with interest.

"Your mother's turning into one of those frustrated females with a cleaning complex!" David shouted. "What about the carload of grain, is it in?"

"I don't know," said Bobby, looking blank.

David glared at him. "Can't you take a message straight, a boy of your age? What did the freight station tell you?"

Bobby continued to look blank.

"Perhaps," Claudia suggested with great reasonableness, "it wasn't the freight station."

David began over again. "Who was on the telephone?"

"Someone for Mother."

This was a different story. She dropped the cane. "For me? Who? Why didn't you say so?"

"I am," said Bobby.

"What's her name?"

"It's a man."

"What's *his* name?"

Bobby thought for a moment. "Gold," he brought out at last.

"Gold? I don't know any Gold," said Claudia.

David's left brow buttoned up his eye. "Wasn't there any more to it than 'Gold'?"

Bobby admitted that there was another part to it, but he hadn't bothered to remember it. "Pardon me," Claudia said, as she shoved him out of her way. "Pardon me," David echoed, shoving him back. "Hey stop it!" Bobby expostulated to empty air.

Sam Goldheart wasted no words. "What in the name of all that's holy do you let a kid answer the telephone for;

it's a waste of a grown man's time!" he bellowed out in answer to Claudia's tremulous "Hello."

"I know it is, we never do," Claudia acknowledged meekly. "We were in the attic when it rang."

"Well don't do it again," he roared. "I don't like to squander money on long-distance calls, it's against my principles!"

"You should have made it person-to-person," Claudia advised.

"Person-to-person costs too much. I've got three million dollars, and that's how I got it, by not spending it . . . How's the weather up there?"

"Raw," said Claudia.

"Down here it's nice.—Jump in your car.—You've got a car, haven't you?"

"Yes," said Claudia, "but I don't jump in it."

"The three minutes are up, sir," the operator interrupted.

Mr. Goldheart's voice showed signs of agitation at the reminder. "It's half-past three now. I'll be waiting for you at my office at half-past five. Good-bye."

He hung up before she could gather her wits. David came back from listening on the extension. He removed the receiver from her nerveless fingers and placed it back on its cradle.

"He sounds crazy, too," he commented.

"He is," said Claudia, "he could be a blood relation—What do you think he wanted?"

"You'll find out," said David, "when you get there."

"Get there!" she echoed. "I have no intention of going!"

Her protest was too vehement. She knew, even as she spoke, that she was already in Mr. Goldheart's office; that nothing, short of illness or death, could keep her away.

David knew it too. They talked about it, driving to the station to catch the three fifty-eight express. "You want to go more than anything you've ever wanted," he said, with his eyes straight ahead on the road.

"How do you know," she murmured, a little guiltily.

"The newspaper, for one thing," he said, swerving from the path of a lunging truck. "You blasted jackass!"

"Who, me?"

"That lunatic truck driver!"

"Maybe he was in a hurry.–What did you mean, 'the newspaper-for-one-thing–' "

"You couldn't wait until I left the house every morning to see if there was something in it about the play."

She was mystified. "How could you tell? I was always so careful to fold it back in every fold."

"I could tell," he said.

They drove a while in silence. "I still don't see why you have to go to New York," Bobby moodily remarked from the rear seat.

"I'll be home tonight," she promised him.

"What train?"

"Never mind what train," David put in. "Your mother doesn't have to ask your permission every time she moves off the place."

"I'll catch the seven-ten," Claudia said. David was right, of course, but nevertheless, she knew how Bobby felt because she'd felt the same way about her own mother. She wished, for his sake, that he had Matthew's sublime engrossment in self. Matthew had been indifferent to her going, he hadn't even wanted to ride down to the station with them. "I'm milking the cows with Edward," he'd told them importantly.

"You dope," Bobby had interpolated. "Mother's going away."

"So you could at least kiss me," Claudia had suggested.

He'd extended an obliging cheek. "Bring me a pony," he instructed her with an eternal optimism.

"Would you like," Claudia asked Bobby, as they waited on the platform while David bought her ticket, "for me to bring you a pony too?"

He kicked a stone. "A boy in school has one," he mumbled, reluctant to reveal his secret hankering. He covered himself at once. "Every minute you have to go to New York," he insisted rebelliously.

"That's a gross exaggeration. The only time I've been to town in a year is when I had my tooth out last week."

"And that, young feller my lad," said David, as he joined them, "was the beginning of our troubles. The next day, Mamma began to sublimate. First she cleaned the cellar, then she cleaned the attic. If we don't let her get this out of her system, she'll begin on us."

"Boy and how," Bobby fervently agreed, on principle.

Claudia breathed a sigh of relief; her frailties were always the cementing tie between them. She sought to make the bond stronger by allying herself against them. "Your father should have been a fashionable psychiatrist," she remarked caustically. "He thinks he knows women . . . This is a parlor car seat," she broke off, looking at the ticket he had given her. "What rank extravagance!"

"I got it cheap, the station master had an old one left over from last year," said David. "Here comes the train."

He kissed her. She kissed Bobby. And then she went back and kissed David again. "Darling, I hate to leave like this, but everything's ready on the stove for supper, and don't bother with the dishes, I'll do them when I get home tonight—"

She thought afterwards of having so glibly said "When I get home tonight." If anyone told her at that moment that she wasn't going to come home for a month, she would have said that such things didn't happen to normal people. Indeed, from the moment she found herself in Sam Goldheart's office, normality ceased to exist.

The secretary seemed to be expecting her. He ushered her down the hall immediately, and announced her at the door. Mr. Goldheart was reading a letter. He kept on reading. The secretary, who looked like a trout with a small blond moustache, swam away with a little flutter of his fins, and left Claudia to fend for herself. After a moment or two, she cleared her throat. Mr. Goldheart continued to read his letter, his mammoth head suspended above the broad expanse of his orderly desk, like the Cheshire Cat in *Alice in Wonderland*. Claudia coughed. "I'm here," she said.

He didn't look up, but he must have heard her, for he reached into his top desk drawer and extended a small package in her general direction. She moved near enough to take it. It turned out to be a five-cent bar of chocolate. As she was hungry and had a weakness for everything with chocolate on or in it, there seemed to be no reason why she should not accept the offering. "I prefer the kind with nuts," she mentioned, "but thank you very much." Still engrossed in his letter, he opened the drawer again and gave her another bar larded with almonds. However, his hand waited until she returned the first bar, which he put into his mouth with a single thrust, rolling the wrapper into a ball. He threw the ball into the scrapbasket, swallowed mightily, and jerked his head up to look at her.

"D'you know who this letter's from?" he demanded. "It's from Mrs. Roosevelt. That's a great woman, eat your candy."

"I am," said Claudia.

"Here's a piece of gum," he said, delving back into the drawer.

"I don't chew unless I have two sticks to make it worth while," she said. "And even then, I don't care for it."

He folded the gum into his own mouth. "Sit down." He motioned to a chair close to his desk, and shifted around to face her. "So you came," he said, with his voice rubbing his hands.

She hated to give him the satisfaction of admitting it. "My husband insisted," she evaded.

He observed her moodily. "That husband business isn't so good," he said.

"I think it's very good," she said.

"What's he do?"

"He's an architect."

"Make a living at it?"

She repressed the impulse to remind him that he was inquiring into their personal problems, but as he was more than old enough to be her father, perhaps he only meant a paternal interest. She gave him the benefit of the doubt.

"David had to close his office while he was overseas," she explained. "He joined up right after Pearl Harbor." She tried to stem the onrushing flow of her pride, David often told her not to brag, but she couldn't help it. "He was one of the first of the construction engineers over in the South Pacific. He was wounded."

"Hero, hm?"

"According to me he is," said Claudia, "but not according to him. The hardest part for him was to be retired, and doing nothing. At least he thinks he's doing nothing," she corrected herself swiftly, "only he isn't. There's not much building going on now, so he puts in twelve hours a day farming."

Mr. Goldheart beetled his brows in such a way as to make David pale into an amateur of brow-work. "What's it doing, raising hell with his masculinity because you want to contribute to the family exchequer?" he shot at her. "I'll fix that." He grabbed the phone. Claudia leaned forward to stop him but he warded her off. "Hey Percy!" he shouted into the instrument, "get me that Eastbrook number again!" He banged up the receiver, got to his feet, opened a blind door in the wall behind his desk, and vanished.

"This is nothing but a nice, foolish dream," Claudia decided, "so I might as well enjoy it." David had once said that it was impossible to dream colors, therefore she must remember to tell him that the leather chair on which she was sitting was distinctly red. She turned to check her memory of Mr. Goldheart as he reappeared through the door. "And your tie is distinctly blue," she affirmed.

Mr. Goldheart accepted her statement with little or no surprise. "The trouble with Sally Evans," he remarked, "she isn't crazy enough to play Cornelia."

Cornelia. It was now quite obvious that she was dreaming David's prophecy. The next thing, Mr. Goldheart would doubtless offer her two hundred dollars to do the part. She was annoyed when the ring of the telephone interrupted them —it would have been nice to get the money before she woke up.

Mr. Goldheart held the receiver to his ear. "David," he shouted, "is that you?"

Presumably David said that it was, and presumably Mr. Goldheart liked David's voice, for as far as Claudia could gather from the one-sided conversation, they might have been lifelong friends. They talked about cigars and the Russians and crops, and it was quite a few minutes before Mr. Goldheart came to the point. "Look old man," he said in his most winning approach, "I don't want to bollix up your domestic life, but I'd like to put your wife into this new show of mine. I don't know a bloody thing about her acting but the author and director seem to think she's the type, and by all that's holy and for all I can tell, she might turn into a great star. And that wouldn't be too bad, now would it?"

Mr. Goldheart paused to listen to David's reply and the disconcerted look of having pushed very hard against nothing, crossed his face. He turned from the phone. "By God, David says you can!" he reported.

The dream was getting out of control. Claudia said nervously, "Ask him who's going to take care of the children."

"Who's going to take care of the children?" Mr. Goldheart repeated obediently. He listened again for a moment, and relayed the answer. "David says you should call Bertha."

Claudia snorted. As if Bertha could rearrange her life to suit their convenience. "Let me talk to him!" she exclaimed.

Mr. Goldheart held her at arm's length. "Good-bye David, old boy," he said hastily. "You sound like you've got a lot of sense." He hung up, and squared around to her. There wasn't anything winning about him now. His eyes were challenging, and his voice was stripped of all its friendliness and warmth. "I suppose you know what the part pays," he said.

Claudia was taken aback by the sudden change in him, and concluded immediately that she might as well finish up the dream to her complete satisfaction. "I couldn't possibly," she responded crisply, "accept the part of Cornelia for less than two hundred dollars."

Mr. Goldheart sank back into his chair, clawing the air. "Get the blazes out of here!" he bellowed. "Who do you think you are, I can get the best names in the business for that money!"

"I guess you'd better," said Claudia, and lost no time in gaining the door. "Come back!" he shouted, as her hand turned the knob.

He was so purple with rage that she was afraid he might be fixing to get a stroke. "You don't have to pay it," she placated him hastily, "because I'm not going to play the part anyway. I wouldn't think of leaving my husband and children to go on the stage."

His face puckered up, and all the roar went out of it. "I'm an old man," he whimpered, "you're taking advantage of an old man." He picked up the telephone. "Percy! Wait a minute, Percy—what's your name dear?"

Claudia thought he must be talking to somebody else. "Mine?" she asked in surprise.

"Yes, dear. Your maiden name, dear, before you were married."

"Brown," said Claudia. "Claudia Brown."

Mr. Goldheart tasted the sound of it before he nodded approbation. "It's a good stage name." He veered back to the telephone. "Percy! Are you there, dammit? Give Miss Brown a script on her way out, she's going to play Cornelia."

It was too pat, even for a dream.

Rain was coming down in diagonal sheets when she reached the street. There were plenty of taxis. She waved and hollered, but after they passed she saw that they all had heads in them. Finally, she felt silly waving for nothing, and started off on a run to the station. A policeman jerked her back to the Forty-second Street curb. He offered to give her the address of the morgue to save her the trouble of being carried there, and embroidered the witticism to such an extent that he made her miss her train by half a minute. It happened to be the last train that stopped at Eastbrook. The dream was beginning to turn into a nightmare. At any minute now she was apt to look down and find she had no clothes on.

She waited in line for a telephone booth, and eventually went in after a woman who wore red pumps without toes. The booth was warm and steamy, like a recently sat-in chair. The woman had also left behind her the smell of sachet, probably the worst of all leftover smells. Claudia tried not to breathe as she gave Long Distance the number. The operator told her that the circuits to Connecticut were busy. "Oh dear," said Claudia, "are you sure?"

The operator said she was sure.

Outside the door, angry faces pressed against the glass. She turned her back, determined to stay where she was until David's voice steadied her against the waves of unreality that were, according to the best formula of nightmare, buffeting her further and further adrift. But David's voice, when she finally heard it, gave her a final push that sent her careening off into space. He said, "I got in touch with Bertha and she's going to try to come out tomorrow. In the meantime, I told her to be at Julia's at half-past seven tonight so you could talk to her. You'd better hurry, it's almost that now. I'll call you later." He rang off before she could tell him that he, like Mr. Goldheart, had gone completely mad.

It was part of the fabric of absurdity that Julia was giving a dinner party when she arrived. Her heart sank when she saw lights in every window, and cars driving up to the door and rolling away. She felt like a wet cat in her damp tweed suit and old felt hat, and Julia would certainly not be overjoyed in claiming her a near relative. The decent thing to do was to go in the service entrance and up the back stairs to the guest room. Lucy might unbend enough to smuggle her a sandwich later on.

Lucy, surprisingly, was already unbent. She presented a welcoming smile, full of teeth, and said that Mrs. Naughton was expecting her, would she please to go straight to the drawing room? It was evident that David had telephoned Julia as well as Bertha.

Julia's opening words left little doubt as to the trail that he had blazed. "It really is the most exciting thing that's ever happened!" she exclaimed.

"Have a cocktail!" Hartley beamed, thrusting one into her hand. He embraced his guests with a broad sweep of arm. "Here's to Broadway's rising star!"

Everyone drank the toast with enthusiasm. Claudia drank too, although a cocktail always reminded her of hair tonic.

She glanced down to make sure that she wasn't standing there without any clothes on, and was so relieved to find that she was still in the tweed suit that she accepted a second cocktail. After a few moments, she stopped caring where she was, and who she was, and why she was. If all these people wanted to think she was wonderful, that was all right with her. If Julia insisted upon turning over the third floor to her, that was all right too; and if Bertha, who was waiting for her when she finally wafted upstairs, assured her that she could manage everything at the farm, Claudia had implicit confidence that she was speaking the truth. "But how can you leave Fritz and your grandchildren on such short notice?" she rallied to ask with a fading shred of reason.

Bertha's plump face, so like an elderly apple, wreathed itself in smiles. "Just like you can leave," she replied with her warm-throated humor. "Everybody can leave, once in a while. Only with me, I don't go on the stage."

"Five years of being part of the Naughton family," Claudia told her, "has left its mark of madness on you too."

"Sometimes," Bertha confessed in a guilty whisper, "I get so lonesome for Bobby and Matthew I can't stand it."

"There's a whole mess of socks I haven't got to darning yet," Claudia warned her, "and the attic is a shambles, and Matthew has to take calcium, and Mr. David should eat a big breakfast whether he wants to or not, and Bobby hates wool."

"You shouldn't have so much on your mind," Bertha ordained. "I take care of everything."

Claudia thought, "This is heaven. Bertha's going to do all my worrying from now on—"

"Also," Bertha continued, "it's time you had a little vacation from the children. Year in year out is not good for anybody." She straightened a pair of Julia's silver mules beside the bed. "Ach, what high heels," she decried. "Be careful

how you walk in them if you have to get up in the middle of the night."

"I will," Claudia promised. Long after Bertha had gone, she lay bathed in the warmth and safety that had seemed to emanate from Bertha's capacious bosom. She began to wish that the dream would never end, for suddenly it was very pleasant to feel free of all responsibility and care. It was the sort of thing that didn't happen outside of dreams. She had said to Bobby that afternoon, "I'll catch the seven-ten back tonight." It had been a safe promise to make to him, because ordinary married people with families always came back when they went away, like the law of gravity turned sideways.

The big difference was that she and David were married people, but not ordinary married people. There was no law that bound them. She had thought that she was tied, but with the magic of his love, he was making it possible for her to go back to being the person that she was before he had come into her life. Claudia Brown—one of the most promising students in the Academy of Dramatic Art. Claudia Brown, playing the Second Mrs. Tanqueray—

The subdued tinkle of the telephone led her hand toward the table by the bed. She lifted the receiver. David's voice came to her from a great distance, as if, suddenly, it were he who had become the dream.

Jerry Seymour was waiting for her at Mr. Goldheart's office the next morning, looking ten years older since his play had gone into rehearsal. "Thank God you've got the part," he greeted her, "I put in five days of sheer hell with that little tramp, and I swear if that old ham tries to teach you any of his tricks, I'm going to knock his damn block off!"

Claudia could not quite figure out who the "old ham" was, although she was reasonably certain that the "little tramp" was Sally Evans. And then, at that very moment, Mr. Goldheart emerged from the elevator looking ten years younger than he was, with his hat on one side, singing a song about his darling Clementine. He came to a halt in front of Jerry, and let the song die off his lips in a slow smile. "Well boy," he said, "she's all yours–" He patted Claudia on the cheek, and marched off down the hall to his office, leaving her with a delayed impression that his smile had carried more venom than Jerry's threat. A prickle of foreboding ran down her spine. "I think Mr. Goldheart thinks you're going to wish you hadn't wanted me," she said.

Jerry linked his arm in hers. "We'll show him," he replied grimly. "Come along, we'll be late for rehearsal."

They walked three blocks uptown to a theatre that housed a play that Claudia had seen the previous season. Or was it two seasons ago? It was. The realization jolted her. Being an actress was like being a wife, you had to stay with what you were doing, for better or for worse, in sickness and in health, until the play died. "Wouldn't it be awful," she thought in fleeting panic, "if I couldn't go back to David and the children for a whole year–"

It was the last time she thought of David and the children all that day. From the moment she and Jerry entered the dark, empty theatre–empty except for a cleaning woman shuttling up and down the rows of vacant seats like a restless ghost–the outside world ceased to exist. Her eyes focused on the stage, lit only by a single brutal light suspended from the curtain, and bare, except for two wooden tables and some kitchen chairs. A half dozen people knotted loosely about. The men wore no coats, and one of the women had her hair rolled up in curlers. They didn't look like actors, but they were. The woman who had her hair rolled in curlers turned out to be Annabel Page, the star of the play. "Hello, lovey!" she called out to Claudia, "Come on up and join us. I hear you don't know from nothing, ain't we got fun, let's start! . . . Hi, Jim, are you directing this dramatic gem or not!"

The man with the granite nose emerged from the wings. He lifted Claudia over the footlights onto the stage. "Remember me? You met me in Sam's office last week."

Claudia said she remembered. He gave her a little book like the ones the others carried.

"Here's your part, honey, you come in from the terrace–" He pointed to a chalk mark on the floor. "This is the terrace," he elucidated, "and you drop your bundles–you have bundles, you've been shopping–and you ring the bell for the maid–the bell's over here, next to the piano, and the piano is this chair, and then you take off your hat and throw it on the sofa and say, 'Oh, what a mess–' have you found it yet?"

Claudia opened the book. He leaned over and riffled the pages. "You're looking at the first act," he said. "We're doing the second act now, we finished the first act yesterday."

"Cornelia's practically been cut out of the first act, anyway," a large and gloomy young man injected. "We both are. We had a swell scene together, the best thing in the whole lousy play but they took it out." He stared at the heavy white gloves that covered his monstrous hands. "I have hives," he volunteered unhappily. "If I don't wear gloves, I scratch."

Miss Page looked up from filing her nails. "Have a heart, Clifton, isn't it enough we've got a stinker for a script, do we have to put with daily bulletins on your hives?"

Claudia wondered if Jerry was still sitting in one of the back rows of the darkened theatre. If he was, he could not help but hear them. She suffered for him. "How can he put up with one thing after another," she thought.

The answer came to her as she stood on the chalk mark, which was the terrace, and read her first speech. In spite of the confusion that thickened her brain and the fear that froze her blood, she felt her heart quicken and lift. This was theatre.

It was after midnight when she let herself in with the latchkey that Julia had given her that morning. The servants were in bed, and Julia and Hartley were out, for which she was profoundly thankful. She was too tired to talk.

The door of her room stood open, and to her astonishment there was David, sound asleep on the chaise longue, with a book across his stomach. She was only half glad to see him. She tiptoed across to the dressing room, but he heard her and opened his eyes.

"A fine time to come home," he said.

"What on earth are you doing here!"

"Who has a better right," he said, "and what kind of a welcome is that?"

She pulled her hat off and sank to the edge of the bed, kicking off her pumps. "When did you get in?"

"This afternoon, about three." He rose and came toward her. "Thanks for the kiss."

She lifted her lips contritely. "Three. And you've been waiting around ever since, that's pathetic. Why didn't you meet me at the theatre?"

"I did," he said. "I sat watching for an hour or two, but it was dark, you couldn't see me. Then I got a haircut, and when I went back to call for you everyone had cleared out."

"We had to move around five, because of the evening performance. We went to some hall down the block to rehearse."

"Where'd you have supper?"

"The stage manager brought me in sandwiches and coffee from the drugstore. I had a lot to catch up on, I'm five days late. I don't even know what the play's about—I only just found out that I'm a flashback."

"What's that?" said David.

"I happen twenty years ago," Claudia wearily explained. "How are the children? Did Bertha get there all right, what did Bobby say, did Matthew remember her, I wish I'd known you were coming, I'd have told you to bring some clothes for me. I haven't a rag."

"Bertha packed a suitcase," said David. "Bridget or Lily or whatever her name is, hung everything up in the closet."

"Her name's Lucy. She'll grow on you."

"Not on me she won't." He eyed the satin trappings of the other twin bed. "And that's a hell of a dressy place to sleep."

"I know," said Claudia, unhappily. "It requires quite a lot of discipline.–You haven't kissed me yet–"

"Never mind kissing," said David. "Get undressed and go to sleep."

"Thanks," said Claudia. "Sometimes it's wonderful not to kiss." She slipped out of her skirt and kicked off her shoes. "Do you think God will mind if I don't brush my teeth? You look different, it must be the haircut. And you have a funny color for New York, nobody here is sunburned. It'll serve me right if Annabel Page falls in love with you, or vice versa."

"If she's the one in curlers," said David, "you need have no worry."

"That's good," said Claudia drowsily. Her lids carried heavy weights that kept pressing down over her eyes. There were a lot of questions she ought to ask him, and she ought to keep telling him how glad she was that he had come– "How are the children–" she murmured politely. She was asleep before he answered.

The next thing she knew, Lucy was at her side with breakfast. Claudia struggled up through layers of delicious slumber, only to find conflict staring her in the face again. "I ought to get up and brush my teeth before I eat–"

"Most ladies don't bother," said Lucy.

"I always have," said Claudia. She sank back on her pillows. "All right, I'll be a lady for once."

"Shall I leave Mr. Naughton's tray on the table for him?"

Claudia sat up, fully awake. She had forgotten about Mr. Naughton. The other bed was empty, its elegant quilt rolled into a ball, and the pillows punched for comfort.

"I hear the shower," said Lucy, modestly averting her gaze from the tumbled covers. "He must be in the shower."

"He must be," Claudia agreed.

"I'd better get out," said Lucy nervously, and whisked away just in time to save her soul, for David appeared a moment later, clothed only in a bath towel. His hair was damp, and his shoulders looked handsome. "I bet you never had hives," said Claudia, "and never will. That's French for 'I love you'."

"I'm going home this morning,' he returned. "And that's also French for 'I love you'."

She could only look at him in mute acknowledgment. "I'll be a human being again after I've learned my lines," she said.

"I won't even phone you," he went on, "unless something important turns up, but you phone me whenever you can get to it."

"I will. And can't you come Sunday again? I don't think we'll rehearse on Sunday."

"That's what I planned." He sat down to his breakfast.

"Isn't it the image of a hotel, with the newspaper and the cracked ice?" Claudia said.

"The image," said David.

"What's the war news?" she asked, trying to remember the mechanics of her second act exit.

"Very good," said David.

"That's good," said Claudia. She squeezed her eyes shut. "Please don't go to the trouble of coming with me," she mumbled—"Cross right, drop handkerchief, wait for him to pick it up—push him away—and say *'Don't!'* "—

"Don't what?" inquired David mildly.

"I haven't found out yet. This is the spot I can't make much sense of . . . What's the matter?" she broke off, as his left eyebrow began to act up.

Silently, he folded the paper into a neat oblong, and gave it to her. There was Sam Goldheart's name, as usual, at the top of the theatrical column. " *'Sam Goldheart',*" she read aloud, " *'Robs Social Register.'* . . . What does that mean?"

"Read on," said David, "you'll see."

She read on, with her jaw gaping:

" 'Claudia Brown, who divides her time between her town house in the Seventies, and her Connecticut farm, has joined the cast of *Sad Ecstasy*. In private life, Miss Brown is the wife of David Naughton, the well-known architect. Mr. Naughton, veteran hero of the Solomons, is regaining his health in the pursuit of his favorite hobby—the building up of his pedigreed herd of Guernsey cattle. Chalk another one up to Mr. Goldheart's indomitable zest for discoveries. He first saw Miss Brown four years ago when she was appearing, for the "lark of it," in a summer try out near the Naughton estate.' "

Claudia looked up with foreboding and dismay. "What a terrible lie. Julia will be furious." She expected David to be furious too, but he only shrugged. "Not really a lie," he said, "just theatre."

She wanted to tell him that he was a very superior person for a variety of reasons, but the reasons were all too subtle to put in words. "You certainly look marvelous in that towel," she said instead. "What time is it?"

"I'm catching the eleven o'clock train back," he said. He glanced at his watch. "It's nine-fifteen."

"And I don't have to be at rehearsal until half-past ten," said Claudia. "We've ages."

The day flew and she felt wonderful. Everyone else in the cast grew fagged and irritable, but she didn't. Her lines came to her without effort, because the things she had to say she might have said to David. Jim said she gave like an angel.

The rehearsal broke at seven, which meant that she got home in time to have dinner with Julia and Hartley. Julia had seen the article in the morning paper, and to Claudia's relief the blatant confusion of the two Mrs. Naughtons merely amused her. "You're more than welcome to all that I am and all that I have," she said, with one of her infrequent flashes of humor. "And to top it off, half of Back Bay will turn out for the Boston opening." As Julia was born in Back Bay, and her family still lived there, Claudia knew that this was no idle threat.

"We'll give a party after the performance," Julia continued. "What have you to wear?"

"My pink," said Claudia.

"That's three years old."

"Five," said Claudia, "but it doesn't look it, I've hardly ever worn it."

"Hartley and I are going to make you a present of a new one," said Julia firmly.

"Don't be silly. I wouldn't hear of it. Thanks just the same."

"If you're too proud, buy it yourself, it'll be an excellent investment of your first week's salary."

"I never have any use for an evening dress. It would just get to be five years old like my pink. Anyway, I have my first week's salary spent."

"On what?" asked Hartley, who, being rich, was always interested in people saving money.

"Bertha's wages, and a pony for the children."

"What does David say?" Hartley inquired.

"To what, the pony?"

"No. Bertha's wages."

Claudia knew what he meant. "David isn't at all like that," she said.

"All men are like that," said Julia shortly.

Claudia helped herself thoughtfully to the impeccable but unexciting dessert of sliced fruit. There was much that lay unsaid beneath Hartley's question and Julia's brief rejoinder. She remembered that Julia had inherited her father's fortune long before Hartley became a successful banker, and she wondered what seed of antagonism had taken root in those early years of their marriage. They seemed happy enough on the surface, yet they were scarcely more than affectionate strangers who met occasionally at the dinner table, and never at breakfast. "That mustn't happen to David and me," thought Claudia in sudden panic. She couldn't wait until she ran up to her room to telephone him.

He was expecting her call. They talked for a shamelessly long while, about everything and nothing. He assured her no less than six times that the children were fine, Bertha was fine and in her element, fattening everybody up. And Candy's Easter vacation was over, she'd just stopped in to say good-bye before going back to college. "Oh," said Claudia, "Let me talk to her."

"It's easy to see," said David, "that you're not paying for this call."

"Julia should be grateful," Claudia replied, "that it's evening rates."

She talked to Candy, and was again reassured that everything was fine. Candy was full of young superlatives and enthusiasms. It was thrilling beyond words about Aunt Claudia going on the stage, and Uncle David was as proud as a peacock about it, and Bobby and Matthew were perfect lambs.

Claudia had always been fond of Candy. Now she felt an added glow of affection—the child was so unspoiled, so sweetly a part of the household. "Candy's a nice youngster," she mentioned appreciatively when David took the telephone again.

"Very," he agreed.

"Elizabeth'll be alone after she goes back to college, and you're alone, so you ought to go over there for dinner," Claudia suggested, feeling very generous . . . "When are you coming down again?"

"Over the weekend."

"That's an awfully long way away," said Claudia.

She was happy for the pain of missing him. It was a living, beautiful pain that Hartley and Julia no longer felt for each other. It must have stayed with her all night, for when she opened her eyes in the morning, it was to the instant thought of him. She blinked at her watch. Seven o'clock. She wished she could break herself of this bucolic habit of waking up so early. Theatre people slept until noon, most of them.

She reached for the telephone. It rang for quite a while before David answered. "You sound wet," she said. "Were you taking a bath?"

He said he was, and while he dried off, she spoke to Matthew, who was hopping up and down so hard she could scarcely hear him. "Hello, hello!" he shouted. "Bertha lives here now!"

"You don't say," said Claudia. "Why doesn't someone tell me these things?"

She heard a scuffle as Bobby took possession of the instrument. "Mother? When are you coming home!" he demanded.

"If we don't rehearse on Sunday, I'll come home instead of Daddy coming down," she decided on an inspiration.

It was something to hope for, something to look forward to. She could have hugged Annabel, who got temperamental the next day and said she wasn't a horse, she needed one day of rest, anyway. Jim said something that sounded almost like "horse" under his breath, and then quickly made peace. "Okay," he said, "we'll skip Sunday, if that's what you call resting."

Claudia telephoned David at once. "I'll be home Saturday night and catch the first train back on Monday morning. What do you think?"

"I think," said David, with his most attractive understatement.

"But don't tell Shakespeare or Bluster that I'm coming, I want to see if they remember me."

"They're probably listening," he said.

She packed her bag on Saturday morning and took it with her to the theatre to save time. She was the first to arrive, except for the stage manager. His name was Kenneth. He was a source of confusion to her, for she could never quite decide whether he was a very young man grown old, or a quite old man who had stayed young. He had a tremulous voice, and many gestures, and called everyone "Lover." This morning he greeted her in a soft frenzy of excitement: everything was simply gruesome! The name of the play had been changed to *Happy Trouble* instead of *Sad Ecstasy*. Jerry had suddenly collapsed with a terrific pain in the stomach and was in bed with the doctor; and Mr. Goldheart was writing a new third act.

"Rehearsals," Kenneth went on in a breathless flurry, "are called off until eight o'clock this evening, so we'll work straight through the night and most of tomorrow. Annabel's wild because she's losing her Sunday, but it can't be helped."

"Oh, dear, I'm wild too," said Claudia, "it means I can't go home." She called David from the pay station in the deserted mezzanine of the theatre. There was no doubt in her mind that he'd come down as they had originally planned, which would at least give them most of today together anyway.

He said, however, that there'd be no sense in his making the trip if she had to rehearse all night. "Besides," he added, "you'd better get as much rest as you can this afternoon. Call me tomorrow if you get the chance."

"Are you in a hurry?" she asked, over the letdown feeling that shot through her.

"No," he said. "Why?"

"No reason. You just seem a little rushed. And your voice sounds funny."

"Nonsense," he said.

She had a sense that she was literally holding on to his coattails to keep him at the telephone. "Will the children be disappointed at my not coming? I mean Bobby, Matthew doesn't know I'm alive."

"I'll explain to them why you couldn't get here," said David. "Good-bye darling—"

He had hung up. She stood staring at the receiver before she put it back on the hook. Something was wrong, it wasn't like David to be so abrupt. It couldn't be that he was angry at her for not coming home, he was too reasonable to be petty. Perhaps he was getting another attack of malaria, and didn't want to tell her. She felt an overwhelming urge to catch the noon train to Eastbrook and look in on her world, if only for an hour. She wouldn't be able to keep her mind on rehearsal, anyway, unless she knew that David and the children were all right.

There wasn't a minute to lose. Fortunately an empty taxicab was passing the theatre as she emerged to the street. She hailed it, and climbed in. "Grand Central Station as fast as you can!"

The cab driver reached behind him to close the door securely. "Take your time, lady," he adjured her with enormous composure. "Take your time."

"Please!" she entreated. "Hurry!"

She liked taxi drivers as a rule, but she knew she wasn't going to like this one. He no sooner got up to a green light than it turned red. Not only that, but he waited until it was good and green again. The last few blocks were a torment, and finally when it came to paying him, she had nothing less than a five-dollar bill, and he had no more than three dollars in change. "Hey Charlie!" he called out to a parked taxi. "Can you break a five?" Charlie could, and did. It was, however, a lengthy transaction involving much pocket-delving and scrutinizing of dimes and pennies. "Take your time, lady, take your time," he again advised her.

"I haven't any time to *take!*" Claudia upbraided him bitterly. "You took it all."

The clock above the information desk told her that she had missed the train by a bare few seconds. She felt that God had played her a dirty trick until she discovered that the express to Eastbrook was late in starting. In a flood of renewed faith and affection, she decided that He was an angel. In fact, He hadn't even let the gates be opened. A great crowd of people milled outside the iron rail, waiting for the moment when they could make a dash for seats.

The crowd kept growing, masses of soldiers, and a large sprinkling of civilians, lured by the first warm weekend of early Spring. Claudia kept her eyes glued to the clock, nervously calculating and recalculating her precious allotment of hours. God was either gilding the lily, or was off on another job. If He didn't hurry up and open those gates, there'd be no sense in going. It was already half-past twelve. Even if she made perfect connections—which she wasn't apt to—it was next to impossible to have any kind of a decent visit at the farm, and be back for a six o'clock rehearsal. David would think she was crazy for attempting it. Maybe she was. Maybe she just imagined that his voice sounded funny.

Finally the gates opened up, and the passengers pushed forward in a solid mass. Claudia was not a pusher: she clung for an instant at the entrance, like a swimmer clutching at a rope in a buffeting surf. "The train's going to start right away, isn't it?" she challenged the ticket collector.

He refused to be pinned down. There was a war on, he reminded her, and troop movements caused delays. "Ticket, please, lady. You're holding up the line—"

"I'm not going," Claudia decided, and disentangled herself from the crowd. God had evidently played along with her to a certain point, and then put it up to her own judgment. "Thanks," she acknowledged disconsolately.

Looking at it from this end, it seemed an eternity to six o'clock. It would be a help if she were the sort of person who could take a nap after lunch, but she never could, except occasionally on Sundays, with David, which wasn't really a matter of napping so much.

She wandered aimlessly toward Fifth Avenue. A city was a lonely place, if you had only a career to keep you busy. She thought of all the women who lived alone, and went to movies alone, and ate alone, and felt sorry for them. When work stopped, it stopped with a bang and left you high and dry. There was nothing like a husband and children to use up spare time.

She ended by riding on top of a bus to Julia's. Above Fifty-ninth Street the traffic tangle cleared into the wide avenue flanking the park, and before she knew it, she had passed her corner. She pulled the bell, and scrambled down the treacherous swirl of steps. The bus stopped when it was ready to, four blocks farther on. "Didn't you hear me signal?" she asked the conductor in seething indignation. He didn't bother to answer her. She stepped to the sidewalk, with no grace, since the step was higher than she expected. A searing pain tore at her ankle. She was sure it couldn't be less than a broken bone, which would take care of everything. She'd go back to the farm and stay there with her foot in a cast.

She hobbled over to clutch the iron railing of a palatial residence. Spitefully, the pain subsided and disappeared. "Damn," she said.

Julia was in Washington, but Hartley was at home with his gall bladder. Claudia found him huddled in the library, waiting for his medicine to work. "I knew it would kick up," he said, "the minute I took cream last night."

It was more likely that the stock market had taken a downward swoop, or that Julia had given him an inferiority complex by running the war, but Claudia gave him the benefit of the doubt, though she didn't see how there could be enough cream in New York cream to bother him. "Is there anything I can do for you?" she offered, glad to have something to fill the empty afternoon.

"Not a thing," said Hartley. "I think I'm better." He straightened himself experimentally. "No, I'm not," she said.

"How about a hot-water bag?" Claudia suggested hopefully.

Hartley studied his watch. "I'll give it another five minutes," he said. "How's the play coming along?"

"Awful," said Claudia.

"That's fine," said Hartley vaguely.

Conversation lagged into an awkward silence. It was not easy to talk to a brother-in-law; in fact, Hartley, being so much older than David, was almost as bad as a father-in-law. She was glad when the medicine ultimately began to take effect, and he went off to play golf, he said. She decided to wash her hair, which would go a long way toward doing her nails. With good management, the afternoon would be practically used up.

Four

When she got to rehearsal, Jim greeted her with the news that she was no longer a flashback, she happened fifty years later. "Aren't you pleased?" he demanded.

"Very," said Claudia, "but how am I going to learn a completely new part one week before we open in Boston?"

"Be glad it isn't one day before we open in New York," said Jim. "That happens, too." He put his arm around her. "Don't worry about it. I'll help you."

He helped her all through the night. It was five o'clock in the morning when he dropped her off at Julia's on his way home. He tried to kiss her. She said, "Please don't do that."

He scowled at her, "Why not? A hell of a lot of women are in love with me. A hell of a lot of women think I'm a right swell guy."

"I think you're a good director," said Claudia.

"Meaning that all you want from me is direction and damn little of that." He looked tired and gaunt and quite interesting in the eerie light of a city dawn. She could imagine a woman falling in love with him. "Good night," she said quickly. "Thanks for letting me share your taxi uptown."

Jim stood where he was, with his arm on the stone pilaster

of the shallow stoop. He did not speak until she had fitted the key into the latch. "If it's of any interest to you," he said, "I live downtown on Washington Square."

He seemed to be saying more than just the words. He had a strange look on his face that made her feel tongue-tied and a little fluttery. "I'm sorry I took you out of your way," she apologized. He didn't answer. He just stood there, staring up at her with that odd grin on his thin lips. She hesitated, and then decided that there wasn't anything to do but close the door.

She tiptoed upstairs, past Julia's room directly below her own. "Come in a minute," Julia called.

"Hello, I thought you were in Washington," Claudia exclaimed.

"I came home," said Julia.

"How's Hartley?"

"All right, I suppose. . . . Why shouldn't he be?"

"He had his gall bladder again this afternoon."

Julia received the news without perturbation. "He's been eating butter."

"Cream," said Claudia, marvelling at Julia's composure. Even in bed, Julia was composed and tailored, with her dark hair as smooth as if no human hand had touched it. She wasn't the sort that tousled easily, and certainly Hartley wasn't the sort to tousle. Claudia could hear him sleeping busily from the adjoining room.

"You ought to be asleep, too, at this hour," she said to Julia.

"I couldn't seem to settle down," said Julia.

Claudia found it a little shocking that Hartley should be oblivious of her wakefulness. David was so different as a husband.

"I was worried," Julia continued, "when you didn't come

home. . . . After all," she excused herself quickly, as if she were ashamed of the emotion, "David left you in my charge."

Claudia assumed an air of nonchalance. "He didn't happen to phone, did he?"

There was the slightest hestiation in Julia's reply. "Not that I know of," she said. "Who brought you home just now?"

"The director. Jim Varney."

"He's very attractive," said Julia. "I met him at a dinner party a few weeks ago. He's got quite a reputation."

"You mean for directing?"

"No," said Julia. "Though probably he's very good at that too."

"He's so homely," said Claudia, "that I'd never thought of him as being attractive."

"That's good," said Julia. "Better go up and get some rest."

The room was full of thin sun by the time she climbed into bed. She wondered how night nurses could settle themselves to sleep throughout the day. She tossed and turned, unable to release herself from strain and apprehension. At seven o'clock, she lifted the receiver and called David. She knew he'd be up—chores on a farm had no respect for Sundays. He might change his mind and run down to see her for a little while.

He was flat in his refusal. "I can't see the sense of it," he said.

"There's a lot of sense in it. We're not rehearsing until three this afternoon, we can have all that time together."

"I wouldn't get there until almost three," he pointed out.

She swallowed her pride. "Why not? There's a new Sunday train at nine o'clock this morning, and you're shaved and everything."

He said, "We've got a hatch of baby chicks to get into the brooder. It'll take until noon, at least."

"I see." Tears of fatigue and hurt thickened her voice. "If you don't want to come, all right."

He didn't seem to notice that she was close to crying, and she'd been fool enough to criticize Hartley for sleeping while Julia was awake. "Don't be unreasonable, darling," he chided her, "of course I'd like to see you–"

"That's nice of you," she broke in caustically. "Are the children there? I'd like to talk to them."

"Bobby's still asleep."

"I forgot, no school–Matthew's up though, isn't he?"

"Matthew?" He seemed to hesitate, as if he were looking around for Matthew, and then he said, "The little monkey was here a minute ago, he must have gone downstairs."

She had an immediate vision of the little monkey, immersed in his own universe, not at all concerned as Bobby was, with the world of elders. Matthew was at a wonderful age, an independent, unaware age, full of sensation without significance. Matthew wouldn't care if she never came home, and neither, she concluded with a rush of self-pity, would David. He had apparently forgotten that she hadn't wanted to accept the part of Cornelia, that he had literally pushed her into it. "Look," she felt like shouting at him, "I can't help it if I had to rehearse all night, I'm not running the theatre business!" However, she controlled herself and said, as civilly as she could, "You seem to be getting along very nicely without me."

"We're fine," he replied obliquely. "Just don't worry about us." At the last moment, he must have had the belated decency to realize that she felt alone and lonely, for he added, "I'll try to get down Tuesday afternoon."

It was on the tip of her tongue to come back with "Why not tomorrow?," but she restrained the impulse. There were limits of eagerness which even a wife ought not transgress. "Tuesday will be fine," she said instead.

Still, she couldn't overcome the feeling that something was wrong. David seemed different; she couldn't pin it down to any one thing, it was just that there was no longer an openness between them. It could be, of course, that he was deliberately assuming a protective armor against this new regime that had invaded their old way of life, and yet she had never known him to function deviously. He was too direct, too healthy in his antagonisms. If he didn't want her to act, he'd come out and say so. Or would he? Male pride was something special and apart. You didn't know how much of it you had until it hit you. Theoretically, David might not resent her turning wage earner, but actually, it could be doing strange things to him . . . Her mind turned a somersault. Malaria did strange things to him, too. He could feel an attack coming on for days ahead, and it always made him irritable and evasive when he found he could not ward it off. She had learned to leave him alone when he was like that.

She pulled the covers over her head, and tried to make herself believe it was nighttime. She closed her eyes, but the children and David were etched against the darkness behind her lids. She felt an hysterical despair, she was so close to them, and so far away. Her hand reached again to the telephone. What excuse could she give for calling up once more? Whatever it was David would most likely see through it. He would tell her that she was mentally undisciplined, always letting her imagination run riot. Very well, then, she acknowledged defiantly, she was a worrier, it was one of her besetting sins, and now was no time to overcome it. She certainly couldn't concentrate on learning lines, if she was upset about David having chills and fever. The thing to do was to call Nancy Riddle, and find out whether he had been over as usual, for much as he disliked the job, he rarely let a day pass without stopping in to check the workmen.

Nancy answered the telephone from the barn. The cows

were mooing so hard she couldn't hear. "Who?" she shouted. "Talk louder!"

"I am!" Claudia shouted back.

"Who?" Nancy screamed above the racket of the cows. "You have to speak up!"

"I am!" Claudia cried hoarsely. "This is Claudia Naughton! I want to know if David's been there, and how he is!"

"How who is? I can't hear you!"

Claudia was sorry she had begun the thing. She was more than willing to let it drop. Besides, Nancy was the last person in the world to tell her how David was, she didn't have very much sense about the human equation. Her own husband had committed suicide under her very eyes, so it wasn't likely that she would be a good judge of the physical or moral status of anyone else's husband. "I wish," thought Claudia impatiently, as she tried to make herself heard, "that she'd shut off those cows."

On the whole, it was a most unsatisfactory conversation, in which she learned nothing except that Nancy had just returned from a cattle sale in Maryland, and intended to go into Aberdeen Angus as soon as she could get some sheds built. Also, that her most valuable Jersey was running a high fever, and wasn't milking. "How's the theatre coming?" Nancy remembered to inquire before she rang off.

"Fine," said Claudia. "Good-bye."

She hung up with a sense of frustration. Could it be, she reflected with a delayed impact, that Nancy was hiding behind her cows, so to speak, and knew more than she was letting on? Once the idea took root she couldn't dismiss it. She lifted the receiver to call Elizabeth Van Doren. She'd ask Elizabeth to run over to the farm and see that everything was as it should be. Elizabeth could take one look at David and know whether it was malaria working in him, or an attack of pride. She was the same sort of person as Claudia, when it came to family.

Elizabeth's maid answered. "Mrs. Van Doren is not at home, who is calling, please?"

Claudia was reluctant to leave her name . . . "When will Mrs. Van Doren be back?"

"She didn't say," the maid replied. "But I have the number where you can reach her, if it's important. It's 164 Ring 4."

"Thank you," said Claudia.

She put the receiver carefully back on its hook. There was no reason why Elizabeth should not be over at the farm. Bertha, who loved to show off her cooking, had probably asked her for Sunday dinner. But why hadn't David mentioned it? It would have been the easiest thing in the world for him to say, "Elizabeth's coming over," instead of putting the blame on a batch of baby chicks. At any rate, one thing was definite and final, she could find no excuse for calling him again. It was the sort of thing one didn't do. She picked up *Happy Trouble* from the floor beside her, and began to study her new lines.

Two days passed in a blur of frantic script changes and endless quarrels and discussions. Jerry haunted the theatre, looking every inch the distracted author. He carried a bottle of paregoric in one hand and held on to his agent with the other. The agent was a dark, short man with bulging eyes, who always seemed about to put his foot down, without doing it. Nobody paid any attention to him.

On Monday night, Annabel Page burst into hysterics and handed in her part, but she had a run-of-the-play contract, so nobody paid any attention to her either. On Tuesday morning, Mr. Goldheart put in an appearance. He wore his hat on the back of his head and handed out sticks of gum, and seemed very pleased with the new title and all of the new funny lines, which turned out to be his. Then he disappeared, but returned at lunch time. Everyone had gone out to eat except Claudia. She was running through a scene with Clifton, whose hives had jumped to his face and spoiled his appetite.

She didn't know Mr. Goldheart had come back until he boomed "Louder, louder, louder!" from the darkness of the orchestra. Then he was clambering up on the stage, yelling "No, no, no, begin over again, put some expression in it!"

"I thought I was putting in too much," said Claudia.

"You're not putting enough, register a lot of surprise when Clifton tells you he met Maggie, give me a nice double-take on it."

"I don't know what a double-take is," said Claudia.

"Jees," Mr. Goldheart whispered in anguish, "and she says she's an actress—"

He showed her. She once had a chiropractor sneak up behind her and twist her neck. Mr. Goldheart gave the same effect, without benefit of the chiropractor. She watched him again and again, trying to achieve the combination of jerk and stare which, properly timed, produced a "double-take." She found herself hopelessly inept. He gave up at last and strode off, muttering something about a bellyful of incompetents, and what was the theatre coming to, shovelling out two hundred dollars to an amateur who had never had her feet in sawdust.

"Pay no attention to the old man," Clifton advised her. "Double-takes went out with vaudeville. Anyway he always sneaks in at the last minute, and mucks up a show by trying to direct it."

So this was what Jerry had feared might happen. She remembered how he had threatened to knock Mr. Goldheart's block off if he tried to teach her any of his tricks. She also remembered how Mr. Goldheart had said to him, with a discomfiting smile, "She's all yours, my boy," but only now did she receive the full impact of the innuendo.

"Mr. Goldheart never really wanted me for the part," she confessed to Clifton, and to her great chagrin and with no warning whatsoever, she burst into tears.

When Jim returned from his sandwich and coffee at the corner drugstore, he knew immediately what had happened. His lips got even thinner than they normally were, and an ivory color came around his nostrils. "If I ever see you give a double-take," he told her furiously, "I'll throw you out on your ear." Then he kissed her like a brother and told her to go out and have some lunch.

For once in her life, she couldn't eat. She sat out in the theatre, blanketing her shame and her tears in the beneficent darkness. In a little while, Jerry stole in with his agent and sat down a few rows away. He kept moaning, "Oh God," as if in pain. She wondered whether it was his stomach that was upsetting him, or the big scene that Mr. Goldheart had written for Annabel and her lover.

Clifton's shadowy form beckoned her from the aisle. "Your husband's on the telephone," he said.

"One of the children—" Claudia thought in panic.

David's voice reassured her at once—nothing was wrong, he was sorry to disturb her during a rehearsal, but was she expecting him down? The question caught her unaware, for it had completely slipped her mind that this was Tuesday, the day he had planned to come in. She could not bring herself to say, "Oh David, this has turned into such a madhouse. I forgot all about you," so she said, "Of course, darling," miserably conscious of the fact that she was not telling him the truth. Relief flooded her when he told her, a little hesitantly, that it was going to be hard for him to get away, because he had to give Edward a hand with some fencing.

"It's just as well," she admitted with honesty, "because I'll have to rehearse until all hours, my part's been changed. Did I tell you I'm not a flash back any longer?"

"Oh really?" said David, only tepidly interested.

Anxiety nagged at her anew. "Are you sure you're all right?"

"Certainly I'm all right."

"I mean, no malaria?"

"No malaria."

"And Bobby's at school?"

"If that's your way of trying to find out if he's sick, yes he's at school," he taunted her. "I'll call you tomorrow. Good-bye."

He rang off, before she could ask about Matthew. "You needn't be in such a hurry to get rid of me," she said coldly to empty air. Fortunately, Matthew wasn't too much of a problem, except that he was subject to colds, but she knew that Bertha bent backwards when it came to rubbers and sweaters.

"Why didn't David come?" Julia asked her that night, with her eyes tactfully averted.

"Spring is a hard time to get away on a farm. If it isn't ploughing it's chickens, if it isn't chickens it's fencing or something else."

Julia was so quick to agree, that it was obvious that she knew how Claudia felt about David's lack of interest. She went out of her way to be nice. "I'm staying home this evening, would you like me to cue you in your lines?" she offered. Claudia shook her head, afraid to trust her voice. Julia bent to kiss her. "Cheer up," she said softly. "Try to get a good night's sleep. You need it."

Probably Julia was right—a good night's sleep might change her jaundiced view on life in general, and husbands in particular. It wasn't so simple as it sounded, though. She lay awake until long past midnight, hoping against hope that

David would telephone again. In the morning, she put off leaving for rehearsal until the last minute, and still he didn't telephone. She swallowed her pride and called him. Bertha answered. "I find Mr. David," she said breathlessly, and rushed away before Claudia had a chance to get her report on the children.

When David came to the telephone, Claudia said, "Bertha's never gotten over thinking the telephone's going to bite her, especially if it's long distance."

Goodness knew it was a generous opening, it gave him all the chance in the world to start off on their old footing, but his reply was as stilted and forced as a stranger. Moreover, he made no pretense of getting to town. "You've got less than a week of rehearsal left," he reasoned. "I might as well save the trip, and join you on the train to Boston. They all stop at Eastbrook. Ask Hartley's secretary to write for accommodations at whatever hotel you want."

She couldn't believe he had the nerve to mean it, but he did. "Very well, if that's the way you want it," she agreed in a dead voice.

"It isn't necessarily the way I want it," he returned, "I'm being sensible."

It was a fine time to pick for being sensible, she reflected bitterly.

She half expected it when he telephoned an hour before she was ready to leave for Boston to say that he wouldn't be able to meet her on the train. He must have felt guilty about it himself, for he smoothed her over by promising to be at the theatre without fail, in time for the opening.

She was past the point of hiding her feelings. "Don't inconvenience yourself," she advised him caustically, with her heart astonished and smarting.

Since she hadn't seen the children for almost three weeks,

she was sure that he'd at least have the decency to bring them down to the station to say hello to her when the train pulled into Eastbrook for its two minute stop. She couldn't wait to dash out to the platform.

There wasn't a sign of them. She scanned the road, praying for the familiar station wagon to turn into the depot square.

"Isn't this where you have your farm?" Jim asked at her elbow.

"Yes," said Claudia.

"Homesick?"

"Pretty."

"Isn't your husband getting on?"

"No. He'll be up this evening."

The train gave a lurch. She turned back into the car. "I see in the Boston paper," Jim went on, "that some Back Bay big shot is throwing a party for you after the performance tonight."

"It's my sister-in-law's aunt," Claudia enlightened him without delight. "Which reminds me, I forgot to tell you that you're invited."

"I never go to parties," said Jim, "but maybe I'll make an exception this once."

Annabel passed them on the way to the diner for her noon breakfast. She had a drawing room to herself and wore dark glasses. "I haven't seen your wife, Jim," she said sweetly. "Didn't she come along?"

"You know damn well she didn't."

"I had no idea you were married," Claudia remarked in surprise. "You don't look married."

"I don't feel married," said Jim.

"Neither do I," said Claudia, with a sigh.

"In that case," said Jim, "let's have some lunch."

She was suffering deeply, but she said, "All right." Eating on a train still carried its irresistible lure.

She had a passion for hotel rooms, too, possibly because she hardly ever had the chance to get away from home overnight. She thought how perfect it would be if only David were with her to share the adventure of walking into a strange place and sizing up the furniture and exploring which door opened to the closet and which to the bath. She had asked for only a double bedroom, but Julia had evidently gone over her head, for the porter ushered her into a sitting room with three windows facing the Commons. In spite of the pervading color of a vigorous but depressing blue, the room was gay with a great basket of roses, the topmost bloom of which bore a card from Julia's aunt, Mrs. J. Gordon Post. "Wishing you a great success tonight," wrote Julia's aunt.

Tonight. The word made her go suddenly sick with panic. She longed for the comforting assurance of David's arms. How could he have deserted her at a time like this? Tears of anger and chagrin blinded her as she stalked into the bedroom, opened her suitcase, and lifted out her old pink evening dress. Surprisingly, Julia had not pressed the issue of a new gown—Julia was no fool, she apparently had the good sense to realize that David would resent it.

She thrust the crumpled mass of chiffon on a hanger. A knock sounded on the sitting-room door. "Come in!" she rasped. The knob rattled and the knock sounded again. She charged back into the room, betting that it was one of those damn doors that locked from the inside. A chair had the audacity to stand in her way. Temper scorched through her as she kicked it out of her way, catching her shinbone a sharp crack. The best of the bad words she had learned from David and the theatre combined were still trembling on her lip when she flung open the door to a startled bellboy, who thrust a square box into her hand, and hot-footed it off without waiting for a tip.

She opened the box, and lifted out a corsage of orchids. She wasn't crazy about orchids, although there was nothing to compare to an orchid for sheer dressiness—they would do wonders for her old pink. She put them on the sill outside the window to keep fresh before she looked at the card. Doubtless another of Julia's punctilious relations had sent them or possibly Nancy Riddle.

To her amazement however, the card said, "Jim." She hadn't dreamed that Jim was the sort of person to send flowers, especially orchids. She was glad that he had, though. It was like a gentle hand laid on the ache in her heart, and yet the flowers from Julia's aunt hadn't touched that ache, in spite of roses being her favorite flower.

His handwriting was very much like himself—each letter as angular and decisive as his taut, thin body. She stood staring at the small sharp impact of his name and then suddenly tore the card in small pieces and threw them in the wastebasket. She must forget that she was lonely. A lonely wife was a dangerous thing to be.

She drew out the business of unpacking so as to have something to do. Jim had told the cast not to report for a run-through until half-past five, and it was barely three o'clock now. She didn't need a bath, but she took one anyway, and put on her nightgown, and flung herself on the bed. She must get into the habit of relaxing before a performance, it was something an actor had to learn. She couldn't have chosen a harder time to learn, though—if she didn't have someone to talk to, she'd jump out of her skin. Solitude was all right in its place, but this was too much of a good thing. She wished Julia were staying at the hotel instead of with her family; it would have even been company if Bobby had been old enough to come along.

She wondered what Bobby and Matthew were doing at this moment. It was windy and bleak. She hoped Bertha hadn't let Matthew go out to the barn to help Edward. It wasn't safe, anyway, because he'd gotten too big for his breeches the last few months, and had his eye on climbing the silo, not to mention running the tractor. Edward had started the tractor idea by letting Matthew ride on the seat beside him. She screamed . . . somehow Edward wasn't on the tractor now, Matthew was driving it alone. . . . Claudia ran to stop him but she was too late, the machine was heading toward a ledge, and Matthew's hands were tiny and ineffectual on the wheel—her limbs turned to lead . . . there was Matthew crashing to his death while she stood rooted to the ground, powerless to save him. . . . She screamed again but this time she couldn't raise her voice . . . the effort to do so caused a loud pounding in her ears . . . pound pound pound . . . she dragged her eyes open . . . the tractor was nothing but a walnut bureau with glass candle stick lamps. She must have dozed off in spite of herself. What a hideous dream. The calves of her legs were watery with the horror of it. Did she imagine it or was the pounding still going on? She lay for a moment, trying to free herself from the aftermath of nightmare before she realized that someone was knocking.

She got to her feet, fishing for her mules. As she started to open the door, she remembered that she was in her nightgown. "Who is it?" she called.

There was no answer. She opened the door cautiously on a crack, and looked out. She couldn't see a soul, but before she could gather her wits, the door pushed open and the figure of a man thrust itself in, and lifted her off the floor. It was another nightmare. She could feel her breath go, and again her strength was puny. She realized in a late flash what a fool she'd always been to have pooh-poohed using a chain on doors. This was the way things happened in the newspapers. "Put me down!" she gasped. "You're holding me so tight, I can't breathe—!"

"You're not supposed to breathe," said David.

"Tell me I'm crazy," she said, half an hour afterwards, as she rose from the stiff and uncooperative damask sofa.

"You're crazy," said David obediently.

She took a few distracted steps and wheeled to face him. "You mean I imagined everything?"

"Everything. You're as temperamental as a star."

"But you can't deny you never came down to New York after the first time," she argued.

"Complete unselfishness on my part. You were head over heels in rehearsal. I'd have been in your way, wouldn't I?"

"Somewhat," she conceded.

Nevertheless, she continued to eye him distrustfully. "So you don't mind my being an actress?"

"I always wanted to run around with an actress," he said.

"Suppose I want to pay Bertha's wages?"

"By all means. I was hoping you'd offer to."

"And suppose the play runs a whole year. Then what?"

"We'd have enough money to live in New York and use the farm for weekends," he replied glibly.

Her cheeks exploded in frustration. "It isn't normal for any one man to be so noble. And I still think there's something funny about the whole thing."

"For instance," he said blandly.

"For one thing, you look as if you haven't slept in a week."

"I haven't," he admitted.

She quickened in apprehension. "Malaria?"

He shook his head.

"Then why haven't you slept?"

"Why do you think?" His eyes did things. She was full of conflict as she thought of the opening only a few hours away. "I oughtn't to be happy," she demurred. "I should be nervous."

"Always be happy first, and nervous afterwards," said David.

He walked over to rehearsal with her toward five o'clock. It was too late in the afternoon for the sun to be out, but it felt like it. At last they came to the theatre. It gave her sweet goose-flesh to see her name on the billboards. True, it was at the bottom of a long list, and the letters weren't very large, but there it was: "Claudia Brown."

"May I have the pleasure of spending the night with you, Miss Brown?" David asked.

"I've always wanted to spend the night with a married man," said Claudia.

They lingered to watch a line of two people at the box-office buying tickets, but it turned out that one of them had come to give his ticket back. "What a nerve," Claudia muttered.

The stage door was hidden away, as stage doors have a way of hiding. Fortunately, Benny, the property man, happened to come along, and led them down an alley to the entrance. "They haven't finished putting up the set yet," he said.

His words were a masterpiece of understatement. They stood in the wings, amid a welter of equipment, and looked out on the stage. Nothing made any sense. There were some trees, and a fireplace and a window and a great many men running back and forth and a carpet being unrolled, and a lot of hammering and turning on and off of lights.

"More amber!" Jim kept yelling from somewhere in the back of the theatre.

"There's Mr. Goldheart," said David.

Mr. Goldheart was yelling louder than anyone else, with

his face too red for health. "You never met him, how did you know who he was?" Claudia demanded.

"It couldn't be anyone else," said David. "Who's the poor devil sitting on the piece of terrace biting his nails?"

"You know perfectly well it's Jerry Seymour," said Claudia. "And he doesn't bite his nails."

"He's next door to it," said David. "I swear I didn't recognize him. Didn't he use to be very dapper?"

"You wouldn't be dapper either if you'd had your title and everything else changed around the way he has."

They waited for half an hour. Nobody paid any attention to them. Finally Jim called the cast together and announced that the set wouldn't be ready for a rehearsal. "Everybody report on stage at eight o'clock in full make-up," he said.

"The set won't be ready then, either," Claudia moaned, as she and David walked back to the hotel. "I don't see how we're ever going to give a performance tonight."

"That's what makes fun and ulcers," said David.

They came to an intersection. He caught her hand to keep her from crossing against the light, and she noticed that his fingers were sticks of ice. He was as nervous as she was.

She felt pleasantly important to find two telegrams stuck in with the key at the desk. She opened them then and there. One was from Roger, all the way from California, and the other from Candy, all the way from college. "What's the matter with Nancy Riddle?" Claudia demanded. "As your client, she really could send me something at least."

"Nancy's up to her ears in mastitis," said David. "Damn near her whole herd's down with it. Which reminds me, Elizabeth's coming tonight, she'll be here on the eight o'clock train."

"Oh," said Claudia. She couldn't quite see why Nancy's cows should have reminded him of Elizabeth. It was far-fetched to say the least. Was it something in the back of his mind that he was trying to get around to? "It's a long trip for Elizabeth to take," she said slowly. "I didn't expect it."

"Elizabeth's a good friend," said David.

"She is," Claudia agreed, and added haltingly, "You saw a lot of her while I was away."

He gave her a quick look. "Not a lot, but some."

"Should I be jealous?"

"If you want to be."

"I don't want to be."

He kissed her. "That's good. It'd only make you feel foolish."

"That's what I reckon," said Claudia.

It was nothing short of a miracle that the curtain was a mere twenty minutes late in going up. It gave the cast a little extra time to get used to props and furniture. "This sofa's too low," Annabel fumed. "For God's sake."

Clifton strode the distance between the terrace and the desk. "It's too far," he announced tragically. "I'll finish my speech before I get there."

"See that you don't, you jackass," Jim advised him tersely. "And take off that mascara, what kind of a guy do you think you're playing?"

Claudia stood behind a chair which had previously existed only in her imagination, and began to mumble her lines. A few words came, and that was all—like the time the faucet sputtered in the kitchen, and there wasn't any more water because the well had gone dry. Now her brain had gone dry, except for panic. Rubber took the place of bone and sinew in her knees. She sank down on the arm of the chair and closed her eyes so that she wouldn't see the floor weave up and down.

From the other side of the curtain, a low rumble that sounded like hungry lions, seeped through the heavy velvet.

Clifton peeped into a hole. "It's a big house," he reported weightily. Claudia wanted to say that most of it was probably Julia's relatives, but her teeth were chattering so that she couldn't speak.

Mr. Goldheart appeared on the stage. He told Annabel she looked beautiful, not a day over forty, which was a compliment merely because he meant it to be a joke. He came up to Claudia and said, "Remember everything I taught you?" She wondered if she ought to tell him that she didn't even remember her lines, but he seemed to know it without her telling him, for he gave her one look and beckoned Jim. He said, without bothering to lower his voice, "Better get your understudy ready in case your wonderful discovery here falls on her face."

He could have chosen no crueller phrasing. Jim tried to head Claudia off as she rushed blindly to the wings. "Don't pay any attention to the old buzzard," he whispered, "you'll be all right. Go in your room and take a whiff of smelling salts."

She shared a dressing room with Gloria Van Tassel, who was playing the servant in the play. Gloria was adjusting her organdy cap. "Hello, sweetie," she said, regarding Claudia through the mirror. "You look like the butterflies were having a field day in your tummy."

"They are. Have you got any smelling salts?"

"No, but I can give you a slug of whiskey," Gloria offered.

Claudia shook her head, battling the tears that threatened her make-up. "Why you poor little fish," said Gloria.

"I never cried in my life until I got into theatre business," Claudia gulped.

Gloria gave her a pat. "Honey, when you've been in this racket as long as me, you won't even blink an eyelash on opening nights. And anyway, what have you personally got to lose, you're married to a rich playboy. But take me now, if this stinker folds up, I wish somebody'd tell me what I'm going to use for money with a sick mother and a couple of kid brothers. Golden-Hearted Sammy knows it, too, just the same as he knows I got five hundred when he had me in *Ladies First.* And what does he give me now? A measly eight-five. 'Remember, dear,' he says, 'it's only a maid's part, dear,' he says. 'Only a maid,' I says to him. 'Tell me what's harder to find than a maid these days–' " Gloria laughed loudly, and Claudia, out of politeness, forced a smile. She envied Gloria her robust spirit and nerves of iron. Gloria was the kind of actress a manager liked to have in a company. She had twenty years of theatre behind her; her feet, as Mr. Goldheart put it, were deep in sawdust.

There was a passing knock on the door. "Curtain!" Kenneth's flutey voice had taken on an organ tone. He passed on to the next door. "Curtain!"

"Well, honey," said Gloria. "This is it. Let's go."

They went out together to the wings. Claudia picked up some packages from the property table. Gloria swooped a dustcloth and ran on the stage. She got down on her hands and knees and began to dust the table which stood in back of the sofa. It was Mr. Goldheart's idea to have Bridget hidden by the furniture, so that when the curtain went up, the audience would think the stage was empty.

"Take the house to half–!" Kenneth intoned to the electrician.

"Take the house to half–" It was like the words of a song, stirring and exciting. Claudia could feel the theatre dim into a hushed silence as the curtain rolled up on a make-believe world. From where she stood, waiting for her entrance, she could see the audience massed in darkness, clapping their hands like children, because they liked the pretty room with its soft lights, and the glimpse of terrace beyond. They would probably laugh when they saw Bridget pop up from behind the sofa. Mr. Goldheart wanted them to laugh. Jerry wanted them to cry. That was where the difficulty lay. Jerry and Mr. Goldheart did not see eye to eye. It was suddenly very clear to Claudia that people who did not see eye to eye could not work together, and for that reason the play could not possibly succeed. Soon she would be back with David and the children. Her heart lifted. A sense of joy and relief suddenly flooded through her, releasing her from fear.

"Now—" Kenneth whispered, and gave her a little push.

"Hey Bridget!" she called exultantly.

She was on the stage before she realized that she shouldn't have said "Hey." It helped, though. It helped her to say "What in the name of heaven are you crawling around under the table for—!" Too late, she remembered that she had forgotten to do a double-take—the little trick of jerking her head that Mr. Goldheart had broken his neck to teach her. But the audience didn't seem to mind what she did or didn't do, they were very friendly. They made her feel at home. It was a pleasant room to be in, and Bridget was obligingly eager to help her open her packages—too eager, in fact, because she got hold of the one that didn't have anything in it, and Claudia had to slap her hand away, as she sometimes did when Bobby had his fingers in everything.

When Bridget realized she would have had to lift a china dog out of an empty box—(the dog was part of the plot)—she lost her head and couldn't speak. She just stood staring at Claudia with her eyes popping. Kenneth threw her the line from the wings, but she was too upset to catch it, so Claudia said, "Bridget, close your mouth, you look like a guppy fish"—and the audience laughed for a long while, and Claudia prayed that before they stopped laughing, Bridget would remember what to say. She didn't, though; her brain was apparently as empty as Claudia's had been before the curtain went up. It was as if they had changed places, for certainly Claudia never felt calmer in her life.

She said, "Run get me a glass of water, will you, Bridget?"

Bridget threw her a look of abject gratitude and scurried off. Claudia rolled the string from the package she had opened, into a neat ball. The string caught on a bit of roughness at the corner of her thumb and she bit at it the way she always did when she had a hangnail. She took her time about it. The audience was very quiet; she had a sense that they would stay with her for as long as she wanted them to. She glanced up as Bridget came back with the water. Bridget was a new woman, brimming with her lines. "Oh, Miss Cornelia!" she carrolled. "Mr. Ned telephoned while you was out—"

"What'd he want?" Claudia asked, as she drank the water. It had a horrid taste as if Bridget had snatched it from any old place. Claudia made a grimace. "Not very cold," she commented. She didn't mean to be as funny as the audience thought she was.

After the act, Annabel went into hysterics and told Jim that Claudia had purposely ruined her entrance with that damn water. Claudia heard every word from her dressing room. "The double-crossing little schemer, I'm going to cut the legs out from under her!" Annabel threatened savagely. "Wait until my big scene with her in the third act, that little upstart's going to wish she'd never been born!"

Claudia was worried. She took Jim aside before the curtain went up. "I'd better be prepared, how does a person cut another person's legs from under them on the stage?"

Jim gave his one-sided grin. "Baby, you should know," he said, and kissed her on both cheeks.

Five

Julia's aunt, Mrs. J. Gordon Post, told Claudia that it was the first time in her life that she had been backstage. "It's fascinating, my dear, like a different world," she said. "And you were charming in the play. Charming."

"Thank you," said Claudia, with her head spinning from the curtain calls. "I'd ask you in my dressing room, but I share it with Gloria Van Tassel."

"We'll wait for you here in the hall," said Julia.

"I'll see if I can find a chair for your aunt," David offered.

"Do," said Julia, for Mrs. Post was handsomely on in years, and walked with a cane. She wore a dogcollar of pearls, and had an enormous rear, which would have been rather dreadful on anyone else, but on Julia's aunt it became a veritable symbol of high breeding—no one short of a blue blood would have dared to go around with it. At the moment, it was pushing everybody up against the wall of the narrow corridor, so David was anxious to find a place for it.

Gloria came along while he was looking for a chair that would hold up under stress. Claudia introduced her. Gloria almost curtsied, for she had read the article in the paper about Claudia's socially prominent connections. "So pleased to make your acquaintance," she said. Agitation got the better of her manners. "Say listen, tell me," she implored, "was it awful when I blew my lines?"

"I'm sure no one noticed," Julia lied.

"You were very good," Hartley chimed in gallantly.

"I thought I'd die," said Gloria, shuddering off the horrible memory. "Imagine me pulling a blank. So help me, I don't know what I'd have done if the kid hadn't jumped in and saved my skin. And what do you think of her having the presence of mind to tell me to close my mouth, I looked like a fish! Don't fool *me* this is her first part, I bet she's holding out on us, I bet she trouped in her cradle."

Mrs. Post was so deeply impressed by Gloria's generous spirit, that she decided on the spot to trade discretion for graciousness, and invited her to join the party. Then Mr. Goldheart strode along and boomed, "Here here, what's the convention!" It soon turned out that he and Hartley knew each other from the steam baths, whereupon Mrs. Post threw all discrimination to the winds and invited him too. "Sure!" he accepted heartily, "I've always wanted to see the inside of one of those Back Bay houses."

Claudia marvelled how Sam could wear his vulgarity with such a flaunting magnificence. He immediately took the party under his wing and in his most beguiling way began to shape it to his liking. He caught sight of Elizabeth as they were about to drive off in Mrs. Post's luxurious limousine, and insisted that she come along. "Mrs. Post has already asked me," Elizabeth declined.

"Oh, please change your mind," Claudia begged her in an undertone. "I know how you hate crowds, but you've gone this far, so you might as well stick with us to the end."

"That's right," said David. "Make an exception this once."

"You're a damn lovely parcel of woman," Mr. Goldheart ruminated, as he eyed Elizabeth up and down. "You're my idea of class." He yanked Claudia from one of the small seats, and wedged her in between himself and Mrs. Post. "Come on now, you can sit next to the guest of honor, Mrs. Van D. Jerry's our guest of honor, eh, Jerry?"

"Don't bring it up," Jerry muttered.

Elizabeth glanced at him quickly as she took her place beside him. "I liked parts of your play," she said in her clear, quiet way. "There was a basic fineness in its concept."

He looked at her gratefully. "There was," he said, "before it got messed up."

They tried to go on talking about the play, but from his vantage point of the rear seat, Mr. Goldheart commandeered the conversation. "Jerry my lad, no post-mortems. All right, so I lose forty or fifty thousand dollars, what's the difference? I'm not kicking, am I? No sir. I say, let's show them, let's roll up our sleeves and do another one together. I believe in you, lad. I think you've got the stuff."

"That's a very thoroughbred attitude," said Mrs. Post.

"It's the only attitude," Mr. Goldheart maintained stoutly. He twisted around to put his arm across Claudia's shoulder. "Besides, I always say that something good comes out of everything. Look at my little discovery here. The old man's getting on in years, but can he still pick 'em!"

Claudia boiled, but again the sense that he really was an old man kept her from giving him a piece of her mind. Jim Varney had no such scruples, however. Every time during the evening that Mr. Goldheart mentioned either Jerry or Claudia, Jim took another drink, and began to say things under his breath in a louder and louder voice. "We'd better get him back to the hotel," David finally whispered to Claudia, and while the party was still at its height, they stole away leaving Mrs. Post to cherish the conviction that theatre folk were a tribe unto themselves—unsullied, loyal, and self-sacrificing.

They escorted Jim to his room, which was on the same floor as theirs, and watched him drop safely across the bed.

"I thought it was Jerry who was falling in love with you," David remarked elliptically as they walked down the hall.

"A playwright having a play produced is about as interested in a love affair as a woman in labor," said Claudia. Then, quite easily, she executed one of the double-takes that Mr. Goldheart had labored so vainly to teach her. "What do you mean?" she demanded.

"It's Jim," said David.

"Don't be an idiot," said Claudia. "He likes my acting, that's all."

They didn't talk about Jim again until David opened the window before climbing into bed. "What's this?" he asked, picking up a square white box from the sill.

Claudia regarded them in dismay. "Orchids. Jim sent them to me, and I forgot all about them."

"That's a hell of a thing to do to the poor guy," said David, but he looked very smug as he put out the light.

The splash of the newspapers against the door the next morning pulled them both out of bed simultaneously. "Shall we each open separate ones or shall we both do one at a time?" Claudia asked unsteadily.

"One at a time," said David.

They needn't have gone on after the first review. "These critics," said David, "must get together and tell each other what to write."

Boston had evidently decided to be equally unkind to both play and cast, but one of the papers mentioned that Claudia Brown, a newcomer, acquitted herself creditably in a confused and thankless part. Carefully, David knifed out the review and put it in his wallet. "For Bobby," he said.

Julia and Hartley stopped on their way to the station while

Claudia and David were eating breakfast, with the table between the beds. "The play really was a stinker," said Julia, whose faultless speech seemed to have absorbed a theatrical tinge from the previous evening.

"The sad part of it is," said Claudia, "Jerry started out with a dignified idea. I committed suicide originally."

"That wouldn't have been any good either," said Hartley. "People want to laugh. Just the same, you were the best thing in it. How about it, David?"

"I'd have wrung her neck if she wasn't," said David, opening a boiled egg with a great deal of unnecessary anguish.

Claudia took it from him. "I'll do it, you're as helpless as Matthew."

"What we came to say–among other things," Julia went on, "we can stop off at Eastbrook and look in on things if you'd like."

"Thanks," said David. "Elizabeth caught an early train back. And I'm planning to go home tonight, and come up again at the end of the week."

The egg slipped from Claudia's fingers and dropped in the cup with a clunk.

"You're no great shakes," David reproved her.

"No," said Julia lightly, "I expected you to handle an egg better than that, Miss Brown."

To Claudia's way of thinking they were making too much fuss about an egg. "What's wrong at the farm?" she asked over a closing throat.

"Nothing that I know of," David said.

"Then why does Julia want to stop off?"

Julia shrugged. "As long as it's on our way, why shouldn't we have?"

"Also," Hartley enlarged, "I haven't seen Bobby in over a year."

"He'll be in school when you get there," Claudia pointed out briefly. Her heart stopped beating. "Or won't he?"

All three of them looked a little blank. Claudia's mind went back over the last few weeks like an octopus, gathering up all the things that had aroused her suspicions: the way David was always too busy to come to town, Elizabeth's visits, Julia's solicitude—and now Hartley's slip of the tongue. "Bobby's been sick," she said in a choked voice.

"Listen to her," said David.

"Really, Claudia, you're a very silly girl," said Julia. She tapped Hartley's arm. "Come dear, we'll miss our train."

Claudia could hardly wait for them to leave. "David, tell me the truth. What's wrong with Bobby?"

"Not a thing," said David.

"Swear?"

"Swear."

"Are you willing for me to die if you're telling me a lie?"

"I'm willing for you to die if I'm telling you a lie," said David.

She was immensely relieved. David might trifle with his own life but not with hers. "We didn't have another fire, did we?" it occurred to her.

"No," said David, "we didn't have another fire."

"Then why do you want to get back to the farm tonight?"

"Because spring waits for no man on a farm. We've got ploughing and seeding and planting to do, and Edward only has two hands—"

"With a finger off of one of them," she amended.

The telephone bell rang. David reached for it quickly,—too quickly, she noted. Was it word from home? "Hello? . . . Yes, this is Mr. Naughton—Oh. Yes—that's too bad—Yes, I'll tell her. I'm sorry, and I know she'll be sorry, too. Good-bye."

"Who was it?" Claudia asked, with her heart beating normally once more. "What's all the sorriness about?"

David put the receiver back on its hook. "It was your stage manager. No rehearsal this afternoon. Mr. Goldheart's closing the play on Saturday night." He leaned over and kissed her. "I *am* sorry, darling, it's a tough break."

"Not for me it's not," said Claudia. "I can't wait to get home."

He kissed her again, a completely different kind of kiss.

It was a wonderful week—like having her cake and eating it at Mr. Goldheart's expense. She had always wanted to act, and now she could have her fill of it without having to pay the price of being too long away from David and the children. She almost enjoyed the pain of missing them because she knew David was coming up to call for her on Saturday to take her home.

The play improved with playing. The cast was optimistic, some of them felt that Mr. Goldheart would change his mind and bring it to New York.

"Not a chance," Jim discouraged them. "He's lost interest. Sam only likes successes."

It was as exciting as a success, the way people kept coming up from New York—directors, producers, agents—to pick over the remains. "I hear Maggie Brewster's going to cover the show Saturday matinee," Gloria told Claudia. "Watch us all get nervous."

"Who's Maggie Brewster?" Claudia inquired.

Gloria snorted. " 'Who's Maggie Brewster?' she asks me. Honestly, baby, don't you know from nothing?"

"I live in the country," said Claudia.

"Maggie Brewster happens to be the dame who wrote and directed *All or Nothing* last season, and she's putting on a new one in the fall. She's casting it now. I hear there's a swell star part in it."

"I suppose she's looking at Annabel," said Claudia.

"Probably," Gloria gloomily agreed. "I'd like to think it was me, but no such luck. I look fine all but my neck. It's hell the way a girl's neck poops out on her."

"There's nothing wrong with your neck."

"It holds my head up, if that's what you mean."

"You spend a week at the farm. Some real milk and butter and cream will do wonders for you."

"It sounds like heaven," said Gloria wistfully.

"It is," said Claudia.

"Got any dogs?"

"A Dane."

Gloria looked awed. "Gee. Those are those big fellers!—and you know what else I love? Just a plain ordinary hammock. None of the fancy contraptions, just a plain hammock between a couple of trees."

"We have one," Claudia said. "Blue and orange, with a hole it in."

"Gee," said Gloria, again. "Are you kidding or do you really mean I should come?"

"I really mean it," said Claudia.

Saturday rolled around before it seemed possible. "It's my last day," Claudia thought, as she wakened. She yawned and blinked at her watch. Eleven o'clock. How easily she had drifted into the habit of rising late—probably because she never got to bed before midnight. It was going to be hard to get back to her old routine. In the world of the farm, she and David usually began to wander upstairs at quarter to nine. In the world of the theatre the evening was just beginning at quarter to nine. It was the magic moment when Kenneth would whisper, "Take the house to half—"

She reached for the telephone and ordered a breakfast big

enough to last her until dinner. Actors never ate three meals like other people. She wondered if she'd ever again get used to getting up for coffee and toast.

She had finished eating and was taking a bath when David announced his arrival by a spirited tattoo upon the door. She jumped out of the tub and wrapped herself in a towel, sticking her head out to make sure that it was he. "Hello! Wait a minute! Come in!"

She edged behind the door. He entered gingerly. "Last week you were in your nightgown," he said. "It's lucky you won't be here another week, or you'd be put out of the hotel for indecency."

Last week was so different, the way he'd swung her off her feet and almost choked the breath out of her. Now they were like strangers as they stood in the middle of the room laughing politely at his rather feeble humour.

"How are the children?" she brought out at last.

"Fine," he said.

"You look a lot better," she said. "Much more rested."

"You look pretty well yourself," he replied. "Earning money for the family agrees with you. How about getting into some clothes and going out for lunch?"

"I just had breakfast. You go on down to the dining room and I'll get dressed and join you. Maybe by then I'll feel like having some dessert."

"I don't doubt it," said David, with the ghost of his old smile.

It was the nearest they came to being themselves. "Something really is wrong this time," she thought unhappily. "I'm not imagining it, either." She was honest enough to recognize that the strangeness that lay between them was no fault of his.

He knew where the fault lay, too. "You're loving all this,

aren't you?" he asked her gently, as the waiter brought dessert and coffee.

"Yes," she confessed. She eyed the miniature blobs of ice cream. "They don't hurt themselves with big portions, do they?"

"No," said David. "Has it been fun?"

"It's been wonderful."

"Sorry to go home?"

"Not sorry to go home, but a little sorry it's over," she admitted. "I mean I wish the play could have run another week or two."

"For your sake, I wish it could have," he said.

Although it was early when they reached the theatre, there was a long line of people at the box office. David's eyes almost popped out of his head.

"Don't get pleased," said Claudia. "It's only paper—department stores and fire departments and people from New York to see the last gasp."

"Oh," said David.

Nevertheless he said he enjoyed the play more than he had the first night. "It could be that you weren't as nervous," Claudia told him.

"Even so," he said, "I thought the story made more sense, and the performance was better."

"Was I better, too?"

"Much. How is it you kept in the ad libbing you did at the opening when Gloria forgot her lines?"

"Jim liked it, he wanted me to keep it in."

"Where is Jim, anyway? I looked for him."

"He had to go back to New York yesterday. His wife's sister died. He was furious with the poor thing. You'd have thought she did it on purpose . . . Where will you wait until I'm ready?"

"I'll take Jerry across the street to get a drink."

She regarded him quizzically. "I think you could get stage-struck quite easily."

"Who couldn't," said David.

She was humming when she went to change into her street clothes. "It's plain to be seen that hubby came," said Gloria. "Did you tell him you asked me to the farm?"

"Yes, and he said he'd adore to have you," Claudia lied. ("I mustn't forget to tell hubby I invited her for a week," she reminded herself apprehensively.)

"It must be swell," said Gloria, "to have your own husband instead of always borrowing somebody else's."

"Extremely swell," Claudia agreed. "Why don't you try it?"

"I might. I know a guy in the army. Nice kid. A couple of years younger than me—maybe six or seven. Think that makes much difference?"

"Not a bit," said Claudia. "David's easily that much older than I am. It's always good to have one of you older in case of an emergency."

"I never looked at it that way," said Gloria thoughtfully.

The wardrobe woman came in. She was monstrously fat, and had to use all her breath to breathe with. "A Miss Brewster waiting," she wheezed.

Gloria's voice went up in a bleat. "Miss Brewster! Oh my God! Tell her I'll be dressed right away, tell her I won't be a minute!"

She was already galloping into her bright green skirt, her hands all thumbs with excitement. "Claudia, button me will you, while I change my shoes. Did you hear that, and can you believe it, Brewster coming in to see me, she must want me for the new play, oh my God, it's an answer to my prayer, if Brewster takes you in a play you're made, it's a legend, everybody who goes into one of Brewster's plays lands in Hollywood or something, oh Christ, where's that rouge, I look like an old hag, how's my hair—?"

"Your hair," Claudia wanted to say, "would be nice if you'd only let it stay the color it wants to be." Instead she said, "Don't put any more make-up on, Gloria, you look lovely just the way you are."

"How's those damn circles under my eyes?"

"They're fine," said Claudia. She straightened the back frill of Gloria's frilly collar. "You'd better let her come in now. I'll get out."

"No don't," said Gloria generously. "Stay a second and meet her, you never can tell what will come of an introduction."

Claudia didn't care about anything coming of it, but Gloria blocked her way and opened the door. "Come in, Miss Brewster," she called with a bright smile in her voice. "I'm so awfully sorry to have kept you waiting!"

On first glance Miss Brewster seemed to be quite young, which was because she wore the intense air of the very young. Actually, she was thickening faintly around the middle, and her neck, as Gloria would have said, was just beginning to "poop out." But she had nice eyes, with slight bags underneath, and a deep voice, and a way of speaking that was pleasantly masculine. "It's a nuisance to have people cluttering up your dressing room," she greeted them with directness.

"Indeed it's *not!*" Gloria effused, reverting to the role of a Duchess many plays ago. "We adore people coming backstage, that's what we live for. I don't dare suppose you remember me in *Ladies First*, do you, Miss Brewster? I played the lead. I mean the bitchy lead."

Miss Brewster hesitated. "I don't think I was in New York at the time. But I did like your performance this afternoon.

Immensely. Maids are so difficult to play with any degree of honesty."

"They're bastards to play," Gloria conceded fervently, forgetting to be the Duchess. "And the worst part of it is, once you play them, you're typed, every dam' manager in town thinks you can't play anything else." She broke off to pull Claudia back by the arm. "Don't go, I'm sure Miss Brewster would like to meet you, Claudia."

Miss Brewster gave Claudia's hand a quick firm pump. "Indeed I would," she said, "that's why I came. I wonder if we couldn't get away to some quiet spot for a cup of tea or a cocktail?"

"You mean me?" Claudia stammered. She could not bear to look at Gloria. If there was glamour and excitement in the theatre, there was also heartbreak. It was unthinkable that she should be the one to destroy the ecstasy in Gloria's tired eyes. She grasped at the first excuse that came into her mind. "I'm sorry, I don't think I can, my husband's waiting for me."

Miss Brewster smiled. "Your husband is invited too," she said.

Gloria administered a sharp pinch to the nearest available surface of Claudia's anatomy. "Go ahead, you chump," she ground out. "It's the chance of your life—"

David liked Miss Brewster, and Miss Brewster liked David. They drank martinis, several apiece, and talked about Claudia as if she weren't there. "Forget her lack of experience, that doesn't disturb me in the least," Miss Brewster said with an earnest crease between her eyes. "It makes it easier for me, in fact. The way I work is to take a piece of putty and mold it to the shading and nuance and variety that I want to get into the character. You see what I mean?"

David saw what she meant, nor did he seem to mind Miss Brewster calling his wife a piece of putty.

"What the girl has," Miss Brewster continued, "is a natural feeling for the theatre, which is fortunately unspoiled thanks to Varney. Jim's a good director, you see. He's had the sense to let her alone, to guide rather than impose, so that she's remained valid and simple. Naturally she doesn't know anything, what she does on the stage is purely instinctive, and with the amateur's composure. She has a tremendous amount of hard work ahead of her. She'll have to study with me all summer, if she wants to do the part of "Emma." But this I promise you, whether the play goes over or fails, one thing is certain—Claudia Brown will emerge a star. It's that kind of a part, you see. It carries the play."

"I still say it's a big order for someone without experience," said David.

"It is," Miss Brewster acknowledged. "But to come back to where we started, that's what I'm looking for, someone completely unknown, yet with stellar potentiality. The combination isn't easy to find. However, it's my formula of success, and I'm willing to put the work in to get what I want."

"In that case, it sounds like the chance of Claudia's life," said David, unconsciously using Gloria's words.

"I'm sure of it," said Miss Brewster.

Claudia cleared her throat. "I have to get back to the theatre for the evening performance," she mentioned in a small voice.

"So you must." Miss Brewster squared around to look at her for the first time. "You've been very quiet. Tell me, what have you got to say about all this?"

"She has nothing to say," David interposed firmly. "She's always loved the theatre, she evidently has a gift for it, and if this is her big opportunity, she's going to take it—Check please, waiter."

Claudia turned to Miss Brewster. "David's so stagestruck

he forgets I have a home and children," she explained, a little apologetically.

"Some of our biggest stars have homes and children," said Miss Brewster. "I have two daughters of my own."

It was something of a shock. Miss Brewster didn't look as if she had two daughters. "You don't even look as if you had a husband!" Claudia exclaimed.

"Thank you!" Miss Brewster laughed, taking it as a compliment, luckily. She grasped Claudia's hand and gave it one of her firm shakes. "We'll consider it settled, shall we? Come to my office on Monday, and I'll give you a script to read. Then we can sit down and have a long talk about it." She gave David the same kind of a shake, and was gone.

Claudia closed her mouth with difficulty, and wet her lips. She wanted to say a lot of things, chiefly that it was all a ridiculous idea, she couldn't possibly leave home and be a star, but the words wouldn't come. "I think you've lost your mind!" she sputtered.

"Could be," said David enigmatically.

It was a mystery how news got around the theatre so fast and so inaccurately. By the time Claudia reached her dressing room, everyone knew that she was going to play the lead in Maggie Brewster's new play. She did her best to protest that nothing was settled, but they preferred to think it was. A Cinderella story had happened in their midst, and according to the age-old tradition of the stage, they intended to make the most of it. Even Annabel was excited about it. "Wait'll Sam hears that Brewster wants you, it'll burn him up," she gloated.

"No it won't," said Gloria. "He'll take all the credit of discovering her."

They had turned out to be nice people. Claudia suddenly realized that she would miss them, even Clifton. Her throat felt tight as the curtain fell for the last time on *Happy*

Trouble but she didn't have time to be sentimental about it because instantly a half dozen burly stage hands shoved her out of the way and began to strike the set to make way for the new play that was moving in the next morning. She saw Jerry watching his world of make-believe come toppling down. He caught her looking at him, and grinned. She almost fell over with surprise. The last thing she expected to see on Jerry's face was a grin. She raised her hand in a small salute.

The property man ran after her as she was leaving the theatre with David, and thrust a box of peppermints in her hands. "They're left over from the second act," he said. "I know you like them."

"Benny, thanks!"

"Don't forget me when you're a great star," he said. "Remember I was always rooting for you."

"I'll remember," Claudia promised, "for as long as I live."

They had planned to stay over in Boston until Sunday but at the last minute they found they could make the midnight train. "Do let's," said Claudia. "It'll be fun to surprise Bertha and the children in the morning."

They made it in the nick of time. The train was chugging to leave as they dashed on to the platform, and they had literally to step on its tail to get on. They staggered down the aisle and collapsed in their chairs, smiling foolishly at each other.

David had left the station wagon parked at the Eastbrook station. "That was smart of you," Claudia complimented him. The headlights scooped up the blackness as they drove along. Dawn was hours away, and here and there an occasional window etched a square of light into the dark night.

"Smell—" Claudia said ecstatically.

"Smell what?" asked David.

"Just air, dressed up for Sunday with a dash of daffodils and manure."

"Don't be whimsical," said David.

The house was cradled in the bend of the road, asleep. They left the car in front of the door so as not to waken Bertha or Edward. The children, they knew, would sleep through an earthquake.

Bluster gave a single sharp bark from his kennel, and then decided that he was mistaken. "Dope," David muttered affectionately.

An infinitesimal pair of lanterns pierced the darkness, heralding Shakespeare's appearance out of nowhere. "Hello darling, we're a surprise, don't tell anyone we're here," Claudia whispered. "My God, I certainly am whimsical," she admitted.

They tiptoed in, and felt their way in the dark. "I'd like just one little peep in the children's room."

"Don't," David stopped her. "Hold your horses until morning."

They undressed without putting on a light. David stubbed his toe getting into bed and cursed softly.

"Dope," Claudia giggled. "Oh what a wonderful mattress," she discovered. "Was it always so wonderful?" She must have fallen asleep before David could answer, because the next thing she knew, there was sun at the windows. It was an early sun, too shy and fragile to burst into the room. She didn't have to look at her watch to know that it wasn't seven o'clock yet. It was nice to wake up at a civilized hour again. She lay still, tasting the sense of home. How clean everything was, how fresh and still. Bertha had waxed the furniture—Bertha was crazy about waxing furniture. The furniture must have been amazed—and pleased.

She looked across to the other bed, to where David was sleeping like mad. His mouth was just next to being open, but not quite, thank goodness. A little more of the strenuous life of the theatre, and he wouldn't wake up until noon.

She tiptoed to the bathroom, and brushed her teeth. They almost fell out with astonishment—it was the first time they had been brushed before breakfast in weeks. She felt like a respectable human being once more.

The bathroom window had a superb view for a bathroom. Now it looked like something on a penny post card, too pretty to be real. Spring had come in the month she had been away. A fuzz of tender green-yellow covered the brown habit of winter, and the maple tree on the terrace was a masterpiece of intricate handiwork, with each furled leaf dangling its necklace of seeds. Funny that she hadn't noticed that it was spring in Boston. She took a deep breath of it. How lovely to get at the air first, before anyone else had a chance to use it. People who slept late, missed the best part of the day.

Across the lawn, a couple of Barred-Rock hens ventured forth from the poultry yard like fat old ladies in polka-dot dresses. Bluster ambled along. He wasn't paying the slightest attention to them, but nevertheless they picked up their skirts and ran screaming to safety. Claudia laughed—a lot of women were that way. Bluster wandered up toward the woods. Claudia gave a low whistle. He lifted his ears, and turned to marble. There was nothing quite so beautiful as a Great Dane, listening. An instant later, he was galloping toward the house. Claudia heard him arguing with Bertha at the kitchen door. He was determined to come in, and Bertha was equally determined to keep him out. He couldn't seem to make her understand that the family was home. She kept saying, "No, no, you wake the children!" Claudia whistled again, a whistle that only Bluster would hear. Then guiltily she stole back to bed.

David was awake when she got there. "You louse, you went in the children's room," he accused her.

"I didn't," she denied. "I wanted to but I didn't."

"Look who's here," said David. He pointed to Shakespeare, sitting on the sill staring in at them. "All the privacy of a barnyard," said Claudia. She opened the screen. He pretended not to notice her, and closed his amber eyes disinterestedly.

"Don't pull that stuff with me," Claudia adjured him tartly. "Make up your mind. In or out."

Shakespeare decided "in," and leapt into the room waving his tail in an airy banner of disdain. He didn't know it, but his purring belied him. It followed him around the room like a small engine, and got louder as he reached the bed. "If we don't pay any attention to him," Claudia enunciated behind wooden lips, "he'll come up."

"I would not," said David coldly, "spell words out for a cat."

"I didn't spell," said Claudia.

"It was the same as," David said. "Can you beat that—" he broke off, as a regiment of heavy paws thundered up the stairs, "how did that pup know we were home!"

"All our animals are brilliant," said Claudia.

"Watch it!" David warned, but it was too late. Bluster was already on the bed, trampling them down, distributing a wholesale slosh of kisses in one great welcoming sweep of tongue. "Not on my mouth! And get off my shinbone!" Claudia besought him in a single breath. "You big old pansy, you, I missed you like blazes! But oh how you smell, you've been out with a skunk!"

The word aroused familiar memories. Bluster barked his acknowledgment and neglected to shut himself off. His barks grew louder and faster. "What's the matter with him!" Claudia shouted over the din.

"He's glad to see us!" David shouted back.

To her tortured ears, another Great Dane seemed to be pounding up the stairs, but it was only Bertha, brandishing a leather leash. "Don't wake up my children, I slap you, you notty boy!" Her anger dissolved abruptly when she saw Claudia's face peering out from under the tent of Bluster's four legs. "Ach!" she cried. "What a smart dog, he told me you were home but I didn't believe him!" She gave him a firm whack on the behind. "Get down, sir!" she commanded, like a buxom Judas.

In half-somersault, Bluster clung with his rear paws to the edge of the bed. Bertha whacked him again. He heaved a great sigh and folded to the floor. Bertha took his place and beamed down upon Claudia. "Mr. David says you were wonderful on the stage, no?"

"You don't know the half of how wonderful," said David. "We'll tell you after breakfast."

Breakfast. The word did to Bertha what the word skunk had done to Bluster. She gave the impression of throwing back her head and barking. "Wait," she cried, "just wait until Miss Claudia tastes our new sausage! I fix some right away with eggs!"

She bustled from the room, only to tread stealthily back with her finger on her lips. "Bobby comes now," she announced in a loud whisper. She lingered at the door to watch what he would do when he caught sight of his mother after so long an absence. She was disappointed. He took a leaf out of Shakespeare's book, with only the immense indifference of his greeting to give him away. "Hello," he said.

"Hello," said Claudia. "Better close your pajama pants."

He tied the cord so tight it almost strangled his belly, but it didn't help the situation. Bertha said, "Come here, I fix." While she fixed, he flung his arms around Bluster and lavished upon him full and rich endearments. Bertha flattened her lips. "He kisses the dog," she observed as an exit line, but

Claudia sighed with happiness, for it was good to be missed as Bobby had missed her. It was good to be welcomed in this strange and beautiful fashion by a son who was growing up.

She wondered how long it would take Matthew to come in. Matthew must know that she was home, but it didn't mean anything to him. He was probably throwing his shoe into the air and pretending it was an airplane. Matthew was like that. It was the benign privilege of being five years old.

David's low voice broke into her thought. "Go get Matthew," he said to Bobby.

Bobby threw him a quick look. "He's still asleep."

"You can wake him up," said David.

Bobby went part way down the hall. "Hey Matthew!" he shouted. "Mother's home! Do you hear me, Matthew? Come on in Daddy's room, Mother's home!"

Claudia heard a quick soft thud and then a rush of feet. Matthew threw himself against her; his arms strained her to him with all of his small strength. "Mother! Don't go away again! Stay here!" he cried.

She held him close and then, still holding him, put him away from her. "Let me look at you," she said. "You've gotten so tall–"

She looked at him. Nobody said anything. Nobody had to. Matthew had traveled into lonely spaces. Matthew had had a long, long dream, he had almost not come back–the dream was still in his eyes.

"Why didn't you let me know?" Claudia whispered.

"Let you know what?" David brazened it out.

"Don't," she said mutely. "What was it?"

"He stepped on a rusty nail. It went through his shoe. He didn't tell us. The day after Bertha came she noticed the inflammation while she was giving him a bath."

Claudia's heart grew sick with fear. "It wasn't blood poisoning?"

"He's over it," David assured her. "No more danger, he's all right."

"But he almost died," Bobby injected importantly. "We had two doctors and Aunt Elizabeth slept here one night."

Anger, sheer and scorching, took the place of fear in Claudia's breast. How dared David keep her in ignorance of Matthew's illness! She was his mother and it was her right to know the pain of motherhood. Did David know her so little as to think an empty ambition was more important than her baby? She turned to him with bitter resentment, and found his eyes waiting for her with a smile.

"That day in Boston," he recalled to her, "you gave me a bad few minutes. You guessed all around the bush. Bobby, a fire, malaria—everyone but Matthew."

She remembered the nightmare she had had about Matthew on the tractor; she remembered the hours of tortured unrest during the weeks of rehearsal, and the desperate effort she had made, one Saturday afternoon, to get back to the farm to look in upon her world. It would seem silly to talk about it now. Besides, these were things she did not want to talk about, they were part of the secret growing of her soul, just as it was part of David's soul to want to protect her from all suffering. Perhaps, it occurred to her, David did not want her to grow up. Her resentment vanished in the brooding knowledge that this was a moment in their lives when their separate entities could not merge.

"Aren't you glad," he continued, "that you didn't know? You'd have gone out of your mind with worry, and what good would it have done?"

For answer, she lifted Matthew on the bed and looked at his foot. It was such a tiny scar, and almost, he wasn't sitting here with his head against her breast.

"You should also be glad," David went on, as if he read her thoughts, "that this is behind us. Now you can start work with Miss Brewster with an easy mind."

Distrust came into Bobby's face. There was a kind of sternness in his voice. "Are you going away to be an actress again?" he asked her.

"Yes," David answered for her.

"I want you to say here!" Matthew repeated on a rising note of urgency.

She put her arms around him. "I'm staying," she said. There was so little time to be needed as they needed her. Heaven was too brief to let it slip away. No one, not even David in his love, could make her trade it for that tinsel paradise where people were puppets, acting out a make-believe life behind a velvet curtain.

Six

The heart of the summer came in April that year, with the lilacs ahead of time, and peace in Europe following close after. Then in July it rained pitch forks all month, and nothing grew except the grass and weeds. "For God's sweet sake I just did you," Claudia addressed a bouquet of stringy blades that sprouted arrogantly in a border of perennials. She yanked it up. A tender cluster of delphinium came along with the clod of earth. She regarded it in dismay —there went the second blooming she'd been slaving over. She set her lips grimly as she thrust the roots back into the soft loam. "It's up to you whether you want to go on growing or not, my dear fellow," she said. "Personally, I've given the best years of my life to this damn garden—"

"You're talking to yourself," Bobby commented at her shoulder.

She jumped. "Why don't you knock?" she demanded testily.

Obediently, with a flicker of humor in his solemnity, Bobby bent to tap the flagged path, which by the way, needed weeding too. She got mad all over again, her ire finding a convenient target in her son. "It wouldn't hurt you to take over a little outside work in the afternoons after school," she upbraided him. "There isn't a boy I know that doesn't look after the grounds."

Bobby accepted the tirade in his stride. "You don't know any boy excepting me and Matthew," he mentioned mildly. "And Matthew's not even a boy, he's still a baby almost."

"Matthew's gotten to be very mature since he's been sick. What's more, he's a bigger help to me than you are." At least, she qualified inwardly, Matthew was still at the age when running errands and answering the telephone were privileges instead of chores.

"I don't like to weed," Bobby reverted, in an attempt to settle the matter once and for all.

"Do you think I like it?" Claudia came back at him. "And do you by any chance think I like to wash dishes and cook and make beds?"

"Aunt Elizabeth's here," he remembered hastily.

Claudia rose to her feet and dusted off the knees of her overalls. "Why didn't you say so?"

"You didn't give me a chance to—I'll weed the walk," he offered in tardy retribution. "I'll do it now."

She patted his shoulder. "No you won't. Don't pay any attention to me, I'm just grousing for the fun of it. I really love to weed and cook and wash dishes."

Bobby regarded her with David's sober eyes. "You don't," he averred.

"So I don't," she agreed. "What's the difference, you're all healthy and happy and Dad's home, and that's all that matters."

"Dad's not home, he's in New York."

She marvelled how a child who was capable of such adult flashes of wit and understanding could be, at times, completely literal. "I meant that Dad's safely out of the war," she clarified punctiliously, "and one of these days it'll be over entirely and everything's going to be wonderful. Everything *is* wonderful," she corrected herself, "and I'm so damn noble, I give myself a pain—where's Aunt Elizabeth?"

"Out front—I guess you're tired," Bobby remarked sagely. He picked up a worm and draped it across his hand. Her nerves curled in a ball. "Don't do that, Bobby! Put it down!"

"Worms can't hurt you. They don't even bite."

"I don't mind being bitten," she said hoarsely. "I just don't like worms."

He held it dangling for an instant of sheer perverseness before he put it back on the ground. It was in his mind to flick it against her neck, they both knew it, and it was a supreme effort for him to overcome the impulse. "Aunt Elizabeth's not a real aunt, is she?" he queried, as he followed her ignominious retreat from the garden.

"You know she's not. We've gone into all that. Must you make conversation?"

He smiled broadly, knowing that she was herself again and therefore all was right with the world. "See you later," he tossed off jauntily, and departed toward the barn.

"Don't you dare climb the silo!" she called after him.

"I'll do some weeding tomorrow," he gave back in answer. "I'll do some edging, too," he added.

"Much obliged," said Claudia. "I'll do my own edging."

"I suppose you think I don't know how!" he shouted, as the distance widened between them. She started to shout back that he certainly did not know how, but she changed her mind. It took too much energy and wasn't worth it.

Elizabeth hadn't gotten out of her car. "I only stopped by for a minute," she explained. "Candy just came back from Maine and couldn't wait to say hello to the children."

"Oh did she? Where is she?"

"Matthew took her off to look at the new calf."

Claudia frowned. "Don't talk to me about that calf. It had

to go and be a bull. Isn't that the limit with feed this high? Belinda hasn't given us one heifer, I could wring her neck."

"Farming isn't easy these days," Elizabeth remarked.

"Easy? Sometimes I wonder why we do it. David and Edward work themselves to death, and there isn't even a living to be got out of it now."

"David loves it though," Elizabeth reminded her. "It's helped him over a bad year."

"Yes, but I think it's beginning to get on his nerves a little," said Claudia slowly. "He doesn't say anything but I can tell. When he left for New York this morning it was like old times—I mean just watching him shave and put on his tie, and rush for the train—by the way, Roger flew in from the coast, did you know it?"

"No, I didn't! When?"

"This morning. That's why David went into town."

"I'm surprised," said Elizabeth. "He wrote me only a few weeks ago that nothing on earth would ever tempt him to come East again."

"Maybe it's his ulcer again."

"California's wonderful for ulcers," said Elizabeth, "it wouldn't be that. Didn't he say what brought him back?"

"No, he just told David to catch the first train in, it was important. And David left the haying in the middle, and bolted. It made me know that a cow could never take the place of architecture in his life. I wish Roger hadn't broken up the firm when the war came. He and David were an awfully good balance for each other, in spite of David's being so much younger."

Elizabeth nodded. "David was less visionary, and had more vision—look at those lunatics," she broke off as Candy came staggering across the lawn with Matthew dragging at her ankles. "You'd think," Claudia smiled, "that Candy was his age, with her hair in pigtails like that, and her pants rolled up."

Elizabeth sighed. "It seems to be the smart get-up for the well-dressed college girl. She couldn't wait to fish out those dreadful old blue jeans. But I drew the line at her going barefoot."

"Still and all, it's becoming," Claudia admitted. "I'd look homely as anything if I got myself up that way, but Candy looks cute. It must be youth."

"Must be," Elizabeth agreed.

"Hello, Aunt Claudia!" Candy landed in a tumble at Claudia's side, while Matthew, helpless with glee, rolled on the ground and waved his legs.

"Get up from the damp grass," Claudia commanded.

She returned Candy's bear-like hug with affection. There was no one who could make Matthew laugh the way Candy could. There had always been a kinship between them from the time he was a baby. "You're the same idiot you always were," said Claudia. "Did you have a nice time in Maine?"

"Marvelous! I'm glad to get home though. It's wonderful to have a month here with Mother before I have to go off to college. Matthew's grown frightfully," she rambled on. "Why do children always grow when they've been sick? Bobby's grown too, though, and he hasn't been sick, so I guess they just grow, it's a habit of children.–He told me Uncle David's in New York. I'm so disappointed not to see him. I could simply eat that little calf–"

"You probably will," said Claudia.

"I'd rather starve."

"I used to be that way," said Claudia. "I wouldn't even eat a chicken off the farm." Strange how one became objective as one grew older. She realized with a little sense of shock that she no longer shared Candy's young idealism.

"Do you know I haven't seen you since you turned into an actress?" it suddenly dawned on Candy.

"I stopped being one. I turned back into chief cook and bottle-washer."

"Yes, and I think it's sickening, I mean I think it was the foulest luck that the play never got further than the tryout. Mother wrote me how simply marvelous you were in it. I bet you'd have made a big hit if it had come into town."

"Your mother was prejudiced."

"Not at all, Jerry Seymour said the same thing."

"How do you happen to know Jerry?"

"Don't you remember, Mother met him when she went up to Boston the night you opened?" Candy grinned. "He called on her in New York right after, he thinks she has a distinguished mind. In fact he was reading her his new play one weekend when I came home. Fancy Mother being an inspiration to the creative soul."

"Oh hush up," said Elizabeth.

"Anyway," Candy continued, "it was all too thrilling for words, and there's no sense in your being so modest about it because you must have been wonderful, or Maggie Brewster wouldn't have wanted you. I mean, everybody knows what a marvelous director she is, I almost died of excitement when I heard about it. I should think it would have broken your heart to give up a chance like that."

Claudia shook her head. "I've forgotten the whole thing," she said. "It's been a dream that never happened."

"I don't believe it," said Candy flatly. "It isn't human nature to forget practically the biggest event in your whole life."

"I've had bigger."

"Oh I'm not talking about husbands and babies," said Candy impatiently. "Everybody has a chance of having those, but how many people turn down an offer to be a star? You'll break out in a rash one of these days, and some psychoanalyst will tell you it's suppressed desires."

"Quoth the sophomore," said Elizabeth dryly. "Come on, Aunt Claudia's got a lot to do, I can see it in her eye."

"I've got supper to start, and David to call for," Claudia acknowledged.

"I'll call for Uncle David," Candy offered. "I'd love to."

"No, I'll have time," said Claudia. It was unthinkable that she should let anyone else meet David at the station—not even if she were a successful actress and they were rich enough to have a chauffeur with a cap. "But of course," she suggested blandly, "if you'd offer to fix supper, I'd be right tempted to accept."

Candy grimaced. "I loathe the art of cooking. I hope when I get married they'll have developed pills for meals."

"I notice, however, that you have no objection to the art of eating," Elizabeth remarked. "Would you care to trade a pill for tonight's lobster?"

"Lobster's different," said Candy.

"I adore lobster too," said Claudia. "I must remind me to get some one of these days. The trouble is, they're so expensive now. We're having kidneys for supper. David keeps on loving them, and the children keep on hating them. So I have to placate them with some obscene dessert like chocolate pudding on sponge cake with whipped cream and nuts."

"That's not obscene, it sounds marvelous!" Candy cried.

"If you want some, you'll find an extra portion in the icebox—all except the nuts."

Elizabeth put out a detaining hand. "Nothing of the kind. You don't need any extra inches around those thighs of yours, young lady."

Candy sighed elaborately. "Oh, all right. My mother wants

me to be beautiful and make a good marriage so she'll be rid of me."

"How'd you guess it?" said Elizabeth.

The train wasn't late for a change. Claudia heard the whistle half a mile from the station. She stepped on the gas, and swerved into the depot square just in time. It was a long while since she had driven at so reckless a speed. She shut off the ignition and tried to look as if she hadn't.

"You went fast," Matthew observed from the back seat.

"You almost tipped over," Bobby added, in one of David's less commendatory voices.

"Nonsense," she denied. "That was only gravel you heard swish up against the wheels. You wouldn't want us not to be waiting here when Daddy came, would you?" she demanded righteously.

"There he is!" Matthew shouted, "I see him!"

"Shh," said Claudia. "Be quiet."

"I see Mrs. Riddle, too," Bobby announced.

"That's why, shh, be quiet," Claudia cautioned. "We don't want Mrs. Riddle to see *us*."

"Why not?"

David came along and saved her answering. "That was a narrow escape," he said. "Quick, slide over before she nabs me."

Claudia slid over. He took the wheel and drove off. A few yards out of the square he stopped the car and kissed her. "Hello!" he said.

"Hello," she kissed him back.

"Hello, boys."

"Hello!" they answered.

Nancy Riddle's car flashed past them. Nancy sat in lonely state, with her eyes closed, and an air of having her shoes off.

"She's using her Rolls and chauffeur again," Claudia noticed. "How come you didn't bump into her on the train?"

"I saw her first," said David.

Claudia turned to the back seat. "Mrs. Riddle is a very lovely person," she impressed upon them sternly. "So don't get any false ideas into your head."

"Then why don't you want to talk to her?" said Bobby.

"Because she never stops," said Claudia, "and Daddy and I have a lot to say to each other." She squared around to David. "Now tell me everything. How is Roger, why did he come, what's happened, and did you call Bertha?"

"I called Bertha," said David. "Fritz's leg will keep him laid up for a while longer. It's phlebitis."

"Oh, dear," said Claudia, "that means she can't come back. She'd never want to be so far away from him and I don't blame her."

"She's trying to get her cousin's sister-in-law to help you out."

"Her sister-in-law's cousin," Claudia corrected him. "I think that's Hilda, probably. I once met her. She's nice. We're lucky."

"Except this isn't Hilda," said David. "It's another one. Hedwig. And she won't be able to come for a week or two, because she wants to rest up after her postoffice job. And after she's rested, it seems she has to take it very easy."

"To rest from resting, I suppose."

"No laundry or cleaning," David specified. "But Bertha says to take her if she'll come, she's better than nothing."

"Will she dust, I wonder?"

"I forgot to ask. She might. The thing that attracts her is that she wants to be on a farm; she feels that plenty of cream, butter and eggs might build her up."

"At least," said Claudia, "she doesn't object to being in the country like the others. I'd better get the guest room ready for her."

Bobby pricked up his ears. "Is company coming?" he asked eagerly.

"Yes," said Claudia. "The new maid. Now be quiet, Daddy and I want to talk, and I don't care if it's going to hurt your psyche or not. Elizabeth and Candy were over, incidentally."

"We played," Matthew inserted. "I like Candy."

Bobby giggled. "Chocolate?"

Matthew looked blank, and then got the point and laughed uproariously.

"All right, children, it's not that funny," Claudia ordered. "Now tell me, David. Everything."

"Somebody's been playing hell with this car," David said.

"It's me," said Claudia. "I take it out every morning after breakfast and play hell with it—*will* you go on?"

"What makes you think I have anything to tell you?"

"Don't be silly, Roger didn't ask you to rush in for nothing. Is it the book he's writing or his ulcer that made him come East? . . . I don't suppose you remembered to bring any nuts?"

"Did you?" Bobby followed up swiftly.

"Don't interrupt," said Claudia. "He didn't."

"That's where you're wrong, I did remember. But I didn't get to it."

"Thanks for the thought," said Claudia. "At least tell me how does Roger look?"

"Just the same," said David. "Only more so."

"How long is he staying?"

"Not long."

"All right. Don't tell me."

David reached for her knee. "Later. When we go to bed."

"I knew it was something important," Claudia exulted, "I felt it in my bones all day."

"You've got the most overworked bones of my acquaintance," said David.

She had no intention of waiting until bedtime. She put a low light under the kidneys when they got home, and followed him up to the bathroom and sat on the tub while he scrubbed the grime of town off his hands. David's hands were always good to look at—even, remarkably, when he was ploughing a field. His hands were one of the things about him that she'd fallen in love with, so few hands managed to be large and capable, along with being sensitive. She sat admiring them, while he wiped them on a towel. She didn't say anything, because she knew he was on the verge of talking. She got up and locked the door. Then they both sat on the tub. "How'd you like to go to New York?" he said, after a moment.

"For what?" she asked. "The day?"

"The winter. Maybe for good."

"You've got a job," she breathed.

"Not so fast. It mightn't go through. It's a big project—a postwar housing development on the lower East side. They wanted Roger for it but he won't leave California. Damn swell of him to come on and put me up for it instead, wasn't it?"

"Oh, it was! Wonderful. But don't fool yourself, they're mighty fortunate to get you."

"Not so fast, there's nothing definite yet. I'm to meet the board tomorrow. But it'd be a great thing for me if it did go through—" His voice trailed off. She could only stare at him, speechless with joy, because his long waiting seemed at last to be ended. "Nothing definite," he repeated. "They mightn't want me. You see, my ideas mightn't qualify." He was like Bobby, insisting that he hadn't passed his arithmetic test when he knew he had.

"You'll qualify," said Claudia.

He looked at her, wanting to believe. "What makes you think so?"

She put her arms around him. "Don't be silly."

The doorknob rattled imperatively. "Where are you?" Matthew demanded.

"In here," Claudia called back. "Go wash for supper!"

"You've got the door locked!" he said, aggrieved. "Where's Daddy?"

"In here," said David.

"What are you doing?"

"Sitting on the tub," said Claudia.

"Oh," said Matthew. He sounded baffled and drifted off.

"The children, too? In New York?"

"Unless you'd leave them here," said David.

"You couldn't commute?"

"Weekends, perhaps. Maybe not even that. This'd be a twenty-four hour job. It's a big thing," he reiterated, as if he could scarcely believe it.

"Then it's New York for all of us. . . . If you want us," she amended politely.

"Delighted to have you and your offspring, Mrs. Naughton," he returned.

"It'd be good for Bobby after three years of a rural school. But what will the city do to Matthew?"

"Matthew's all right. He'll build up an immunity to germs. Now answer me this: what will it be like for you?"

It was her impulse to tell him that it would be sheer bliss to get a respite from housekeeping in the country, with its endless round of cellar, attic, stairs and grounds. But suppose he didn't get the commission, and things had to go on as they were? "Me? Fine!" she answered with careless enthusiasm.

"Is that all? Just fine?"

"What's better than 'fine'?" she evaded. "It isn't as if we'd ever really stopped being New Yorkers. I mean, if I ever have another baby—" she paused to knock on wood, "I'd certainly go back to Dr. Rowland, instead of to a doctor in Eastbrook."

"We'll have to get after that baby one of these days," said David. "In the meantime, do you know the first thing I want you to do when we get back in town?"

"Get a manicure," she said promptly. She held out her hands. "Look at those nails, will you? Now I know why a lot of women wear red polish. It hides a multitude of sins, especially when you're weeding."

"I want you," David continued levelly, as if he hadn't heard her long harangue, "to lose no time in getting in touch with Maggie Brewster."

His invasion of her innermost daydreams both startled and confused her. "You're crazy," she could only stammer. "What do I want with Maggie Brewster?"

"Tell her that you'll have us all on your apron strings around the corner, and you can play 'Emma' with an easy mind."

It occurred to her, through the turmoil of her thoughts, that he must be pretty sure of the building project, for he had neglected to knock on wood or make some similar appeasement to fate.

"But what if Maggie Brewster's changed her mind about me?" she rejoined with deliberate indifference.

He pooh-poohed the idea. "Though," he conceded reluctantly, "there's a possibility you might be too late, the play might be in rehearsal already."

"It isn't," said Claudia eagerly. "There hasn't been a word in the paper about it since the first announcement weeks and weeks ago, of a fall production. Miss Brewster's still up in Nantucket."

She did not need the quirk of his eyebrow to tell her that she had given herself away. She could have bitten her tongue out. "Naturally, I read the papers," she covered herself. "Why not?"

"You poor old little slob," he said. "I hope to God for your sake that this deal goes through."

It was foolhardy to let him think that her happiness depended on going to New York. "Hope for your own sake," she adjured him crisply. "I gave up Maggie Brewster's offer because I wanted to, and I've never regretted it. Even if we do go to New York, I don't think I'll bother to follow it up."

"The hell you won't," said he.

They talked until late into the night, with their hands linked across the beds. There was so much to decide—where they would live in New York, what would happen to the farm, how they would be able to afford the maintenance of two places. "If we cut down on our foundation stock," David planned, "Edward can swing the farm by himself this winter, and the milk check alone should pay his wages."

"That's a relief," said Claudia. "It's wonderful to know that the farm is always behind us, like an anchor. Maybe we can come home for Thanksgiving and Christmas."

"Maybe," said David.

"Suppose we didn't though. Suppose we saved money and took an unfurnished apartment and used our own stuff?"

"That would be a gamble," said David, "until we see how things turn out. We'd better stick to a furnished place, even if it costs a little more—but don't count your chickens," he protested in tardy superstition, "this thing hasn't gone through yet. They mightn't want me."

Claudia smiled into the darkness. "Whoever 'they' is, 'they' will," she affirmed.

"Be sure not to say anything about it until it's settled," he warned her. "I don't mind Elizabeth knowing, but not Nancy, she'd have it all over town."

"Oh, and will Nancy be upset when she does hear about it," Claudia gloated. "She thinks you've got your life's work cut out in designing some sort of fancy business for her Angus cattle. What do they use, anyway, that's different from cows?"

"A type of shed. Nancy wants an open courtyard effect." David yawned. "Thank the Lord I'm through with that sort of thing." Claudia could feel his arm reach up to the back of the bed and tap it.

"Careful to hit the wood," she advised him. She caught his wrist on the way down, and turned his watch around. "Is that quarter of twelve, or nine? All watches look alike in the dark to me."

"Quarter of twelve," he said. "Better get to sleep."

"I'm too excited."

"So am I."

"I want an apartment overlooking the park, if it isn't too expensive, and if possible a room for each of the children—and a double bed in our room."

"By all means," said David.

"By all means, what?"

"A room for each of the children," said David.

"That's what I thought you meant," said Claudia.

Nevertheless, he wouldn't let her start looking for apartments until, almost two weeks later, Roger came up to see them before leaving for California, and told them that the deal was as good as set. Roger's hair looked beautifully white against his sunburned face, and he was very proud of his good health and kept taking pills for it. "Vegetable compounds," he explained. "I go to a perf'ly amazing man out there." He said that if Claudia and David sent a drop of blood, the doctor, who was a biochemist, could make extraordinary diagnoses.

"But we're feeling fine," Claudia demurred. She hoped that

Roger wasn't going to stay overnight as it would mean a lot of conversation along with good sheets and guest towels and scrubbing up the bathroom. "*Please* stay," she begged, going overboard with cordiality.

"No dear," he said, "thanks ever so much, but really." He drank three glasses of milk and took the evening train back to town. After he'd gone, Claudia found that he had left an exquisite pair of old Chinese libation bowls for the living room. "Roger mightn't be the most virile man in the world," she commented, "but he's very civilized and sweet."

"He is that," said David. "Not that I'd have minded," he added loyally, "if he'd stayed over."

"Neither would I." They looked at each other and knew they weren't telling the truth. "It's a good thing we're going back to New York," said Claudia. "We'll be forced to develop a little normal herd instinct."

As if to get them into training, Gloria Van Tassel telephoned the next morning, and sounded wistful. "I promised her she could come up some time so how could I help myself," Claudia apologized to David. "I thought she'd forgotten about it, though."

"No such luck," said David. "Don't expect me to be nice to her."

He was darling, of course, as Claudia had known he would be, because Gloria was well-meaning and half starved. She kept brimming over with appreciation, larding her boundless enthusiasm with spurts of news about the "gang." Did they hear about poor old Kenneth being involved in a scandal of all things? And Annabel Page was in the hospital, and it wasn't an appendix, either. Oh, and Clifton was married, a girl must certainly be hard up to marry that goop. And of course Claudia knew, didn't she, that Jim Varney was casting a new play. "I'm going to see him on Monday, for old time's sake, he might have something for me. Why don't you come along? You never can tell. Anyway I know he'd love to see you. I thought he was quite gone on you for a while there—Have you heard from him?"

"No," said Claudia. "But I can't take the time to go with you, I have to look for an apartment."

"Pardon me for laughing," said Gloria.

They all went into town together on Monday morning. Candy came over to stay with Matthew. "Isn't she a cunning kid," said Gloria. "Gee you have everything so nice, nice neighbors and all, I don't see what more you could want."

"Nothing more," said Claudia.

"Except," Gloria amended dubiously, "I don't think you're going to find a place to live in New York, the way you're counting on."

"I don't see why not," said Claudia.

Gloria kissed her good-bye when they parted at the Grand Central Station and almost managed to kiss David, but he was too quick for her. "Good-bye," he said, and was lost in the crowd.

"I think he's grand," Gloria sighed, looking after him. "I only hope no dame steals him away from you."

"I only hope not too," Claudia agreed without concern.

Gloria patted the bulky bundle of eggs and butter and vegetables that Edward had packed up for her. "Gee I certainly had a swell weekend," she said for the tenth time. "It was all like you read in a book. I wouldn't want to ever leave such a lovely place if I was you, but as long as you have to on account of business, I'm sure going to keep my fingers crossed for you to find an apartment."

"You do that," said Claudia, still without concern.

It was a distinct shock to discover that Gloria knew what she was talking about. Hour after hour, Claudia trudged the streets, feeling like Rip Van Winkle. What had happened to all the vacancy signs she remembered five years ago when they'd rented a furnished place for the winter? She'd read about the housing shortage of course, but, like death, she had an idea that it only happened to other people.

"Would you believe it, Gloria was right," she told David when she met him for lunch after a futile tour. "There isn't a single vacancy anywhere!"

"Nonsense," said David largely. "You've scarcely looked."

"I've looked all I need to look. There just aren't any apartments to be had. I passed some hotels too, and stopped to inquire. Not that we can afford a hotel, but I was curious."

"Well?"

"They practically snickered in my face. Waiting lists a mile long."

"That's ridiculous," said David. He was like an ostrich, hiding his head under the menu. "Order your lunch," he said, refusing to be perturbed. "What would you like?"

She was momentarily diverted. "What are *you* going to have?"

"Now don't begin that business again," he said. "What I order has nothing whatever to do with you."

"You mean you won't order separate things and divide?"

"No, I will not divide," he stated firmly. "I am having corned-beef hash entirely on my own."

"Why hash? You can have hash home."

"The waiter is waiting," said David ominously.

"I think you're mean," she reproached him. "I hate hash—"

"Order a lobster, and be done with it."

"Two-seventy-five and up, what do you think I am?" She studied the menu again. "I'll have the pork chops," she said.

The waiter vanished. David glowered. "Why pork chops? You can have pork chops home too."

"I know, and I don't particularly like them, but it said applesauce with it, and I'm always weak-minded when it comes to anything with applesauce."

"I suppose," said David bitterly, "that you feel you're getting something for nothing."

"A little," she confessed.

The waiter returned. "No more pork chops," he announced.

"Serves you right," said David. "Have a steak."

"No steak," said the waiter, which saved her the trouble of looking at the price. Nevertheless, she had to start from scratch again. She scanned the entrees and the roasts, some of which were included in the table d'hote luncheon, so it would have been foolish to order them separately. On the other hand, she didn't want the soup or the coffee, and the table d'hote desserts were all of the rice-pudding variety. She glanced at David apprehensively. He was drumming two fingers on the table, looking crucified.

"I'll have a mixed salad," she decided with dignity. "And iced tea."

"That's no lunch," said David. "And will you stop looking at the right hand side!—Madame will have a lobster," he told the waiter.

"I won't!"

"Then make up your mind," he said, with much too much control.

She studied the menu frantically. "Corned-beef hash," she decided in despair.

They arranged to meet again at the station. "I'll wait for you in front of the information desk right under the clock," David made clear, "and see that you're on time."

She made it by the barest fraction. David looked as if he hadn't changed his expression since the restaurant. "What are you looking so gritted-teeth about?" she panted, as they raced down the ramp. "The train hasn't gone yet, it's only chugging!"

They passed coach after coach, all crowded. Her heart sank. She was hoping that they'd find two seats together—it was always so nice to look out of the window. "See what you get for being late," he threw up to her. "We'll have to stand all the way."

"We'll probably find one seat somewhere, and you can have it," she said generously.

"It'll be next to a woman with a baby and oranges," he said, "and you can have it, thank you."

"All aboard!" the conductor shouted.

"We'd better get on," said Claudia nervously.

They walked through three more coaches, jammed to the utmost. "Where do all the people come from," Claudia bemoaned.

"The same place you come from," said David.

In the last car there were two seats riding backwards, but there was a sailor's hat on one of them, and a purse on the other. "Do you think that could be a typographical error?" Claudia murmured hopefully.

David gave her an ungentle shove. "Keep moving," he said heartlessly.

"But this is the last car," she discovered unhappily. "I guess we'll have to stand after all."

It developed then, that he had Pullman seats in his pocket the whole time. "You beast," she cried.

"That's the thanks I get."

"Rank extravagance," she scolded.

Secretly, she was grateful beyond words. A day in New York always gave her the feeling of having two feet in each shoe, and the prospect of standing for a couple of hours had filled her with dismay. She sank back in the commodious green chair and closed her eyes wearily. "Darling, do you mind if I put my legs up on your seat?"

"I'm not enthusiastic about it, I've just had these trousers pressed." However, he held on to her ankles, and the pressure of his hand was like a kiss; it made a little shiver run through her. It was immoral to feel that way toward a man you'd been married to for almost ten years.

"What luck did you have this afternoon?" he asked. "Did you find an apartment?"

He was so happy about the commission, that she hated to dampen his spirits by telling him that in all probability, it looked as if she and the children would have to spend the winter on the farm. "Yes, there were two vacancies," she said brightly. "A two-room walk-up, and an eighteen-room duplex. Take your choice."

"If there are those, there are others," he declared. She could have thrown something at him. He could be as illogical as a woman at times. "I'll bet you twenty cents," he continued, "that an apartment will turn up that will be perfect for us."

She wanted to believe him. "Why do you say so?"

"You're not the only one to have bones to feel in," he returned.

"I don't put any faith in men's feelings," she said. . . . "Must you read the paper?"

"Yes." He put the paper aside. "Must you talk?"

"Yes."

"Well?"

"I can't think of anything to say at the moment—except that the back of that man's head over there looks familiar. I think it's Jerry Seymour."

"What would Jerry Seymour be doing on the train to Eastbrook?" said David, deep in his paper again.

"I don't know," said Claudia. "Unless he's on his way to New Haven to see some tryout or other—anyway, I'm going to go to the washroom just to pass by and see if it really is Jerry."

"Go ahead," David urged her.

"You want to be rid of me."

"I'd like to finish this article."

She swung down the aisle, not being as graceful about it as she had thought she'd be. "Excuse me," she apologized, as she careened against a chair and knocked a woman's hat askew. The woman favored her with a stony stare, and righted her hat, trying to look dignified about it.

She was afraid she'd lose her balance again by turning around, so she kept on to the washroom. On the way back, she had plenty of time to see that it actually was Jerry, a little thinner than when she'd seen him in Boston, but as good-looking as ever. She wished she weren't coming from the washroom, it placed one under a certain disadvantage. "Why Jerry," she said as nonchalantly as she could, "what are you doing here?"

He was deep in a manuscript. He had to stare at her a moment before he came out of his absorption. "Hello there!" He tried to rise. "Don't bother," said Claudia hastily, "The car's swaying too much."

"Where are you sitting?"

"A few chairs down. David's with me."

"Good. I'd like to see him." He gathered his manuscript and put it in his brief case.

Claudia eyed it. "Another play?"

"Just finished the last act."

"That took quite some character."

"After the panning I got with the last one, it did take guts," he admitted.

"Well, I hope you get a better break with this one. You deserve it."

"The odd thing is," he said, " I don't care whether I do or not. I don't even care whether it's produced. I had to write it, you see—it freed me of the need of writing—I suppose I'm talking so much jibberish."

"No, you're not," said Claudia reflectively. "As long as you've done a thing, you don't have to do it—that's jibberish, too."

They looked at each other and smiled. "Let's go find David," he suggested, "and have a highball in the Club car."

It was a shame, Claudia repined, to waste good parlor car seats by riding in the club car. She ordered a lemonade. "I see you're still a heavy drinker," Jerry teased her.

"Do you know what's happened to Maggie Brewster's new play?" David asked abruptly.

"Nothing, so far," said Jerry. "Maggie's been having trouble casting it."

"Good," said David, "that's what I was hoping."

"I'm going to tell Jerry about your commission," said Claudia, "so that he doesn't think you're plain nasty."

Jerry listened attentively, and was gratifyingly impressed on all accounts. "David's right, don't waste any time in getting in touch with Maggie," he advised. "She's due back in town some time next week."

"There's not much sense in seeing her until I know where I'll be. I've been apartment hunting all day."

Jerry gave a doubtful whistle.

"I wish you'd whistle again," Claudia said triumphantly. "David thinks it's so easy, he thinks it's going to be the simplest thing in the world to house two children, a Great Dane dog that barks, a cat that sheds, and us. All in a nice neighborhood for very little rent, with lovely furnishings, preferably Eighteenth Century, and opposite the park."

"We're coming into Eastbrook," said David. "We'd better get back to our seats."

Claudia rose. "He has a convenient way of changing the subject," she remarked to Jerry. "Where do you get off?"

"Eastbrook," said Jerry, rising too.

"Really? Have you rented a cottage there again?"

"No, I'm visiting Nancy Riddle," he said.

Nancy's chauffeur was waiting at the station. "I'm sure he wouldn't mind dropping you off at your place," Jerry offered.

"We always leave our car parked at the depot garage," said Claudia. "Thanks anyway."

"It can't be Nancy that's bringing him to Eastbrook," said David, as they drove home. "Has he by any chance been harbouring a secret passion for you all these months?"

"I don't see why you should say, 'by any chance' as if it were so awfully improbable," Claudia replied stiffly. "I'm not that unattractive. In fact, when I live in New York–*if* I find an apartment and live in New York–I'm going to step out and have one affair after another."

"That's nice," said David. "Does that mean I can do the same?"

"Certainly not," said Claudia. "Getting back to Jerry, I wouldn't be surprised if he really was in love, he's changed such a lot for the better. Something's done it. Do you think it could be Nancy?"

"Nonsense. She's old enough to be his mother."

"That could happen," said Claudia."–Wait!" she digressed importunately. "Turn at the traffic light, I have to go into the village and get some chopped meat for supper. It's the quickest thing to fix."

"Have eggs."

"The children hate eggs."

"Too bad about them."

"How would you like to have your mother and father gone all day and then have eggs?"

"Candy's more than compensated for our absence," David assured her.

"I know. She plays with them like a hoodlum. I've been worried all day about leaving them with her. Do you think everything's all right?"

"You'll soon see," said David.

"Don't be so detached," said Claudia, fidgeting.

"Look here," he reminded her. "Candy's not such a youngster, she's eighteen–you were married at her age."

"I was more mature."

"You were not," said David.

"Then you were a fool."

"I was," he agreed. "And still am."

"Kissing's dangerous while you're driving," she admonished him. "We could have gone into a ditch."

There were lights in the kitchen window when they turned into the driveway. David honked the horn, and immediately Candy and the children burst from the house and dashed across the lawn to meet them. "Any luck?" Candy called.

"Not yet–how've they been?"

"Angels," Candy said. "Isn't it awful about apartments, suppose you had to stay out here away from Uncle David all winter?"

"Don't even think it," said Claudia.

"Did you bring me a pony?" Matthew demanded.

"Two of them," said David.

"Do we have to have chopped meat for supper?" Bobby whined.

"No," said Claudia. "Eggs."

He pouted extravagantly. "I won't eat eggs!" he rebelled.

"Oh you won't, won't you. We'll see about that," said David.

"Oh we will, will we," Bobby mimicked, and went off into a howl of laughter. Matthew howled with laughter, too. "I won't eat eggs either," he announced.

Candy frowned at them. Claudia knew that some sort of

surprise was under way, for Bobby and Matthew were no masters of innuendo.

The surprise turned out to be four handsome lobsters set out on the dining room table—split, garnished, and ready to eat. "Mother brought them over," said Candy. "She thought you'd be too tired to fix supper."

"I am," said Claudia gratefully. It was like Elizabeth to blanket her gift in an excuse.

"Now aren't you glad," said David brazenly, "that I didn't let you order lobster for lunch?" He pulled one of Candy's braids. "Stay and eat with us."

"I was hoping you'd invite me," said Candy. "It's our cook's night off, and Mother went to bed early with a book."

It was one of those pleasantly messy suppers, full of paper napkins and long periods of intense preoccupation with the business in hand.

Matthew dutifully swallowed a soft-boiled egg, with his eye on a plateful of spindly crimson legs. "He doesn't know he's not getting any lobster out of them," Bobby whispered in a loud voice.

"Don't upset the applecart," Claudia reproved him severely. "You've only just graduated from legs yourself." The telephone bell rang. "Go answer."

He poked at an elusive morsel for a moment longer, and then reluctantly tore himself away. "It's Aunt Elizabeth, she wants to speak to Candy," he reported, dashing back to his plate.

"Tell your mother I'll phone her in the morning and thank her properly," said Claudia.

"Somebody crack my claw for me while I'm gone," Candy called back over her shoulder.

David cracked it. He laid it on Candy's plate with an additional claw of his own. Candy came back. She looked amused, but it wasn't because of the extra claw.

"What's the joke?" David asked.

"I guess Mother's not going to bed with a book after all. Jerry Seymour's turned up with the end of his play. He's coming over after supper to read it. Mother says I have to come home and listen too." Candy giggled. "Chaperone."

Claudia's eyes met David's above Candy's head, bent in renewed absorption over her plate of lobster. "Someone," she remarked to David after Candy had gone home, "is going to be terribly hurt."

"I'm afraid so," said David soberly.

They didn't have a chance to say any more because Edward burst in from the kitchen in great exictement. "I just heard over the radio," he cried, "that we attacked Japan with an atomic bomb!"

How strange, it occurred to Claudia in some odd correlation of thought, that it should have been Edward who had turned the radio on that Sunday afternoon, when Japan had attacked Pearl Harbor.

It was all a little like the time that war was declared. David and Edward sat, far into the night, glued to the radio. Only now the word peace was in their hearts and on their lips.

Seven

Nancy Riddle was pacing nervously up and down the station platform in riding breeches, looking, thought Claudia, rather pathetic with her elderly pink hair and bumps. Nancy didn't ride, but she had horses in her barn.

"Yoohoo!" Claudia called. "Hello!"

Nancy turned and squinted through her nearsighted eyes. "It's you," she said. "Hello. What brings you down to meet a morning train?"

"I'm expecting a maid," said Claudia.

"I'm expecting a man-and-wife, I hope," said Nancy. "Agency?"

"No. Bertha's sending her sister-in-law's cousin. She was supposed to come last week, but she couldn't get an appointment for a permanent wave."

"Isn't it the limit," said Nancy. "Anyway you're very lucky with help," she added enviously.

"When I do get them, I keep them, if that's what you mean. But I haven't had anybody for ages."

"You've got that wonderful farmer," said Nancy. "What's his name again?"

Nancy knew perfectly well what Edward's name was. "Where did you get him?" she continued.

"He's Bertha's son-in-law," said Claudia. "But of course, he only does the outside work."

"I know," said Nancy. "It beats me how you manage."

"It's beginning to beat me, too," Claudia confessed. "It's especially hard now, because I have no one to leave the children with when I go in town. Candy's been coming over—you know, little Candace Van Doren—but she's leaving for college in a few days." She broke off as a train whistle tore the air. "There we are," she said. She and Nancy looked at each other and laughed a little sheepishly. There was nothing quite so much like an unopened Christmas package as waiting for a new maid.

The train turned out to be a freight. It rumbled endlessly past. Nancy grew impatient. "What about that job of David's!" she shouted above the din. "I thought you were going to live in New York this winter!"

"He's got it!" Claudia shouted back. "We are!"

"Then why do you have to begin with a new maid!" Nancy screamed. The freight car ended abruptly and left her straining her lungs into the quiet sunshine.

"I haven't found an apartment yet!" Claudia screamed back. She cleared her throat self-consciously. "Listen to me yell—I don't know," she lowered her voice discreetly, "where we're going to live yet."

Nancy got her voice back to normal too. "I hear apartments are hell to find," she said hoarsely.

"They are. I've looked until I don't know where to look any more."

"It serves David right," Nancy grumbled. "He should stay here and design my new barn unit. Where am I going to put my Angus cattle?"

"I'm much more interested in where I'm going to put my

children," Claudia returned. "If we don't find something, I'll have to spend the winter up here, and David will come up weekends, when he can manage it. But we'll both hate it. It's going to spoil the whole wonderful break of his getting this new commission."

"Not only that, but I hear you want to go on acting too," said Nancy.

"That's David's idea," said Claudia, "not mine. . . . Who told you, anyway?"

"Jerry Seymour. He was up last weekend. Also the one before that, and he's coming up again this weekend." Nancy paused to twist her lips into a wry smile. "I couldn't get him near my place when I first built it, and now I can't keep him away. I suppose with the girl going back to college, I won't see him again until it's time for another vacation."

"What are you talking about, what girl?"

"Your 'little' Candace Van Doren," said Nancy ironically. "Little, my eye."

"You mean you think Jerry Seymour's in love with Candy?" Claudia snorted, "Don't be ridiculous, Candy's only a baby!"

"Eighteen," said Nancy, "is not a baby. It's the oldest age of all."

"But Jerry's over forty!"

"No fool like an old fool." Nancy laughed shortly. "I ought to know."

The arrival of the train cut off further discussion. Not that there was anything to discuss, for Nancy was certainly barking up the wrong tree. If Jerry Seymour was interested in anyone, it wasn't Candy, it was Candy's mother; and that was just too bad for Jerry, because Elizabeth was married, and always would be married, to the memory of Candy's father.

However, the last thing Claudia wanted to do, was to discuss Elizabeth Van Doren's private affairs with Nancy. She was glad to change the subject. "I see someone with a suitcase," she announced. "I think she might be mine."

Claudia's first impression was that Bertha's sister-in-law's cousin looked a little like a lobster. She remembered years ago, meeting a new maid at the train and thinking that she had a face like a halibut. The maid hadn't stayed, and as Claudia didn't care for halibut, it was no great loss. But the disconcerting thing about Hedwig was, that Claudia was extremely fond of lobster, and almost immediately she knew that she would never grow fond of Hedwig. Her face was too long and sharp, her green eyes set too close and high against her bridgeless nose, and her lips too thin for warmth. All this Claudia had a chance to see while Hedwig craned her neck, peering off down the platform. She gazed at, and through Claudia, not expecting, apparently, that her future employer would be standing by a truck, in overalls. No. Hedwig's eye had fastened on to Nancy's chauffeured limousine.

"How do you do," Claudia inserted herself into Hedwig's line of vision. "I think it's probably I you're looking for."

"I am looking for Mrs. Naughton," Hedwig returned in equally perfect English, but with a German father lurking somewhere in her gutterals.

"I'm Mrs. Naughton," said Claudia. "I had to bring the truck down," she hastened to explain, "because there was some grain to pick up."

Hedwig did not look pleased at the prospect of riding in a truck. "I love trucks," Claudia commented brightly, "it's much more fun than riding in the station wagon." (That fixes it so that she knows we've got a station wagon, too.) She kept an ingratiating smile on her face, conscious of the fact that the train had started on, leaving Nancy alone and desolate on the platform. Claudia went over to her. "Didn't your couple come?"

"No," said Nancy in a lost voice. "Did your girl?"

Claudia nodded and motioned toward Hedwig who was regarding the high step of the truck with disapproval. Nancy's eyes raked her jealously. "She looks nice," she said. "She looks wonderful." Anger and disappointment sharpened her voice. "It's those agencies," she decried. "You can't depend on them. I wish you'd ask Bertha if she has any more cousins."

"I will," Claudia promised.

"I only hope," said Nancy fervently, "that now that the war is practically over, we'll be able to get decent help again."

Poor Nancy, thought Claudia, how little she had suffered during these rich and turbulent years. She went back to Hedwig feeling pity and contempt.

Conversation was difficult to keep alive on the way home. Hedwig's face looked straight ahead of her, stolid and forbidding beneath her brand new permanent wave. "I hope you like the country," Claudia murmured.

Hedwig didn't say she did and she didn't say she didn't. "The doctor said I need it," she replied obliquely.

Claudia bit back a retort. "Do you like children?" she asked instead.

Hedwig continued to be wary. "How old are they?"

"Nine and five."

"They go to school, I guess."

"Not Matthew," Claudia apologized. "I'm starting him soon, though."

Hedwig made the best of a bad bargain. "I rather have boys anyway than girls," she said.

Claudia patted herself on the back. "I'm so glad," she said. "Although," she reminded some divine Beneficence, "I wouldn't mind a daughter—for the third one—"

"Have you got movies?" Hedwig demanded after a long pause.

"Yes," said Claudia, "all the new ones," but forbore to add that the nearest movie-house was thirteen miles away. She sought to take Hedwig's mind off the subject. "Have you seen Bertha recently?"

"I don't see Bertha," Hedwig stated.

Claudia recalled that Bertha's recommendation of Hedwig had been equally remote. "I don't know her so good," Bertha had made clear, "I only know she's looking for a place in the country, but she should be all right because her family is very nice. Her family is all right, that much I know."

Claudia hadn't argued with fortune. Anyone, she felt, even vaguely attached to Bertha's orbit, was bound to have some superior attributes. Perhaps Hedwig would boil her dish towels, and never use her fingers in cooking. That would be something to be grateful for.

Matthew and Candy were throwing sticks for Bluster to catch when the car turned in at the driveway. He was making a tremendous to-do about it, behind in air, and barking ferociously.

"This is it!" Claudia chirped, wishing that she had had the sense to lock Bluster up. She glanced at Hedwig's profile apprehensively. Hedwig's little green lobster eyes showed plainly that she was no lover of animals. "Is that your dog?" she asked coldly.

"We've had him for years," Claudia confessed. "His brother died last year," she went on hastily, and caught herself in horror. (Am I actually holding out hope to this fishy-eyed creature?)—"I only pray," she said, and was immediately restored to her own good graces, "that Bluster lives forever and a day."

To this fervent toast, Hedwig made no direct reply. She turned her attention from Bluster and regarded Candy in sudden suspicion. "Is she belong to you, too?" she inquired.

Was the girl being spiteful or just stupid? Or was it possible that Candy in her rolled-up pants and stiff little braids, really did look young enough to be Claudia's daughter—or Claudia old enough to be Candy's mother? "Miss Van Doren is a neighbor of ours," she elucidated tartly. "I'll show you to your room."

"You got a cat too," Hedwig remarked in growing disapproval.

Shakespeare gave Hedwig one look, and moved away from her with lifted tail. "I don't like cats," said Hedwig.

"That's too bad," said Claudia shortly. She knew at this point that she didn't care for Hedwig and never would. Which simply showed that fish, even the best of them, had no right to look like people.

Hedwig must have sensed that the worm had turned. She favored Claudia with a palliating smile. "I rather have a cat anyway," she conceded, "than a monkey. I worked once with a lady that had a monkey. He had nasty habits. I didn't stay."

They had reached the threshold of Hedwig's room, sunny and pretty, as nice as any room in the house. Hedwig surveyed it with grudging approval. "Three windows," she observed merely. "I hope in winter it's not cold."

"I hope not to be here this winter," Claudia replied, and left Hedwig to unpack and think that one out for herself.

Candy was waiting on the terrace. "Do you like her?" she asked doubtfully, and went on, taking the answer for granted. "If you don't want to leave the children with her, I could call for Uncle David at the station this evening—that is if it would help out any."

"No thanks," said Claudia. "Edward can keep an eye open." Candy laughed. "I might have known it. You'd never let anyone call for Uncle David even if ten new maids came and you were half dead."

Claudia nodded. "It's the perfect ending to the day."

"Mother and Dad were like that," Candy said, a little wistfully. "I was only twelve when he died but I remember Mother's face, toward evening. She never cried, but there was something so awful about evening coming, and being alone."

"It's the loneliest feeling in the world," said Claudia, thinking of the long months when David was overseas.

Partly because of what Candy had said, but chiefly because it was never far from her consciousness, she was more than ever sentient of the crowning blessing of David's home-coming that evening. "Are you going out?" Bobby demanded, as she powdered her nose, and put on a dress for a change.

"Yes," said Claudia.

He scowled. "Where?"

"To meet an old sweetheart of mine. He's coming up to spend the night."

Bobby's face lighted with anticipation. He loved company and the advent of both Hedwig and a visitor all within a few hours, was indeed a red-letter day in the quiet annals of the farm. "Is it Uncle Roger again?"

"No."

"Who then?"

"You'll see."

"How long will he stay?"

"Indefinitely," said Claudia.

"You mean more than just tonight?"

"Much more."

"But where'll he sleep?"

"With me," said Claudia demurely.

After the first quick shock of it, Bobby exploded in chagrin. "It's only Daddy!—I'll go down to the station with you."

"No, you'd better stay here. Hedwig's new to Matthew and the place."

"Do you like Hedwig?"

"Oh, very much," Claudia lied.

Bobby looked uncertain. "She says she can play baseball," he offered.

"That's a godsend, indeed," said Claudia. "Go bring the car around to the front for me."

"All right. And I will, too, in another year," he gave out in sultry promise. "I can drive the tractor already. Almost."

"You stay off the tractor," she adjured him sharply. "And don't *dare* go up the silo."

"It would be a load off my mind," she reflected, as she climbed into the car, and looked all around to see that no stray animals or children were behind her, "to get back into New York away from the dangers of a farm–" And then she passed Mrs. Cootz's house down the road, and remembered how little Joey had fallen from the hayloft and broken his neck, and the bitter irony of the thought burned into her. Yet Mrs. Cootz was out in her garden now, picking the last of the string beans, and going on with life as if there were not a scar slit deep across her heart.

She passed Elizabeth's house too, on the way to the station. It was a lovely house, and seemed to grow lovelier as Elizabeth continued to live in it. It was probably the loveliest house that David had ever designed–perhaps because he had made it to fit Elizabeth–quiet, and spacious and clear. Claudia wondered what Elizabeth's life would be like if Candy got married. Then she'd be alone in the house–alone in the world. Elizabeth would take that too, the same as she'd taken her husband's death. Women were quite wonderful, Claudia concluded with a degree of awe. Even Nancy Riddle was wonderful, in a way, making do with the few little odds and ends of left-over happiness that life had bestowed upon her –chief of which was money, and least of all. Claudia wondered why she, Claudia Naughton, was so blessed beyond all the other women she knew—why her life should be so replete with happiness and fulfillment. "If I could only find an apartment," she threw in to sweeten the bargain, "I wouldn't have another thing in the world to ask for."

David jumped off the train before it stopped. She shook her finger at him, frowning her reproval. He waggled his head in return, being silly about it. It was a joy to see him that way again after the subtle torture of inactivity. He went to New York for conferences almost every day now, and always came back in high good humour, with a roll of blueprints beneath his arm. His mood, this evening, reminded her of the day he tried on his Captain's uniform at the tailor's; Claudia recalled how she had sat in the corner watching him, and remembered thinking, with heartbreak, that he was like a bride trying on a wedding gown. Once more, she was sitting in the corner watching him—this time without heartbreak—thinking that he was in love with living all over again. Only yesterday he had found a small office for himself, not far from the old offices that he and Rogers had shared. He had lined up a draftsman, too—young but eager. "John reminds me of me when I first started," David described him to Claudia.

"John must be nice," said Claudia.

Tonight he had another surprise for her. Before he started the car, he handed her an envelope. She opened it, and withdrew a blank sheet of paper. Then she turned it over, and saw the engraved lettering at the top of it. "*David Naughton. Architect*," and in smaller letters, "*John Payne*."

"It's only the proof. Do you like it?"

She smiled at how little time he'd wasted. "I love it. Now you're all set."

"All set," said David. "All I have to do is make good."

"You'll make good," said Claudia.

She prayed that the years of war would not come back to

stalk him, that he had had his last attack of malaria, that pride and despondency would no longer tear him to pieces, but that his courage would remain pinned firmly to his flying hopes. "No matter how hard he works," she warned herself, "I mustn't nag him to take care of himself."

She was aware that he was saying something—"I've asked you twice, did the new maid come?"

"Oh—Yes," she said.

"Good. Then you'd better go in town with me tomorrow and start looking for apartments again, because now that we're starting work on the plans, I won't be able to commute much longer. Besides, you've got an acting career to think of this winter."

"I know." She felt like telling him, "Never mind about me. This is your winter. You're the bride, I'm only the matron of honor."

Hedwig was frying meat balls in a cold pan when they arrived home. She looked very expensive in a lavender uniform, and had taken down the finger bowls from the top shelf and arranged them on plates across the kitchen table with little doilies underneath. "Oh dear," thought Claudia, "this is going to be quite a strain." She decided that as soon as she found an apartment—*if* she found an apartment, she amended automatically—she would tie Hedwig up in lavender bows, and send her over to Nancy Riddle.

Dinner was punctiliously served, plate by plate, but breakfast the next morning, was not served at all. Hedwig failed to put in an appearance until after the children had had their cereal and David had begun on his second cup of coffee. "She needs her rest, she's delicate," Claudia explained.

Hedwig wandered into the kitchen, yawning, just as Claudia was leaving to drive David to the station. She controlled the impulse to ask her guest to find another hotel.

"Matthew's playing on the terrace," she said, "please keep an eye on him until I get back."

Hedwig peered into the coffee pot. "I didn't know I was expected to be a nurse," she remarked.

"I'll take him with me," said Claudia shortly.

"What's the matter?" David asked, opening the car door for her.

"I could bust," said Claudia. "I'd rather do my own work."

David knew exactly what she meant. "Better swallow your pride until we're settled," he advised.

"I am," she said, "but it's choking me."

They passed the school bus, and waved to Bobby, who looked self-conscious and appeared not to recognize them. "That'll learn us," said David.

A little further on, they came in sight of Elizabeth's house. "I see Candy!" Matthew exclaimed. "I want to stop!"

"We haven't got time to stop, Daddy'll miss his train," said Claudia.

"Isn't Candy coming over to play with me?"

Claudia turned to David. "I wish to goodness she was, then I could have gone to New York with you, but I didn't have the nerve to ask her again."

"She sees us," said David.

Candy came galloping across the lawn, brandishing her arms like a young colt. David laughed. "Doesn't she ever roll her pants down and fix her hair like a human being?"

"No," said Claudia. "Isn't it wonderful to be as young as that, and not care how you look?" She had forgotten to tell David what Nancy had said about Jerry and Candy. Not that it was worth repeating. As if Jerry could possibly be in love with a schoolgirl hoyden.

Candy stopped the car by the sheer weight of her ebullience. She bounced up on the running board, leaned through the window and bestowed a resounding kiss on David's cheek.

"Hello, Uncle David, I haven't seen you for ages—hello and goodbye."

"Good-bye? Where are you going?"

"To spend a week with my father's family before I leave for college. Isn't it foul? I'll miss you all like blazes."

"Don't think I won't miss you like blazes too," said Claudia. "I don't know what I'd have done without you this last month."

"Aren't you going apartment hunting today?"

Claudia shook her head. Candy needed no explanation. "I'll come over and stay with Matthew."

"I wouldn't dream of it, you're packing. Also, it's the last day you'll have with your mother."

"That's true," said Candy. "The packing isn't anything, but I would like the time with Mother. And look, keep an eye on her, will you? She doesn't admit it, but it gets awfully lonesome for her with me gone. If she'd only have company or belong to garden clubs or play bridge like other women—why don't you leave Matthew here with us," she interrupted herself, "we'd adore to have him."

"I want to stay," Matthew accepted at once, "I want to stay with Candy and Aunt Elizabeth."

Elizabeth came out of the house, trim and firm around the middle, in a pleated skirt and white blouse. She looked her age, not beautiful, not stylish, not even oppressingly well-bred. "Of course, Matthew stays," she said. "We can even phone Bobby at school to get off the bus here on his way home."

"It sounds perfect," said Claudia, "only I didn't expect to go, and I'm not dressed for town."

"Run back and change," said Elizabeth.

"No time, David will miss his train."

"We'll drive in," said David.

Half an hour later, they were speeding along the parkway. Claudia stretched luxuriously. "This is like an unexpected holiday. Elizabeth's an angel. An angel without being so blamed good about it, either."

"She's quite a rare person, all in all," David said. "I don't know anyone I admire more."

"Do you think she's pretty?"

"No, but the sort of face that wears well."

"She's the only other woman I know besides me who doesn't use make-up in the morning. Why do a lot of women look so puffy when they wake up?"

"There's usually a reason," said David.

"I was jealous of Elizabeth when you first started designing her house. Oh dear, I used to think, they're going over blue-prints together. I used to think, if you were only a dentist, or an obstetrician, it wouldn't be so bad, a woman doesn't look her best with her mouth full of cotton—"

"You've gone far enough," David interrupted. "I get the general idea. Where shall I drop you off?"

"Anywhere uptown. I've stopped being choosy. I'll work down and across like a crab."

It turned out to be still another day of futile search. She telephoned David at his office at four. "Not a thing," she said wearily. "Where do you want me to meet you?"

"Where are you now?"

"At Sixty-eighth and Third."

"You're not too far from Hartley and Julia. Suppose I meet you there?"

"Why this sudden demonstration of family feeling?"

"Julia wants me to look at some Eighteenth Century panelling."

"That's fine with me," said Claudia. "I'm hungry."

Julia could usually be counted on for food at any hour, particularly at cocktail time, but today Claudia found the house taken over by an army of carpenters and painters. Julia was putting in a boisserie. Claudia had never heard the word, but with 'bois', meaning 'wood', in French, she put two and two together, and kept her mouth discreetly closed. Personally, she didn't see why Julia wanted to live with a lot of dingy oak, and neither did Hartley, but David thought the panelling was magnificent, and kept running his hand over it in an awe-struck way. Every once in a while, the architect in him would come out in great splotches, and make Claudia feel as if she were married to a stranger.

Julia, of course, was much pleased at his enthusiasm. She said she was having a thrilling time doing over the house, now that the war was over, and she wished, as long as they were in such a mess anyway, that Hartley would put in an elevator for his high blood pressure.

"Nonsense," said Hartley, who had reached the age when he didn't like to admit that stairs were too much for him. "However, if Julia wants an elevator, she can have it."

"Not for me," said Julia, a little sharply. "Running up and down has helped me keep my figure."

That, Claudia amended silently, plus massage three times a week, and fruit for dessert. "Talking of houses," she said aloud, "maybe that's our solution, we could rent a house."

"I doubt it. Come and live with us," Hartley suggested largely. "Plenty of room for the whole lot of you."

"Hartley," Julia expostulated, "with the place a shambles—!"

Claudia felt sorry for Julia, who was always at the mercy of Hartley's prodigal generosity. "Shambles or not," she said quickly, "no roof is big enough for two families." What she was really thinking of, was the formidable grandeur of the twin beds in the guest room. David must have had the same thought, because he said at once, "It's out of the question, thanks just the same."

Julia relaxed, relieved that Hartley's invitation was not to be pigeonholed away for future use. "As soon as we're in shape again," she planned, "I'm going to give you a big dinner party. A lot of your old friends have been asking for you."

"I didn't know I had any," said Claudia. "Who, for instance?"

"Oh, Philip Dexter among others," said Julia with a little laugh.

A gratifying warmth stirred around Claudia's heart. "My one romance."

"And I met Jim Varney the other night," Julia continued. "He wanted to know what happened to you. He's going into rehearsal, incidentally, with a new play. You ought to call him up, he might have a part for you."

"There's no use," said Claudia, "until we find a place to live."

"What'll you do if you don't?"

Claudia glanced at David, and lowered her voice. "David won't face it, but he'll probably have to live in a hotel by himself, and I'll stay out on the farm with the children. I'm sick over the thought of it."

"I don't blame you," said Julia. "It's no fun to be stranded out there winter after winter."

"It isn't the lack of fun. It's being away from David."

Julia regarded her with puzzled eyes. "You two seem as much in love as ever," she said.

"More," said Claudia. "Much more."

"Do you think?" she asked David thoughtfully, on the way home, "that a boisserie—a boisserie really is a room made of wood, isn't it?"

"Yes, ignoramus. If you're going to be married to a famous architect, you'll have to get up on some of these things."

"If you're going to be married to a famous actress, you'll have to get used to my not being so damn intellectual."

"I've been used to that for many years," said David. "What about the boisserie?"

"Do you think it could take the place of passion in a woman's life?"

"A lot of things take the place of passion," said David, "and a boisserie's as good as any."

They stopped off at Elizabeth's to pick up Bobby and Matthew. Candy had company—a splendid looking young man in a bow tie and eyeglasses on his way to Harvard. She had kindly let him keep an eye on the children all afternoon while she finished her packing, and he seemed to be glad that they were at last going home.

"I don't like college boys," Candy said, as she followed them out to the car. "They bore me. I like men around thirty-five. At least, they're mature."

"Thank you," said David. He pulled her braids and tweaked her nose and said good-bye. "Behave yourself at college," he adjured her.

"You and Aunt Claudia be sure to keep an eye on Mother, especially when you get to New York. See that she goes out and has a nice time and doesn't stick in the house so much."

"Stop worrying about me," Elizabeth commanded. "You've gotten to be a dreadful little Mamma-baby."

The phrase stirred an ache in Claudia. She had been a Mamma-baby, too, even after she was married. She knew how Candy felt.

"We will, Candy," she promised. "That is," she added, like the refrain of a chorus, "if I ever get to New York, which looks more and more doubtful."

She knew before David said it, that he was going to say, "Ridiculous. You'll find something." But when another fortnight passed without so much as a single possibility opening up, he was forced to admit that the housing shortage was a grim reality.

"I'm sure you'll be able to get back to the farm for week-ends," Claudia planned, with optimism laid over a heavy heart. "I'm not crazy about New York, anyway."

"No, but I'm crazy about you," said David gloomily. "This is a hell of a mess."

"It's two hells of a mess," said Claudia, "because I happen to be crazy about you, too."

Then, at the last minute, when they had given up all hope of being together, the impossible happened. Quietly, one evening, Elizabeth announced that she was going to marry Jerry Seymour the following week. Claudia and David could only gape at her in astonishment.

Elizabeth made no attempt to explain her position. "Jerry's a fine person," she said. "I think you'll like him when you know him. I'm sure Candy will learn to like him too."

"How did Candy take it?" David asked.

Claudia noticed that for once, Elizabeth evaded a direct reply. "It's a little of a surprise to all of us," she said, "including Jerry and me. You see, I never thought I'd marry again."

"Neither did I," said Claudia frankly.

"It's healthy," said David. "It's right."

Elizabeth turned to look at him. "You helped me realize that," she said, "years ago, when I first met you."

"I'm glad," said David. "It's good for Candy, also. It might take her a little while to find it out, but it's the best thing that could happen, as far as she's concerned."

"I know that," said Elizabeth.

There were implications in Elizabeth's brief avowal that made Claudia know that her second marriage was a decision to which she had not come lightly. It had happened fast, of course, but looking back over the past, Claudia reflected that things that happened fast were sometimes years long in the making.

It happened, fast, too, that a short while after their simple wedding, Jerry's mother died in England, and Jerry had to go to London to settle the estate. Elizabeth sought Claudia out, asking a favor. "There's no telling how long we'll be gone," she said, "and leaving Candy alone is the one thing that worries me. Would you and David consider living in my apartment, and having her come home for the holidays as usual? You know how she adores you and the children, it would be almost the same as if I were there—even a little better, possibly, until she gets used to the idea of Jerry."

Claudia stared at Elizabeth incredulously. "You mean you'd actually rent your lovely place to us, dog and cat and children?"

"Not rent," Elizabeth specified. "It would be an even exchange for taking Candy, and keeping Mary and Katie on for me. Besides, there is no rent. It's co-operative, just the upkeep."

"Which we'll pay," said Claudia firmly. "And Mary and Katie too—Oh it's much too good to be true, are you *sure* you really mean it?"

"All you have to do is move in," said Elizabeth. "Talk it over with David, and see what he says."

Claudia could hardly wait until David came home that evening. He saw at once that she was bursting with news.

"You look smug," he said. "What is it?"

It was too wonderful not to string out. She took a long breath. "How would you like to live in a beautiful but comfortable apartment, with spacious rooms and big armchairs, and a marvelous old Chippendale double bed in the bedroom, and four windows overlooking the East River?"

"Elizabeth's?"

She was furious. "You're too smart. How did you guess so fast?"

"I recognized the bed," he said.

The move into town was simple and painless beyond belief. There was nothing to do except pack some suitcases, and dispatch Hedwig over to Nancy Riddle's. In the short time that they had enjoyed her services, Hedwig had gained three pounds, and had displayed a fanatical talent in making soggy baking powder biscuits at the slightest provocation. However, Nancy was taken in completely by the lavender uniform, and in return for Hedwig (on whom she had had her eye from the start) she sent an elaborate basket of fruit, which turned out to be chiefly a pineapple in the bottom. It looked so deceivingly beautiful from the top, though, that Claudia didn't have the heart to disturb it, so after filching two gold-papered prunes for the children, she sent it over to Mrs. Cootz and let her worry about it.

At the last minute there was more baggage than they thought, so Edward had to strap things behind and on the roof of the car. "Will the day ever come when we won't travel like immigrants," Claudia bemoaned.

"Children make it that way," said Edward. He put his hand on Matthew's head. "I'll miss them."

"We'll be back for Thanksgiving," Claudia promised.

"We'll be taking a run up before that to call for Bluster," said David.

"And Shakespeare," Claudia added.

They all shook hands, like friends. Bobby swallowed hard, and talked very loud, and a little fresh. Claudia could see that he was trying not to cry. He would probably feel like crying when he left New York to come back to the farm. Children were like that, and it was good, in a way, to keep them moving. It kept their roots from getting a strangle hold on their lives. The move was good for her too, for the same reason. She would, at this moment, gladly have changed an adventurous future for the gentle past.

It was not until she heard the river noises that night, and saw the lights of boats go past the window, that she felt excitement stir within her. She lay awake, staring into the darkness and realizing, with a sense of awe, that there wasn't a single cloud upon the glowing horizon of her life. Everything was working out just right. David was coming into his own, professionally; the children would be starting in good schools, and Bertha, who lived only a few blocks away, was arranging her household so that she could take them out in the afternoons. It was pleasant, too, to think of Candy's vacations. It would be fun to plan little parties for her; to take her to the theatre; to try and fill Elizabeth's place. Perhaps Claudia would be rehearsing—Candy would adore to watch a real rehearsal, she had said so many times.

"Time for you to get to sleep," said David, out of the blue.

"I was lying still, how did you know I was awake?"

"I could feel you thinking," he said.

"The lights are lovely on the river, aren't they?"

"Yes. This has always been my favorite part of New York."

"Do you remember the furnished apartment we had five years ago?"

"There was a mirror over the kitchen sink," said David.

She shuddered. "And knickknacks on all the mantels. And a buffet in the dinning room with drawers that stuck."

"Is that what you were thinking about?" he reverted. "Somebody's old buffet that stuck."

"No," she said, "I'm thinking that everything is so perfect, I'm almost afraid.

"Afraid of what?"

"The future," said Claudia. "It's smiling at me like a hypocrite, I don't trust it."

Eight

Even David, who didn't have much sense about those things, agreed with Julia when she said that Claudia simply must not go to see Maggie Brewster in that six-year-old tweed suit, and that god-awful felt hat.

"I don't know why not," Claudia grumbled. "Tweed doesn't go out of style and I feel at home in the hat."

"You forget you're the wife of an architect who will be more or less in the public eye," Julia reminded her.

"Leave me out of it," David injected crisply.

Claudia disregarded him. "I'll go shopping first thing in the morning," she said.

Foreboding dampened Julia's victory. "And just where do you intend to shop?" she inquired ominously.

"Wherever there's a sale."

"That's what I was afraid of. I'll meet you at 'Irene's' at eleven."

"You will not!" Claudia's voice went into a bleat. "I've never been to Irene's, but I know you can't touch anything there under a small fortune."

"Irene has sales too," David put in blandly. "Hasn't she, Julia?"

Julia nodded. "Also original models that you can buy at the end of the season for almost nothing."

"I saw you wink at each other," said Claudia. "No monkey business. And anyway, since when is early fall the end of the season?"

"Irene begins a new season every month," said Julia.

"Oh," said Claudia, "that's different."

She arrived at "Irene's" half an hour early. She wanted to look over the models by herself, try on the least expensive of them, and then merely have Julia approve her choice. Cheating showed, however, because there was not only not a sign of a dress on view, but no one to wait on her in the bargain. The elegant expanse of "Irene's" spacious main floor might have been the foyer of a private residence.

She sat down on a velvet bench and waited for someone to discover that she was there. "I ought to make a noise like a customer," she thought uncomfortably. She rose eventually, and accosted a golden-haired lady who wafted past with a mist of chiffon blouses across her arm.

"Could you wait on me please?"

It was an expression that had always done very well at the grocer's and the butcher's, but apparently it wasn't the sort of thing one said at "Irene's." The saleslady winced. She looked at and through the tweed suit. "I'm engaged," she replied off the top of a very wavy voice, and went on her way.

Claudia bided her time until another golden-haired beauty crossed her path. "I'd like to look at dresses," she said. Too late, she realized that the word "dresses" was ill chosen. There was nothing to do but to try again. This time she accosted a dapper little man who wore his accent in his moustache. "May I see your gowns?" she asked him.

She knew the effect she was aiming at, but it didn't sound quite right. She braced herself to meet his shattering contempt.

"Have you an appointment?" he asked her, and without waiting for an answer disappeared into thin air before her very eyes.

Then Julia came, and immediately things began to happen. She moved toward Claudia like a female Pied Piper with a swelling procession of salesladies in her wake. "Hello, darling!" she called, loud enough for everyone to hear. "Am I late?" She shot a slim wrist from an immaculate tailored sleeve and studied her watch. "Two minutes early." She turned to the hovering group at her elbow. "This is my sister-in-law, Mrs. David Naughton."

A murmur of interest swelled the air. Julia raised an invisible hand for silence. "Mrs. Naughton is extremely pressed for time," she continued. "We'll start on a dinner gown and a street ensemble." She paused to smile at Claudia. "Since you're not going to be able to spend much time on the farm this winter, darling, let's stay away from tweed, shall we?"

Claudia's confidence came flowing back as Julia, with a single touch of magic, elevated her to country-gentry, and transformed the pumpkin of her shabby suit into a coach and four of irreproachable good taste. Nevertheless, she was glad that she'd worn the silk underwear she'd been saving for her next pregnancy, because even Julia couldn't have glorified the substantial rayons that had weathered, without grace, the repeated rigors of a washing machine.

As it turned out however, nobody saw what she looked like underneath, for buying a dress at Irene's was in the nature of an immaculate conception, in which Claudia's sole participation consisted of looking at swatches of material and watching mannequins of an unearthly frailty drift across her vision. She soon tired of the performance. "Why can't I get something ready-made?" she demanded.

It was as if a bombshell had exploded against the mirror-lined salon. Julia gathered up the pieces in her calm contralto. "No, darling, it won't be necessary. Irene will stretch a point and put your things in work at once."

The dapper little man who turned out to be Irene himself, assured them that every possible point would be stretched to the utmost.

"Good," said Julia. "I think the brown satin in turquoise velvet for the dinner gown, and the green faille in black for the street dress."

"I never wear black," said Claudia, "and anyway, what I'm really interested in are your original models."

Another bombshell exploded, and again Julia gathered up the pieces. "Mrs. Naughton is quite right. By all means, let her try on the originals so that we can see exactly what we've got to work with."

"Ah yes, but she will not be able to get into the originals," Irene regretted. "Our mannequins are all size twelve."

"I'm a size twelve," said Claudia.

Irene shook his head and let his words slip slowly through his lips like syrup. "Unfortunately, no. According to the measurements we have taken, you are a size fourteen."

"Not on my tape measure," said Claudia with asperity.

Irene shrugged. "Very well–"

She shouldn't have done it. Something that was very live and young died within her as the green faille skirt balked stubbornly up her side.

"Our girls are very slender," the fitter mentioned kindly. The fitter was a pleasant, elderly woman with probably white hair.

"I used to be very slender," Claudia told her in a puzzled voice.

"Madame has children?" The fitter gave a gentle smile without waiting for an answer. "That makes a difference," she said.

Everyone was waiting to see how she looked in the model.

Claudia had to face them with her hand clutching at her hip to hide the gaping, but Julia's generalship was admirable. "The style," she declared with approval, "is excellent. I'm glad you tried it on, don't hesitate for a moment." She turned to Irene. "Mrs. Naughton will open a charge, of course. Beekman House."

The address turned the trick. It delivered the finished portrait of one slightly eccentric but entirely acceptable Naughton to the exclusive list of Irene's patrons. Claudia didn't feel decent about it. She would have liked to explain that it wasn't her own apartment, but Julia must have known what she was up to, because she very quickly jumped in and said, "We're late for luncheon. Come along."

There was no luncheon, of course. Once outside, she stole Claudia's thunder by getting angry first. "It takes a ton of brick to fall on you. What you've put me through!" she exclaimed.

Claudia made an effort to keep her voice from shaking. "Would you mind telling me the prices?"

"None of your business," said Julia. "I only opened the charge for background. Hartley and I will take care of the bill."

"Don't be an idiot," Claudia protested. "You're awfully generous, but David would be wild."

"Let him be wild," said Julia. "It's too bad about him if he can't accept a present from his own brother once in a blue moon. Now no more talk. Go buy yourself a pair of black suede pumps. With high heels, mind you. You can't wear oxfords with an Irene costume."

"I know," said Claudia morosely.

"I'm ten minutes overdue at the hairdressers. Drop me off in your taxi on the way down," Julia suggested in a magnanimous squaring of accounts.

Claudia had no intention of taking a taxi, but in the face

of all that Julia had done for her, it seemed a little niggardly not to.

Julia continued to keep an iron hand on Claudia's wardrobe from hat to stockings, and when the street dress was finished, she selected, from her own commodious cedar storeroom, a slender sable scarf. "Take it," she commanded. "It's a good excuse for me to get a new one."

"I've never owned furs," said Claudia, "since a squirrel coat when I was twelve."

"It's high time you began," said Julia. "No costume is complete without a neck piece–tomorrow you can go to see Maggie Brewster."

"Thank you," said Claudia.

No one was home when she started forth the next day–Matthew had gone to the park with Bertha, Bobby was in school and David had left earlier than usual that morning for an important conference. She had tried to set a definite time with Miss Brewster, but an impersonal secretary told her that no special appointments could be made for casting–Miss Brewster was seeing people between one and four. Claudia presented herself at two but already the businesslike ante-office was crowded. She observed at once that there wasn't a tweed suit in the whole room. Most of the women were dripping with mink, even though the day was unseasonably warm. Perhaps Julia was right, she reflected.

Promptly at four, a door at the farther end of the corridor opened, and Miss Brewster emerged, wearing tweed. "I'll be at the theatre!" she called out to her secretary, and swung out, looking neither right nor left.

There was an immediate move to the elevator. Claudia happened to be sitting near the hall, so she was among those fortunate enough to ride down to the street floor in Miss Brewster's company. To her chagrin it took a few moments for

Miss Brewster to remember who she was. "I've seen so many girls . . . I do recall the incident, though, and I remember your husband," Miss Brewster admitted in a puzzled voice, "but I can't understand why I saw you as 'Emma.' You're not at all the type."

Directors weren't very bright, Claudia concluded. "It's only my clothes," she explained. "You really did like me."

Miss Brewster could have received no stronger letter of recommendation. "In that case, come and see me at the Forty-seventh Street Theatre at ten-thirty tomorrow," she said.

Claudia would have walked home on air if it weren't for her high heels. As she stood debating whether or not to, a gust of wind unsettled her silly hat. She reached up to hold it; her sable scarf slithered off. She bent to catch it before it touched the ground. The glove-tight perfection of her faille skirt emitted a threatening squeak of splitting seams. Life was suddenly too complicated. She hailed a cab. Within it's steamy leatherette privacy, she held the scarf and hat in her lap and kicked off her shoes and felt like Nancy Riddle.

All too soon, the cab turned into the landscaped courtyard of Beekman House. Claudia put herself together again, and drew a bill from her purse. The meter did it's usual dirty trick of dropping another nickel, making the fare an even seventy-five cents, and placing her in the awkward position of asking the driver to break the quarter he so optimistically held out to her. She knew a moment of conflict and then decided, with a degree of bitterness, that there was a certain amount of necessary upkeep to wearing an Irene suit and living in Beekman House. She waved the quarter away.

The doorman leaped to assist her. It was time to tip him, too—he'd leaped at least half a dozen times in the last twenty-four hours. Besides, he was nice to the children. She gave him a dollar.

"Thank you very much," he said, and added, free of charge, "The boys are in the East garden with the nurse."

It was sheer gallantry on his part to dignify Bertha's two hundred pounds with the sleek-sounding title of "nurse." Claudia stood watching the trio as they gazed, fascinated, at the boats going down the river. She gave up a little prayer that the novelty would not soon wear off. Quietly, so that they should remain oblivious of her presence, she stood behind them. Suppose, she thought, that they didn't belong to her, would she consider them good-looking, well-mannered, engaging? Bobby turned before she could arrive at an honest answer. He regarded her with eyes as impartial as her own. "You look funny," he announced at length.

"I consider you neither good-looking, well-mannered *or* engaging," she replied. Curiosity got the better of her. "Where do I look funny?"

"All over," he said. "I got an A in arithmetic."

"Good," said Claudia, "You're a better man than I am—hello, Matthew, no kiss? . . . Hello Bertha."

"Ach, the new clothes!" Bertha exclaimed.

"I like New York," said Matthew.

"I don't," said Bobby.

"Would you care to go back to Connecticut?" Claudia inquired. "It can be arranged, you know, very easily." He preferred to be deaf at that point. "I don't want to go out with Matthew in the afternoons," he rebelled. "It's sissy."

"We're investigating 'Groups,'" said Claudia, "hold your horses. What do you think, Bertha?"

Bertha was an old hand at Claudia's mental short cuts. "It's very stylish," she hedged. "Different from what you always wear. You have only to get used to it. I think I'll take the children in now. It's getting damp."

"One more boat," cried Matthew.

"All right," Bertha granted. "We wait for one more boat to go by."

"Coming in with me or waiting?" Claudia asked Bobby.

"I'll wait," said Bobby sheepishly.

Claudia turned away to hide a smile—he was as much of a baby as Matthew. She must take them both to the zoo one of these days. She loved the zoo, herself. She'd talk to David about it. They might all go next Sunday morning.

Her thoughts were everywhere and nowhere, and into them a voice came. "Well of all people, Claudia Brown!"

She started. Who, outside a handful of theatre people, would know her as Claudia Brown? Then, as she stared at the smooth figure of the woman who had spoken to her, the years miraculously dropped away, and she was back in school. "Helen Drew!" she exclaimed. "Where did you drop from?"

"I'm on my way up to cocktails at the Spencer Reeds. You don't live here, do you, I thought you had a farm or something?"

"We do. We have. Yes, we are living here. I was just going up too. Won't you stop in for a minute?"

Helen glanced at her watch. "I suppose I could, it's only five-thirty. I'd love to."

They stepped into the elevator together, surreptitiously sizing each other up. The years caught up with them, and they were back in the present. Claudia could see that beneath Helen's enamelled face, a decade of living had decided to leave its mark.

"You haven't changed a bit," said Helen.

"Neither have you," said Claudia, faintly. She thought, "We're both fooling each other."

They stepped out into Elizabeth's private foyer, with its lovely Adam console and mirror. Claudia rang the bell, and Mary was there, as if she had nothing to do all day long but open doors in a black uniform and white apron. "Would you care for some tea, or sherry, Mrs. Naughton?" she asked, when she saw that Claudia had brought a guest.

"I'd love some tea. What about you Helen?"

"Sherry would be nice," said Helen. She smiled at Mary. "Or could you wangle me a martini?"

"I could," said Mary. "Cook makes them nicely."

Claudia led the way to the living room. Helen's knowing eyes took in the comfortable aristocracy of old Chippendale and Sheraton, and the expansive River view. "You've certainly come up in the world," she said frankly. "I remember the little walk-up you had around the corner from here the first year you were married."

"This isn't our apartment," Claudia said. "It's Elizabeth Van Doren's."

"Oh, I know who she is," Helen digressed with interest. "She married Jerry Seymour, didn't she? He's frightfully good-looking and much younger, but she's terribly rich, I hear."

"He is not much younger," Claudia contradicted hotly, "and he didn't marry her for her money. He fell in love with her the first time he saw her. I ought to know, because it happened at a party that was given for me after the Boston opening of Jerry's play."

Helen's avidity for gossip again took command of the conversation. "Why given for you?" she demanded.

"I was in the play."

"Go on, you weren't. I mean don't tell me you've actually kept on with your acting?"

"On and off. I've an appointment with Maggie Brewster in the morning."

"You don't say," said Helen, quite impressed. "I must have been in Reno when your play opened.—My fourth," she paused to elucidate. "My second died, though, this is only my third divorce as far as divorces go."

"Oh," said Claudia. The eventfulness of her own life paled into nothingness beside the swift panorama of Helen's marital affairs.

"Well, where are they now?" Helen reverted. "Elizabeth and her husband, I mean. On their honeymoon?"

"Yes," said Claudia. "We're looking out for Candy."

"Candy being Elizabeth's offspring, I gather." Helen shrugged. "Well, every silver lining has its cloud."

"Only Candy's no cloud. David and I are devoted to the child."

"Where is she, at school?"

"College."

"How old is she, anyway?"

"Eighteen."

"That's no child."

"Yes it is," said Claudia.

"Like fun it is," said Helen. "I was on the way to my first divorce when I was eighteen. How'd she take her mother's marriage?"

"It was a little of a shock," Claudia admitted. "But she was fine about it."

"Elizabeth happy?" Helen pursued, inordinately occupied, Claudia thought, with other people's business.

"Very," she took pleasure in saying. "We got our first long letter from her the other day." She decided that Helen had pried sufficiently into Elizabeth's affairs. "How's your mother?" she inquired. "I remember she was in politics, which always made me sort of stand in awe of her. I mean she was so different from my mother."

"She certainly was," Helen agreed enigmatically. "I remember how we used to have cookies and milk at your house after school, and your getting home early when you went to parties." She laughed. "My mother never gave a damn. I could come in at dawn and she wouldn't know the difference. As a matter of fact, she never approved of me. Still doesn't. Your mother died, didn't she?"

"Five years ago," said Claudia. She didn't want to talk about it to Helen. She was glad when she heard the elevator door close. "These are mine," she announced, as Bobby and Matthew paused at the threshold. "Come on in, boys. This is Mrs. –" She hesitated.

"It's too complicated," said Helen good-naturedly. "Just call me 'Helen.' Tell me," she went on, "what's happened to your husband? He didn't get killed in the war or anything, did he?"

"Run along," Claudia told the children.

They did not linger, even for cinnamon toast. Bobby bestowed upon Helen a disapproving stare and said, "Come on, Matthew."

"They're cute," Helen mentioned dutifully, as they departed. "What about David–that's his name, or wasn't it?"

"Yes. He was in the war, of course. Now he's back in architecture. Very successful."

"He must be," said Helen. She eyed Claudia's suit. "Jenny's?"

"No, Irene's." She was glad now that David had refused, pleasantly but firmly, to allow Julia and Hartley to pay for her new outfits. "I can't think of any better way to use a savings account," he had said.

"He was awfully handsome, as I remember," Helen went on thoughtfully.

"He's gotten handsomer," said Claudia.

Helen was still there when David came home. Claudia went out into the hall to meet him. He whistled when he saw her. "I thought you were company," he said.

"There is company," she replied, "but I'm not it." She turned around. "How do you like it?"

He pulled her into the small library off the foyer, and moved her to the light. "You don't like it," she anticipated him disconsolately. "Don't be afraid to tell me, I don't either, and Bobby said I looked funny."

"I'll knock his block off," said David. "You don't look funny, you just look funny for you. I have to get used to it."

"That's what Bertha said."

"Bertha, Bobby and I are in solid agreement, and doubtless laboring under our own limitations." He kissed her. "Cheer up. How did the evening gown turn out?"

"That's not finished yet. It'll be ready the end of the week for Julia's dinner party—Helen Drew's inside. You remember, I went to school with her—I think she's been waiting for you. Anyway, she was on her way to a cocktail party, but she seems to have forgotten to go to it. Come on in."

"Do I have to?"

"Yes, or she won't leave—What kind of a day did you have, how was the conference, we could go to the zoo on Sunday."

"Or up to the farm to call for the pup—hey, tell me, did you see Maggie Brewster, what happened?"

"Nothing. I'm to see her tomorrow."

"Is the part filled?"

"I don't know yet. I don't think so, she wouldn't have told me to come back if it was—Would she?"

"I imagine not," said David. He wrinkled his nose. "God, is that you smelling like that?"

"No, it's Helen. She even puts perfume on her palms, so that when she shakes hands with you, it sticks."

"Thanks for warning me," said David.

The warning didn't help him very much because Helen got hold of not only one hand but both, and held on for dear life.

She held on to him with her eyes, too. "As if she were looking at him with all her insides," Claudia thought. "No wonder she had four husbands, I only hope she doesn't get mine."

"May I have another teeny weeny little cocktail?" Helen begged.

"Of course," said Claudia, on pins and needles. She glanced at David apprehensively, but he didn't seem annoyed, he was mixing the cocktails himself, and apparently enjoying it.

"I ought to drink," Claudia decided. "I'll have one too," she said abruptly.

"What," David asked, after Helen had finally taken her departure, "was the idea of wasting two of my good cigarettes and an ounce of gin?"

"I'm trying to hold you. A man doesn't like to come home and drink alone, and smoke alone."

He looked at her for a long moment. "Or do a lot of other things alone," he said slowly. He turned his back on her and walked to the window, staring silently at the lights on the river.

"Dinner's been ready for half an hour," Claudia reminded him.

"I'm not hungry," he told her in a muffled voice. "I'm going out for a walk—"

He strode to the door, and then wheeled around and caught her shoulders. "Look, Claudia. There's no use in soiling our marriage with lies. I still love you, I'll always love you, I suppose. But it's happened. Sometimes it does happen, as quickly as it happened this evening, in this room, before your very eyes. The touch of a woman's hand, a whiff of fragrance, the rustle of her skirt—God only knows what makes it happen, but it does."

She wet her lips. "Are you trying to tell me that you've fallen in love with Helen?"

He bent his head.

"I'll never let you go!" she cried out in anguished protest. "It can't be love, it's only infatuation! I'll fight to keep you, I'll drink myself to the bone! But never, never will I let you go!"

"You can't hold me!" he shouted. "You little fool, don't you realize that you're trying to fight the most primitive, the most powerful urge in man!" He picked her up in his arms, as if she were so much fluff, and swung her clockwise, fastening his lips upon hers with savage passion. "That's what I mean," he cried harshly. "But what do you know about love? Nothing—nothing—" He put her back on her feet, and gave her a whack on the backside. "Come on, let's eat. Doesn't that dame know when it's time to leave?"

Claudia sighed. "You're such a fool. Shall we to a movie after supper, or shall we go to bed?"

"Both," said David.

"That's one of the nice things about New York," she said. "There's a movie and a drugstore on almost every corner."

It wasn't a very good movie—the good one was coming the following week as it invariably did—but they enjoyed it anyway. They walked home. Claudia took a soda in the drugstore while David bought some things.

They emerged into the street again. "Look at the stars," she said.

Obediently, David looked up. The sky was full of heavy clouds. "It's a mistake," she explained. "It should be full of stars."

"Is that the way you feel?"

"Yes," she said, "stars in the sky because I'm glad you're the father of my children, both born and unborn, and butterflies in my stomach because I'm seeing Maggie Brewster tomorrow—I don't want to bore God," she inserted apologetically, "but I still say I don't see why He should let one person have so much, and be so happy—I hope you like my dinner gown."

"I hope so too," said David. "Why does a woman with a big hat on always have to sit in front of me in the movies?" he reflected moodily.

"They'll continue to," said Claudia, "until you develop the courage to ask them to take it off."

They stood by the river for a while and watched for ships. "You're as bad as Bobby," she told him.

"Some day," said David, "we'll buy a boat, and just go off."

"Where?"

"Anywhere. Everywhere."

"With the children?"

"Of course with the children."

"I wonder if we're that kind of people," Claudia pondered.

"We could find out," said David.

They saw a light shining in the living room when they opened the door. "That's funny," said Claudia. "Mary usually leaves the light in the bedroom. Don't bother, I'll put it out."

She hurried into the room while David hung his coat up. She stepped short on the threshold in amazement.

"Come and see what we've got!" she called back to David.

"I hope I didn't scare you," said Candy.

"You're so grown-up, I almost didn't recognize you at first," Claudia marvelled. "Is anything wrong?" she added in quick alarm.

"No," said Candy. "I just got lonesome. And I haven't any classes tomorrow, so I thought I'd come home and have a visit with you and Uncle David. And Bobby and Matthew. I got so awfully lonesome for them, all at once—" she repeated lamely.

"Do they know you're here? I simply can't get over the change in you!"

"No, they were asleep. I haven't changed, I look the same as always, except you've never seen me except in the country with overalls rolled up to my knees."

"And pigtails sticking out from behind each ear," David tacked on. He came up behind her and tweaked her hair which fell in straight rich pleats beneath her brown felt beret. "Take off your hat and coat and stay awhile."

"Am I invited?" she asked a little timidly.

To Claudia, the old Candy came back in spite of her smooth, long-legged loveliness. "What do you mean, are you invited, this is your home and we're terribly glad to see you. Aren't we David?"

"You bet we are," said David.

Candy pulled off her hat. Claudia thought, "She's quite beautiful." She said aloud, "You look like your mother must have looked when she was your age."

"I do," said Candy. "I have an old picture of her."

David turned to Claudia. "She reminds me of you when I first met you," he said.

"I wasn't as good-looking."

"You were," said David.

Candy laughed. "Oh, you're both so nice and silly." She stretched her arms. "I'm so glad to be home. I didn't think I'd like it. I wanted to find out how it would be with Mother gone."

"She hasn't gone," Claudia remarked. "You talk like she's walked out of your life."

"I feel that way." The bruised, lost look came back into Candy's eyes. "I just can't realize it, I mean that she belongs to someone else."

"Now you're talking like the bad movie we just saw," said David.

"Oh, it's not that I'm not glad she's happy," Candy explained. "And she does seem to be, really. Her last letter was awfully full of happiness. It's just that there's only been the two of us for so long—look, I didn't come home to weep all over the place, you and Aunt Claudia are so wonderful to me, I just wanted to see you, that's all."

"We know just how you feel," said Claudia. "There's some peach shortcake left in the icebox, would you like some?"

"I think so," Candy said. "Are Mary and Katie working out all right for you?"

"Perfect," said Claudia. "I'll be spoiled forever after."

They went together to the kitchen, and Claudia found the shortcake, and also some cold steak and half an alligator pear. In a little while David joined them, and drank a glass of beer. "I guess my soda's pretty much out of the way," Claudia decided, and drank the rest of the bottle.

"This is so nice," Candy said again. "I think I'll have another glass of milk."

"God bless your appetite," said David.

Candy bridled. "It's the first time I've been hungry—" She had started to say, "since Mother got married," but she changed it swiftly to, "since I've been to college."

"I wonder if your room is ready," Claudia remembered. "I'd better see."

Later, when they were going to bed, she said to David, "You had the look of being paternal when I came back to the kitchen."

"I was," said David. "Candy's in a stew. I didn't realize how strong an attachment she had for Elizabeth."

"I wonder how I'd have felt if Mamma had married again," said Claudia thoughtfully. "I'm sure it would have been a blow."

"The thing that bothers her most," said David, "is that

she thinks Jerry's not good enough for Elizabeth, she thinks he's a playboy."

"I was afraid of the same thing," Claudia confessed. "Jerry does give that impression, you know, but probably it's because he's so good-looking and writes bad plays."

"No matter how the marriage turns out," David insisted, "I felt from the start that it was the best thing that could have happened to Candy. Elizabeth felt it, too. She knew that Candy had a pretty strong mother-image and that's nothing to fool around with."

"I ought to know," said Claudia. "I had a pretty hard time adjusting myself to Mamma's death." She looked at David soberly. "You must have gone through quite something with me."

"I did."

"Sometimes I think I'm not over it yet."

"You are."

"Are you sure?"

He kissed her. She held him close, with all her being. "I'm sure," he said softly. "I'm very sure."

The children discovered Candy at breakfast the next morning, and tore the house down with excitement. She wore a soft negligee of Elizabeth's that inflated her slim young figure into a subtle completion, but they did not notice that she had grown up—to them she was the same gay hoyden that had romped with them all summer. "I wish I didn't have to go to school," Bobby rebelled. "I'd rather stay home with Candy."

"Me, too," Matthew chimed in. "I want to stay with Candy, too."

"Such popularity," said Claudia.

"Isn't it grand?" Candy glowed.

"For two cents," said David, "I'd stay home myself." He kissed Claudia, and laid his hand for an instant on Candy's head as he passed her chair. "I'd like to take you two girls out for lunch, but I'm tied up at the office."

"I thought I'd take Candy with me when I go to see Maggie Brewster, she can see what backstage is like."

"Oh, I'd love it," said Candy.

"Phone me," David ordered. "Let me know what happened."

"Nothing's going to happen," said Claudia, but she didn't believe it for a moment, she was placating Fate—turning her back, as it were, and letting Fate surprise her when she wasn't looking.

At the last moment, just as they were ready to leave, it began to rain. Candy regarded Claudia's "Irene" costume in dismay. "Suppose we can't get taxis, it'll be ruined," she deplored. "And yet it's so frightfully stunning. I hate to see you not wear it."

Claudia looked out of the window. "It's getting worse. The sky last night looked stormy, I bet it rains all day. I'm going to change to my tweed."

"Oh dear," said Candy. "That same old suit? It seems to me I've seen it for years."

"Well, you're going to see it once more," Claudia decided. "Anyway, Maggie Brewster saw my 'Irene' yesterday, so it's just as well."

It was a welcome relief to settle into the easy comfort of the roomy skirt, and loose-fitting jacket, although beside Candy's smart young plaid, she suddenly felt a little plump and dowdy. She frowned. "Am I getting fat, do you think?"

"Aunt Claudia, don't be ridiculous," Candy scoffed. "You're just right."

Claudia didn't particularly like the expression, "just right," for it didn't allow sufficient leeway in either direction. She was mulling it over when the telephone rang. It was Helen Drew. Her heart sank. Helen was going to be a pest.

"What about lunch today?" Helen began immediately.

"I can't," said Claudia.

"I know, I know, you've an appointment with Maggie Brewster, but that's why I thought we could meet at Petro's, it's right across the street."

"I still can't," said Claudia. "Candy came home last night for a day or two. We were going to get some shopping done for her."

"Fine," said Helen. "Bring her along. I'd love to meet her, and besides it'll be fun for her, she'll see a lot of celebrities at Petro's."

Claudia hesitated. Lunching out might indeed be fun for Candy, the sort of fun that would make her look forward to coming home on vacations, which was what Elizabeth so wanted to have happen. Also it would be pleasant to go with Helen, who was doubtless an old habitué of the restaurant. She covered the transmitter with her hand. "Lunch at Petro's," she suggested, to which Candy nodded violently.

Claudia had forgotten that youth could be so perpetually thrilled. Even going up to the stage door of the theatre thrilled her. A young man however told them to wait out in front until Miss Brewster was through with her scene. "Who's he?" Candy whispered eagerly. "An actor?"

"Probably."

"Can we really watch a rehearsal?"

"It seems so."

She was as bad as Candy, she was shaky with excitement as they felt their way across the dim lobby into a row of empty seats at the rear of the orchestra. The single brutal light on the bare stage, the little group of actors—who looked so little like actors without their make-up—plunged her back into the world behind the footlights.

Candy's whisper reached her again. "Miss Brewster's terribly young, I thought she'd be about forty-five or so."

"She is," Claudia said, "but it's dark, and she's wearing slacks. She's awfully nice, though. A little mannish, but quite stunning."

"I wonder if she'll give you the part."

"I don't know. She seems to be reading quite a lot of people."

It was a shock when Miss Brewster's clear voice announced, "All right, everyone, we'll break now, Marcia, Freddie and Miss Lawton come back at two o'clock."

Claudia peered at her watch. "It's five of one already!" she discovered incredulously.

"She might have forgotten she told you to come," said Candy anxiously. "I think you ought to go backstage again."

"I suppose I should," said Claudia.

"I won't tag along this time, I'll wait for you on the street."

"It might be better," Claudia agreed.

She met Miss Brewster in the wings. Miss Brewster looked vague. Claudia had to refresh her memory. "You told me to come to see you at half-past ten today, Miss Brewster. I'm Claudia Brown."

"Oh yes—" Miss Brewster dragged her thoughts back from the morning's work. "Oh yes. Yes." She put her hand on Claudia's shoulder in a friendly way. "Come back tomorrow around three, will you?" she said brightly. "I remember quite well, now. I did like you. By all means come in to see me." She was gone before Claudia could say that she wouldn't be able to make it the following afternoon.

Candy's face fell when she saw her appear so quickly. "Nothing happened," she concluded.

"Not yet. She wants to see me tomorrow at three, but I can't because Bertha's off. She has to go with Fritz to the doctor."

"Don't be silly, I'll take care of the children. I'd adore to, I'll take them to the zoo."

Claudia started to say, "David and I wanted to take them to the zoo this Sunday," but she didn't have the heart to deprive Candy of the pleasure. They could go to the farm instead. "Didn't you have to go back to college tomorrow, though?"

"I'm having such a good time," Candy pleaded, "what's the sense of going back before the weekend—I mean tomorrow's Friday already, and there aren't any classes until Monday, so really what's the sense?"

"No sense," said Claudia. She remembered suddenly, that Julia's dinner party was Saturday night. "I must remind me to call Julia in the morning and ask if we can bring Candy along with us," she thought.

The small outer entrance of the restaurant was crowded when they got there. Helen was waiting for them. She looked harassed. She said, "You can get us a table, can't you, Claudia?" She gave a little laugh. "I tried to make a reservation over the telephone, but they didn't know me. I used your name, but it seems they couldn't place you either. Maybe if they see you—"

Claudia shrank from the mere thought of forcing the headwaiter's attention. She had come in to Petro's once or twice with Jim Varney during rehearsals, but that was all. "I'm afraid we'll just have to wait our turn," she said. She was acutely uncomfortable—one of the first pacts that she and David had made when they were married was that no dinner on earth was worth standing in line for, and they'd stuck to it. "Let's go some place else," she said.

"Every place is crowded at this hour," Helen argued. She realized Candy's presence for the first time, "Hello," she said.

"Hello," said Candy. "I hope when we do get a table, it'll be where I can see the names under the pictures on the wall. Maybe Aunt Claudia will have hers up there one day."

"I wouldn't count on it," said Claudia. "There's Jim Varney."

"Where!" Candy exclaimed. "On the wall?"

"No, over there in the corner."

Helen jogged her impatiently. "Well, why don't you wave to him!"

"He doesn't see me."

"Make him see you," Helen urged. "The only way we can get a table is if you know somebody important."

Sam Goldheart pushed his way through the coatroom at that moment. Claudia died a thousand deaths, but because she didn't want to spoil Candy's luncheon, she said boldly, "Hello, Mr. Goldheart."

"Hello!" Mr. Goldheart boomed out, on general principles. He eyed her up and down. He must have recognized the tweed suit—she'd never worn anything else during rehearsals—because he said, "Well, well, well! Looking for a job? Come and see me tomorrow."

Helen was vastly impressed. Candy said, "Now they'll both want you!"

Claudia smiled grimly to herself. Mr. Goldheart's glib invitation did not mean as much as they thought it did. It was better than nothing, certainly, but it was one of the oldest refrains in the theatre—"*Come and see me tomorrow*—"

It might have been a coincidence, but they were signalled to a table ahead of others who had been there before them. "He means us!" Candy exclaimed incredulously.

She took time off from looking around to order a cup of vichysoisse, a portion of spaghetti and ravioli mixed, and a piece of cocoanut pie. Helen ordered a salad and tea, with melba toast. "And you'd better take the same," she advised Claudia briefly.

Claudia was affronted. "Why should I, I'll have the same as Candy," she said.

Helen shrugged. "You'll be sorry. We're crowding thirty, my pet. That's a smart suit."

"Mine?" asked Claudia, surprised, and partially mollified.

"Very good-looking," Helen approved.

The tweed was obviously basking in the reflected glory of the Irene ensemble that Helen had seen the day before. "Two smart costumes for the price of one," Claudia reflected with satisfaction.

"Oh and by the way, watch that husband of yours," Helen mentioned casually.

"Why?"

"Because I'm mad about him. I'm going to get him away from you if it's the last thing I do."

"Go ahead," said Claudia, with an inward smile. "You have my full permission."

"You're awfully sure of him, aren't you?" said Helen.

Candy came up from her cup of vichysoisse. "I don't blame Miss Drew," she said. "I think he's wonderful, too."

Helen studied Candy with a quizzical smile. "Oh? What have we here?" she murmured.

Claudia got the implication of Helen's lifted brows. "What a pathetic fool she is," she thought, as she tackled her spaghetti.

At dinner that night, it was Candy who recounted to David everything that happened. "I suppose Aunt Claudia doesn't want to talk about it because she's superstitious, she's afraid to get excited about it, but really and truly, David, you should have been there, Mr. Goldheart remembered her right away—"

Claudia didn't hear what David said in return. She had noticed with a small, strange shock that Candy had kept the 'Aunt' and dropped the 'Uncle.'

Before she went to bed she got out the tape measure. She

put it around her waist and peered down at it. She took a deep breath, drew herself in, and looked again.

David was amused. "What it is?"

"Twenty-seven," she said grimly. "I've eaten my last spaghetti."

"I thought twenty-seven was pretty good for an old married lady," he said.

It wasn't good enough. She happened to know that Candy's waist was twenty-four.

Nine

Julia said by all means to bring Candy. "Although I don't think it'll be much fun for her," she said. "A middle-aged dinner party isn't very amusing for the young."

Claudia felt like saying that if it was going to be as middle-aged as all that, it wouldn't be very amusing for her either, but Julia didn't have that kind of a sense of humour. "It wouldn't be a bad idea," she went on, with the matchmaker's look in her eye, "to ask John Payne for Candy."

"I know David would like it," said Claudia. "He thinks John's an awfully fine boy besides being the best draftsman he's ever had."

"Also, he comes from very good family," Julia added. "We'll have him by all means."

Candy was excited about the party, but not particularly interested in meeting John Payne. "Aunt Claudia, it's so silly to have anyone special for me. As long as you and David are there, I'll have a wonderful time."

"Look," said Claudia abruptly, "why do you call me 'Aunt' and not David, 'Uncle'?"

Candy got a little red. "Do you think he minds?"

"No," said Claudia, "but I mind. You make me feel doddering."

Candy thought about it. "I don't know why, but leaving off the 'Uncle' just came naturally."

"Well kindly leave off the 'Aunt'," said Claudia.

"I'd love to if you don't think it's fresh."

"If your Uncle David didn't think it was fresh, why should I?"

Candy giggled. "'My Uncle David'—that sounded so funny."

"No funnier than my 'Aunt' Claudia," Claudia was tempted to retort, but it was the sort of conversation that could have gone on endlessly, without logic, into indefinite and therefore dangerous channels.

They were sitting in Candy's room. It was a sweet room, a conglomeration of child and womanhood, with its collection of Copenhagen dogs on the mantel, a wooly panda on the commode between a pair of crystal perfume bottles, innumerable pictures of Elizabeth, and a copy of Havelock Ellis on the bedside table. Candy was manicuring her nails. Claudia studied her own with a frown. "I'll certainly have to get another manicure before Julia's dinner," she announced.

"It's easier to do them yourself," said Candy.

"Not mine it's not," said Claudia. "Living on the farm has made them problem children."

"I used to be a problem child," Candy volunteered cheerfully. "Mother told me I used to bite my nails."

"Thank goodness Bobby and Matthew never have."

"I wouldn't marry a man who bit his nails," Candy proclaimed, "or who didn't like dogs, or have a nice back-of-the-neck and a sense of the ridiculous."

It occurred to Claudia that she might have been talking about David, so completely did he fill her qualifications for a husband. Judiciously, however, she avoided the obvious, and bestowed the attributes where they would do more good. "I suppose those were some of the reasons that made your mother marry Jerry," she said.

Candy's soft young lips set into a hard line. "I don't like him," she burst out. "I never will."

Claudia knew that Candy resented Jerry, but she hadn't realized quite how much. "You're being unfair," she protested. "You ought to be glad for Elizabeth; her letters are so happy."

"I know it," Candy mumbled.

"And think how alone she'd be when you got married," Claudia quickly followed up.

"I wouldn't have gotten married," Candy said.

"Perhaps that was one of the things she was afraid of," Claudia pointed out gently. "People have to learn not to cling to anyone, or anything. Whether it's a husband, a mother, a house, or even just an idea."

Candy looked at Claudia a little in awe. "I didn't know you knew so much."

"I know it with my mind," said Claudia, "but I'm not so good at applying it."

"I think you are. Look what you've been through—aside from David going to war, I mean. Your mother died, and you lost a baby and David almost got killed in an automobile accident and so did Bobby, didn't he?"

"Yes, David in Eastbrook, and Bobby in New York. So it just goes to show that it doesn't make much difference where you are. Life catches up with you."

"It seems that way," said Candy thoughtfully. "You're lucky Matthew hasn't been much trouble though. Except last spring with his blood poisoning."

"And pneumonia. And a convulsion when he was a baby—"

"How did I never hear about the convulsion?" Candy interrupted.

"I don't know," said Claudia. "It was that same winter we were in New York. I was alone with him. Bertha had gone to a funeral. Fortunately Edith Dexter happened to come in."

Candy sat up and took notice. "Edith Dexter. She was the woman who was jealous of you because her husband was in love with you!"

A gratifying warmth mingled with the chilling memories of past catastrophes. "Who told you any such thing?" she queried curiously.

"It's a little vague, but I remember some friend of Mother's coming to the house and spilling the whole story. I remember Mother shushing her up and saying it was no one's business."

"I don't think he was really so much in love with me, he was just in love with youth. I mean Edith had gone a little fat around the hips, and sloppy, and she'd lost her son and wouldn't snap out of it, and when Phil first met me—at a dinner-party of Julia's, incidentally—I must have looked rather attractive. I wore a pink dress and he said I was like a morning in spring."

"My dress is pink," said Candy, "do you think I'll have the same luck?—No, seriously, is it true that Mrs. Dexter threatened to jump out of the window, or was that just silly gossip?"

"No, it was true," said Claudia. "She was in a frightful state the day she came to see me, and in the middle of it Matthew blew his convulsion, and Edith snapped out of her histronics like nobody's business, and helped me pull him through."

"What happened to Phil and Edith?"

"I don't know. We went back to Eastbrook, and stayed there ever since. But they'll be at Julia's too. I'm looking forward to seeing them again."

"So am I," said Candy. "It must have been fun having a married man like you like that. Did you really like him?"

"I did," Claudia admitted. "He reminded me of what David would probably be at that age. Come to think of it, David's getting along to that age now. Life is funny, isn't it?"

"Awfully funny," Candy agreed. "But frightfully interesting." She squinted at two small bottles filled with almost identical shades of crimson fluid. "Shall I use 'Sunrise' or 'Intoxication'?"

"I wouldn't know," said Claudia. "I never use color on my nails, David hates it."

"Oh," said Candy. She chose 'Intoxication,' but at supper that evening Claudia noticed that she had taken it off.

Her gown from Irene's came promptly at noon on Saturday. Candy begged to see it, but Claudia was obdurate. She hung it away in her closet until it was time to dress. "It's the actress in me," she said. "I want to make an entrance."

She sat in her panties, and watched David wrestle with a stiff shirt. He was in a vile mood. He hadn't worn his tuxedo since before the war, and he didn't see why in Hades he had to begin. He was somewhat appeased, however, when he found that he could slip two fingers beneath the belt with no difficulty whatsoever. "The old man has kept his shape," he discovered smugly.

"I wish the old lady could say the same," Claudia returned gloomily. "I'm two inches more than I was."

"Nonsense," said David, refusing to face facts. He slipped on his jacket, and immediately he became a stranger, new to her eyes, and stimulating to her senses.

"Why can't you always be so handsome?" she murmured.

"I am," he said. "Oughtn't you to dress?"

"I'll be ready in a minute, I'm all done from the inside out, teeth washed, neck powdered, and everything." She whisked into Elizabeth's commodious dressing room and closed the door behind her.

He opened it, and poked his head through. "Why the modesty?"

"It's not modesty. I want to burst upon your vision."

"See that you burst fast," he adjured her. "It's almost seven."

"That's lots of time, don't hurry me."

Not the least of Irene's expensive artistry lay in the simple miracle of a sheath of velvet that molded sheer perfection as it cascaded from shoulder to floor in a single liquid motion. David was lighting a cigarette when she came back into the room. He stared at her with the match burning in his hand, and gave a low whistle—whether of approval or disapproval, she could not be sure. She waited for him to say something. He whistled again. "Turn around," he said. She turned around. "Quite a figger of a woman," he said at last. He was going to say more, but the children wandered in. "Is that a new dress?" Bobby demanded at once.

She nodded. "Do you like it?"

"You look tall in it."

She knew that was as much as she was going to get from him. She turned to Matthew. "And what's your opinion, sir?"

Matthew hedged. "What's that color?"

"Turquoise."

"What's turquoise?"

"Just blue. At twice the price."

"It's green," Bobby denied.

"That's why it's turquoise," said Claudia.

Then Candy stood in the doorway. There was nothing subtle about her dress, or about the way she looked. "Candy looks pretty," Bobby announced immediately, and David said, "Haven't you got a pink dress something like that, Claudia?"

"Yes," said Claudia.

"I like pink," said Matthew firmly. "Pink looks nice."

Candy was oblivious of their comments. Her eyes were glued on Claudia's gown. "It's too stunning for words," she declared. "You look simply divine, so frightfully sophisticated!"

Claudia smoothed the folds of chiffon against Candy's flat young hips. "You look pretty beautiful yourself," she said.

"This old thing? I hate it, but Mother insists that it has"—Candy made a moue—" 'grace and fragrance'."

"It has," said David.

"I'd rather have style," said Candy.

"Don't be silly," said Claudia. "You begin to have style when you start losing other things. I think we'd better go."

With the flurry of departure, Bobby received the delayed impact of an evening alone. "Cheer up," said Claudia, "I can see your security shaking."

He wasn't quite sure what she meant, so he ignored the remark. "I wish you didn't have to go out all the time," he grumbled.

David said, "You're rotten spoiled, young man. Suppose you had parents who went gallivanting every night."

"And separately," Claudia put in.

"I was lucky too, Bobby," Candy told him. "Mother hardly ever went out and when she did, I'd hate it as much as you do. Just think, though, what fun we'll have tomorrow when we go up to the farm to bring Bluster down."

"But you'll have to go back to college in the night," Bobby complained.

Claudia knew him so well—he wanted to keep his small universe intact, and already Candy had become a part of that universe. She had become, in these few days, a part of all their lives. "I can feel my own security shaking," thought Claudia grimly. It was shameful to admit it, but she was glad that in another twenty-four hours, she and David would be alone again. She felt a loathing of herself, when, as the cab drew up in front of the festive lights of Julia's house, Candy's lips brushed her cheek in a quick, shy kiss. "Thanks," she breathed, "for giving me such a wonderful time—"

They were the first to arrive. "I could wring your neck," Claudia hissed in David's ear, "you're always so damned early."

"Julia said a quarter of eight," David insisted doggedly, "and that's exactly what it is now."

"How many times have I told you that quarter of eight always means a quarter past."

Hartley met them in the hall and led them to the library, where he immediately produced a big black cigar and gave it to David. Big black cigars did not look well on David, but Hartley always gave him one the minute he saw him. This accomplished, he turned to Candy and put a fatherly arm around her. "Well, well, well, so you're Candy," he said. Claudia could see how uncomfortable Candy felt held up against Hartley's portly side, so she said, "How's your gall bladder, Hartley?" and he promptly released Candy and moved toward Claudia as to a magnet. "Kicking up," he said, "kicking up."

Julia came in—thin but not willowy, in rippling black satin. She frowned when she saw that they were making themselves at home in the library. "Hartley I told you we were serving cocktails upstairs in the boisserie," she said.

Hartley gave Claudia a broad wink. "Don't let Julia put anything over on you," he advised. "She's not giving this party for you or David, she's giving it to show off her Eighteenth Century panelling."

"Don't be absurd," said Julia shortly. Claudia wondered if she ever said, "Don't be silly," like ordinary people.

It was eight o'clock before another soul showed up. John

Payne was fashionably late, too, but only because he had gone to Fourteen West, instead of Fourteen East. He stood in the doorway, mopping his moist young face with a silk handkerchief, and looking miserable. Then he caught sight of Claudia, and sought haven at her side. Claudia turned him over to Candy.

"Isn't it a lovely room?" said Candy.

"Very nice," John conceded frugally. He ran a pleasantly bony hand across the panelling. "I doubt very much whether it's a Period Louis Quinze."

"Oh," said Candy, quite bored. "Do you?"

"Yes," said John, "and I'll show you why—"

"If he's not careful," Claudia thought, "he's going to earn Julia's undying animosity." Her eyes swept the quickly filling room. Phil hadn't come yet. Neither had Jim Varney. Julia was right—it was a very middle-aged party. And then, suddenly, Phil did come, and though he was still distinguished, he had lost the look of steel that Claudia remembered him to have. He, too, was middle-aged, with the faintest suggestion of a paunch.

For a moment neither of them could find anything to say to each other. At last Phil broke the silence. "Well, well, well," he said, and Claudia knew at once that there was nothing more between them. He must have felt it at the same instant, for his smile went a little blank. "How've you been?" he finished lamely.

"Oh fine," said Claudia.

"You're looking exceptionally well," he went on, without really looking at her.

"I feel exceptionally well," she said. "How's Edith?"

"Very well. She'll be along in a moment, she stopped to powder her nose."

From what Claudia remembered of Edith, she wasn't the sort to care much about her nose, and with the passing of minutes, it became increasingly obvious that not even a very particular nose could take that long to powder. Edith had always had a little trouble with her stomach, and it was probably bothering her before seeing a lot of people.

"Your husband," Phil's voice came from a distance, "looks exceedingly fit."

"He is," said Claudia.

"Julia tells me he's the architect for this big housing project downtown."

"He is," said Claudia. ("I mustn't say 'he is,' again," she told herself.)

"Who's the young thing in pink?" Phil asked.

"She's Elizabeth Van Doren's daughter."

"Ah," said Phil, with great meaning and meaning nothing. "Fresh as a summer evening," he added, as an afterthought.

Spring morning. Summer evening. Phil was moving on to twilight and toward warmer seasons. They looked at each other, a little uncomfortable, and again words forsook them utterly. She hoped that Julia would not put them side by side at dinner. She wondered if there'd be oysters. Phil had given her his oysters that night they'd first met. Not because they didn't agree with him, but because he preferred to see her enjoy them.

She might have known that Julia would pair them off; and there were oysters. Phil started to eat one, but Edith sitting opposite, wagged her finger playfully and said, "Ah, ah— mustn't touch—"

Phil laid his fork down with a sigh, "I like them, but they don't like me," he said.

"Time can be so cruel," thought Claudia. "And so mischievous." Time had certainly played tricks with Edith and Phil. Apparently, Edith didn't know she had a stomach any longer, and her hips were gone, too, and quite a lot of her rear. She was as straight up and down as Candy, and far more vivacious. Candy had taken a fleeting moment to whisper in Claudia's ear, "That can't be the woman you told me about–" and Claudia had nodded, baffled.

Later, Julia told her that Edith was going to a doctor who was giving her some sort of injections. "Personally," said Julia, in brooding conflict, "I wouldn't trifle with nature. She might be ten years younger now, but in ten years she's going to be twenty years older." Claudia wasn't too good at mathematics, but as far as she could figure out, Edith was eventually going to break even, and she and Phil would catch up with each other again, for better or for worse.

In the meantime, Edith appeared to be enjoying her span of borrowed time. She reminded Claudia of Helen Drew the way she fastened her attention on John during dinner. He was sitting next to Candy, crossways down the table, but it didn't make any difference to Edith, she monopolized him just the same. Candy willingly dropped out of the competition, and returned to her oysters with relish. Across the empty place that Julia was still saving hopefully for Jim Varney, Claudia saw David slip one of his own oysters on to Candy's plate. David loved oysters, they agreed with him magnificently. Claudia looked away quickly. There was a sickness in her heart. She thought, "Tomorrow at this time Candy will be back at college, and I'll be well again."

She was glad when Jim finally came. He wore an old brown suit and needed a haircut, and didn't apologize for either. Julia smiled away his oddities. "Mr. Varney's in rehearsal, directing a new play," she explained.

Edith's sparkling gaze wondered to the newcomer. She cried, with her voice clapping its hands, "What fun! May I come and watch sometime?"

"No," said Jim. He pulled out his chair at Claudia's side. "Hello," he said, just as if he had seen her only yesterday.

"I suppose you know you're the only reason I came to this damn party."

Claudia said, "The food's wonderful."

"That's a help," said Jim. "How've you been? You look like a million dollars. I hear you're living in New York and going back on the stage—the food *is* good, by God—any luck so far?"

"You mean with a job?" She shook her head. "I've seen Maggie Brewster twice. I don't know whether she's still interested in me or not."

"I doubt it," said Jim. "She's found a girl to play the lead." He made a wry face. "Maggie and her discoveries. It seems this new find is the daughter of a little upholsterer in her neighborhood. Maggie's been coaching her up at her country place all summer—didn't she tell you?"

"No, she just said to come back, something might turn up. I'm sure nothing will, but as long as she liked me last spring, she has such a lot of respect for her own judgment that she doesn't want to insult herself."

"That's Maggie," said Jim with an appreciative guffaw. "Tell me, have you seen Sam Goldheart?"

"Yes, I ran into him at lunch the day I saw Miss Brewster. He said to come in and see him. I did. But I didn't see him."

"You're cutting your teeth in the theatre business in a big way," Jim chortled, "and it's a long tough road, baby, believe me. Well, you had your chance, you didn't take it, and the theatre forgets fast. Now you'll have to begin from scratch like everybody else."

"I'm not so sure I want to," said Claudia.

"Too proud, too lazy or just plain garden variety sour grapes?"

"I don't think any of those reasons. The theatre isn't my world."

He looked at her shrewdly. "How do you know it isn't?"

"I just know. People should stay where they belong."

"Smart girl. Where'd you get your philosophy?"

"It must have come on me gradually—like old age."

"Well, if you find yourself getting youthful again"—he grinned at her—"come in and see me."

"I don't believe a word of it," she said. "But thanks just the same."

"That's where you're wrong." He covered her hand with his, and the grin faded from his lips. "I mean it, baby. Any time that philosophy of yours goes back on you, you come to Uncle Jim. Remember it."

Something in his voice made her know that he did mean it. "I'll remember it," she said gratefully, "but I don't imagine I'll change my mind."

"You will," he said.

She was curious. "What makes you say so?"

"Because," he replied, "you're too young to be that old."

She found him provocative, as always. It was too bad that the hostess in Julia decided that Claudia was monopolizing the one interesting guest of the evening. "Candy's aching to get a word in edgewise with Jim," she suggested gayly, from the head of the table.

Candy didn't deny it. She said, full of excitement, "We saw you at lunch the other day, Mr. Varney, but you didn't see us."

Jim turned in his chair to look at her. "Why didn't you do something about it?" he demanded. He turned back to Claudia. "Who is this luminous young female?"

"I thought you knew. Candace Van Doren. Elizabeth's daughter." She held her breath lest he was going to say, "Well, well, well," but he didn't, of course. He said, "And by all that's holy, Jerry's step-daughter!"

The joy went out of Candy's face, and some magic that might have existed between Jim and herself was destroyed.

Jim didn't know what it was all about, he was aware only that after a limping exchange of formalities, Candy bored him. "Dull girl," he commented to Claudia through a mouthful of squab.

"You're wrong," said Claudia. "She's an enchanting child."

Jim shrugged. "Maybe I just don't like enchanting children," he said.

Claudia tried not to be glad.

"It wasn't too bad an evening," David said as they went to bed.

"Not too bad."

"You seem to like that fellow."

"What fellow?"

"Jim Varney."

"I can't make up my mind whether he bites his nails or whether they're just grubby from backstage dust."

"Ask him," David advised.

"I'd rather not know."

"Your friend, Phil, is getting slightly bald around the temples," David continued with a degree of complacence. "And for God's sake, what happened to Edith?"

"Glands."

"She should lay off of John. She invited him to the opera with her damn glands. And the poor devil likes music."

"Candy didn't seem to mind his not paying much attention to her." Claudia stuck a lot of things into a drawer, she liked a tidy room to sleep in. "In fact, Candy doesn't know anyone else is around when you're there," she elaborated in a voice that she hoped sounded casual.

"Candy's a nice youngster," said David. He put out the light. "Shall we go to sleep?"

"Yes," she said. She didn't feel too well, though it was probably only an attack of bad character.

Before they knew it, Bobby was at the door, whispering in a loud voice, "Wake up, it's time to go to the farm!"

"Go away," said David.

"But it's late," Bobby insisted. "It's eight o'clock!"

"Go wake Candy," Claudia suggested. "That'll give you something to do."

"Candy's up," he announced. "She went to the garage already to bring the car around."

"That's the youngness of it all," said David glumly.

"I used to be like that," said Claudia. "I used to be awake before I opened my eyes. Now I open my eyes before I'm awake."

"Nevertheless," David remarked, "you're one of the few women I know who wake up looking human."

"How many women are you in the habit of seeing when they wake up?"

"I'd hate to look at Edith Dexter early in the morning."

"You should stop talking," Bobby injected mutinously.

"If you get out, we'll get up," said Claudia.

He vanished without further ado. They looked at each other and smiled. "Wouldn't it be nice if it were tonight," said David.

"Perfect," said Claudia devoutly. Could it be that he remembered that they were going to drop Candy at the train on the way home from the farm? She reached for his hand. "I'm an awful fool," she told him contritely.

He didn't ask her why. He merely agreed, serenely, that she was. "But you're a nice girl anyway," he said.

She felt cleansed, relaxed. She had made her confession, and was forgiven.

Bobby came stomping back a few minutes later. "You're still in bed!" he discovered in outrage.

"If you get out," said David mildly, "we'll get up."

Bobby whimpered in frustration. "You said that before!"

"Did you wash your teeth?" Claudia asked.

"When?" Bobby evaded.

"Go wash them," she said sternly. "At once." She took pity on him. "We'll be ready in two minutes!" she called after him.

Candy was in the driver's seat when they went downstairs. She wore her tweed suit and a felt hat. She laughed when she saw Claudia. "We look like twins," she said.

"Niece-and-aunt twins," said Claudia.

"Don't be silly," said Candy. "I look as old as you do."

"That may be," said Claudia, "but I don't look as young as you."

"When you two girls get finished talking double talk," said David, "I'd like to have my seat, please."

"Oh, I thought I'd drive," said Candy innocently.

"Oh, you did, did you," said David. "Get back there with the children where you belong."

"What a wonderful day!" Claudia breathed, as she took her place beside David, "I can smell the smell of burning leaves in the air."

"People don't burn leaves in New York," said David. When they turned into the farm, Edward was burning leaves in the orchard. "I told you!" Claudia exulted.

"I see Bluster!" Bobby shouted. Bluster was a speck in the distance, going off on one of his forbidden trips. He stopped dead at the sound of a car. It took a long moment for him to register that the family had come home, but when he finally did, there was no holding him. He almost knocked Edward over. Edward said, "Hey!" Then he saw what it was all about, and dropped his rake and came over to them. He was all smiles, but he could hardly talk.

"Where did you get that cold?" David frowned.

"I'm over it now. Down Bluster! Be quiet, boy!"

"He'll get a stroke," said Claudia. "Do dogs get strokes?"

"You ought to be in bed instead of out here on a Sunday raking leaves," David persisted.

"I'm all right," Edward said, "but the children oughtn't to come too near me."

There wasn't a chance of the children catching his cold. They had already disappeared with Candy toward the pond. Claudia looked around. "Where's Shakespeare?"

"He's hiding someplace," said Edward. "I have his basket ready for you to take him to the city. He's a smart cat. I bet maybe he knows."

"The ungrateful hussy," said Claudia.

"He'll come out when he hears you," said Edward.

"How's everything else?" David broke in. "Let's start with the barn."

"I'll meet you there, I want to see the garden first," said Claudia. It seemed as if they couldn't talk fast enough, couldn't do enough things at once.

The dahlias and chrysanthemums were at their most beautiful. She picked great bunches of them. She would always remember this clear fall day, with the smell of leaves in the air. David had come home from the war on just such a day. "Thanks, God, for giving him back to me," she whispered. "And keep on helping me to be a nice girl, and not a jealous old hag."

A pickup stopped in front of the door; she wondered who it was, for no one could have known that they had come home. "It would be nice," she hinted to God, "if it were a man to buy a pig."

It wasn't, though, it was Nancy Riddle, large and ruddy in her riding breeches, talking at the top of her voice to someone she had brought along with her. "The family's away" Claudia could hear her distinctly—"so we'll tell Edward we want to see the cows, we're interested in a young heifer or two that might fit in with our bloodline. That'll give us enough chance—" Nancy laughed, but her laughter trickled off when she caught sight of Claudia coming from the garden, and red polka dots came out on her neck and gave her away. "What a surprise!" she exclaimed. "I didn't know you were back!" She looked at her escort with the effect of stepping on his foot. "This is Mrs. Naughton. Claudia, this is Mr. Bradford, my new superintendent."

"Pleased to meet you, I'm sure," Mr. Bradford said civilly. "Nice little place you got here."

"Something," thought Claudia, "is at the back of this visit."

"How is Hedwig working out?" she asked pointedly.

Nancy didn't get the connection. "Quite nicely," she said. "My cook doesn't like her, but she gets along very well with the chauffeur."

"Perhaps Edward will get along well with the cook," Claudia amended inwardly, "and then everything would be fine."

Nancy didn't stay long, and she was no more interested in a heifer than the man in the moon. After she left, Claudia and David wandered through the alfalfa field toward the knoll. "That old girl had a guilty conscience if ever I saw one," David said.

"She should know by this time that Edward wouldn't leave us," said Claudia.

"We'd be in a fix if he did. Running a place like this on an absentee basis is a bad business. I wish I could see my way clear to getting back this spring, but I can't. I mightn't even be able to get here at Christmas."

"Edward's kept everything up, hasn't he?"

"He's done wonders," said David. "But if his cold had turned into something serious, there'd have been no one to take over."

"That's true. Hadn't we better put an extra man on?"

"I don't see how we can swing it financially, now that we've cut down on our milk and egg production. The trouble is, we can't afford to get in any deeper than we are. Feed and labor's too high."

"Well, let's let things ride awhile," said Claudia. "Maybe Edward's had his cold for the winter, like Matthew's foot."

"Maybe," said David.

They had reached the knoll, where they could see the farm lying like a toy, within its circle of maples. "Always," Claudia murmured, "in the big moments of our lives, we've come up here."

"What's the big moment now?" David smiled. He was watching Bluster dissolve beneath a fence, and then spring back to bone and muscle. "You great big smart boy," he commended, as Bluster came panting up to them, full of achievement.

"Keep your tail to yourself," Claudia said.

Not to be outdone, Shakespeare suddenly performed his special trick of coming out of nowhere. Claudia swooped him up. "How do you do, it's about time you said hello to us. Now the whole family's here, except the children. Where'd they disappear to, I wonder?"

"Down to the pond with Candy," said David.

"I know, but didn't they come back?"

"I haven't seen them."

Visions of drowning flashed through Claudia's mind. "I think we ought to call them."

"We really should," David agreed. "I don't think Candy's ever caught the view from up here."

Claudia buried her face in Shakespeare's orange fur. She didn't want David to see her at that moment, for she felt that her lips had set into an unlovely line. Shakespeare's paw lay lightly against her cheek, his claws sheathed in velvet, his amber eyes indifferent but alert. "It's a good thing I trust you," she said, "or I could be torn to pieces."

"Trust who?" said David.

"Whom," Claudia corrected. "The cat."

"Oh," said David. "What's the big moment you were talking about?" he asked after a pause.

She wanted to say, "In a little while we'll be taking Candy to her train," but she was ashamed. "Coming home to the farm," she said, "is a very big moment." She was ignobly determined that Candy should not invade the knoll, the one remaining place that was their's alone. "Let's find the children," she said.

They walked back slowly, with David stopping every now and again to pick up a stone, or test a fence post. He was pleased to see what the cows had done. "Best fertilizer in the world," he said. "This'll be fine pasture. Do you remember how worthless this piece was when we bought the place?"

She remembered. "New York seems a million miles away," she said.

Suddenly Bobby raced across the lawn. "Mother!" he shouted. "Daddy!"

Claudia's heart stopped beating. "It's Matthew," she cried. "Something's happened to him—"

She started on a run. David pulled her back. "Don't be so edgy, he's just looking for us that's all."

"Bobby! Here we are! What's the matter?" she called.

"It's Candy!" Bobby called back. "She's killed herself almost, you'd better come quick!"

David was ahead of her. She ran after him, with her breath cutting her chest. They found Candy huddled on the rocky path to the pond. Matthew was squatted beside her, full of solicitude. "Candy fell down," he said.

Candy's voice was shaky. "It's nothing. I told Bobby not to call you."

"How'd you fall?" David demanded.

"I tripped over a log."

He turned to Claudia, glowering. She recognized the fury that always masked his tenderness. "That girl's as bad as you are. Always tripping."

"I haven't tripped in a year," Claudia indignantly denied.

David said gruffly, "Can you stand up?"

"Of course," said Candy.

He helped her to her feet. "I'm fine," she said, but she winced as she tried to walk. David swooped her up in his arms. "I'm too heavy!" she protested.

"Shut up," he said. He carried her to the house. The children followed with Claudia. "Candy's hurt," Matthew announced in awe.

"Not too badly," said Claudia shortly.

"She fell hard, her knees were all bleeding from the stones," Bobby volunteered. "She cried. She said she wasn't crying, but it looked like crying."

"I've fallen down lots of times," said Claudia. She wanted to add, "and I didn't cry." She bit back a rush of anger. She hated Candy for being in David's arms, she didn't believe for one instant that it was necessary for him to carry her. "Run and play," she told the children, "until it's time to leave."

In the living room David put Candy down on the sofa. "Stay there until I get the iodine," he said.

"Ouch, don't," Candy wailed. "It's going to sting!"

"You big baby. How'd you like a nice infection?"

"I'd love it," said Candy. "Anything but iodine."

Claudia felt as if she were listening to herself, as if Candy had taken over a role that had been played at sweet and exciting intervals in their marriage. She stole a glance at David. He was seemingly unaware that a shift had been made in the central character. "There," he said, as he gently cleansed the jagged bruises on her knees, "that ought to feel better."

"It does," said Candy. "You should have studied medicine."

On the way home, he took the long road through the village, and drew up in front of Dr. Barry's rambling brown house across from the post office. Candy was vehement when she discovered his intention. "But this is assinine," she cried. "I'm perfectly all right, I don't need a doctor!"

"No back talk," said David.

"Your mother left you in our care," said Claudia. She knew she sounded prim, and a sense of sedateness increased as she accompanied them up the gravel path. "Don't budge!" she called back to the children, who were staying in the car. "And don't dare touch the brakes or anything!"

"Don't be such a fuss-box," said David. "You're putting ideas in their heads."

"They've got ideas," Claudia told him shortly. She was nothing but a third wheel while they waited for someone to answer the doctor's bell.

"Nobody home," Candy crowed, but after a few minutes, a light went up in the hall, and Mrs. Barry opened the door. Her neat brown dress looked as if she had just whisked off an apron, and she wore the freshly innocent look of someone who had been eating. "Well, I declare, come right in!" she beamed. "It's nice to see you all back in Eastbrook again. I hope this isn't a professional call."

"It is, rather," said David.

Mrs. Barry dropped her sewing-circle air and at once became the physician's wife. "I'll tell Doctor," she said. "Just step into the waiting room."

Miraculously, as if he had been there all the time and not having supper in the kitchen, Dr. Barry opened the sliding doors of his office. "How do you do, how do you do!" he said. "Nobody ill, I hope?"

"I scratched my knees," Candy said scornfully. "David thinks I'm made of sugar."

"Well, we'll take a look at them," said Dr. Barry, gesturing her ahead of him.

David said, "You'd better go with her, Claudia." He picked up an old magazine on hygiene, and sat down in a chair.

Dr. Barry examined the ugly bruises on Candy's knees. "You must have had quite a fall," he conceded. He felt her kneecaps, "It doesn't seem to be anything very serious however. It's better to let the air get to them. No bandages, let the air get at them.–How's your mother?"

"Very well," said Candy.

"Still in England on her wedding trip?"

"Yes."

"A fine woman. A fine woman, and a lovely one."

"Did you see very much of her while I was at college?" Candy asked in quick suspicion.

Dr. Barry was slightly taken aback. Again Claudia felt that inexplicable identification with Candy's mental processes. "Candy's not afraid you were carrying on an affair with her mother," she explained lightly. "She was being a detective to find out if Elizabeth needed a doctor, and didn't tell her."

"That's it," Candy murmured. "I'm a fool when it comes to mother."

Dr. Barry smiled. "If all my patients were as healthy as Mrs. Van Doren," he said, "I'd be poorer than I am."

Candy surreptitiously reached for wood and knocked on it. "She's got a mother image as bad as mine was," thought Claudia, "and I thought I took the cake."

"As a matter of fact," Dr. Barry continued, "I saw quite a bit of her when Matthew was so sick last spring. She was over there a good part of the time."

Claudia recalled what a pillar of strength Elizabeth had been during those dark days. "Nothing," she resolved firmly, "that David and I can do for Candy can be too much, and I've got to stop being a jealous fool."

"Anything else besides your knees hurt you?" Dr. Barry queried, as Candy rolled up her stockings.

"No," said Candy. "Except a little pain around here." She pointed to an area in her chest. "But it only hurts when I breathe," she added hastily.

"As you'll have to do considerable breathing," Claudia advised, "you'd better let Dr. Barry see what it is."

"It isn't anything, just sore," Candy insisted. "No wonder, I fell flat on my stomach against those hard stones."

"Slip your blouse off," said Dr. Barry.

Candy slipped her blouse off. She looked heart-breakingly young and vulnerable. Unconsciously, Claudia's hand strayed to her own firm hips and waistline. "Ten years, and having children does make a difference," she thought. She knew with a sense of loss, that her body would never again be like Candy's. She wished, for David's sake, that it could be.

"Ouch!" Candy cried out suddenly. "That's where I feel it."

Claudia came out of her reverie. Candy's "ouch" was in earnest this time. She watched Dr. Barry's fingers move with expert precision along the slender torso. "Ouch," Candy cried again. A little white line etched itself around her lips. "That does hurt," she admitted.

"Humph," said Dr. Barry.

"Is it anything?" Claudia asked quickly.

"Yes. She's broken a couple of ribs."

"Broken?" Candy echoed, half in alarm, and half in pride. "Oh, no, it can't be! I'm on my way back to college, I'm catching the train in an hour!"

"You'll go home to bed," Dr. Barry ordered, "and have some X-rays taken in the morning."

Claudia was stunned. "Broken ribs are pretty serious, aren't they?"

"Not often. Troublesome, perhaps, and extremely painful, but usually no complications arise. I'll strap her so she'll be more comfortable, and give her something to make her sleep tonight." He turned to his cabinet, and squinted along a row of bottles.

Candy stared at Claudia, "Isn't it funny," she said in a muted voice, "no matter how old you are, you miss your mother when something happens to you."

"I know," said Claudia.

"It's the first time I've ever broken anything." She reached for Claudia's hand. "I'm awfully glad you came in with me," she said with a watery smile.

"I'm glad too," said Claudia. "It must have hurt awfully."

"It did," Candy confessed, "but I hated to make any trouble for you and David."

Dr. Barry bandaged her up, and gave her a white pellet to swallow. "There are two more in the envelope. Take then when you get home." They went out to the waiting room. David said, "You were a long time. What's wrong?"

"Just a couple of scratched knees," said Candy.

"Don't be so noble," Claudia broke in crisply. "Just a couple of broken ribs, David."

David regarded Candy with incredulous eyes. "Well, why the hell didn't you yell about it?"

"Claudia told you I was being noble."

"Let her sit in the front seat going home," Dr. Barry said, "and drive as smoothly as you can."

"It's a good thing," said David, "we decided not to bring the dog and the cat back with us this time."

The children didn't see anything good about it. They were doubly disappointed because Candy was going to ride in front. "Why can't she ride with us?" Matthew complained.

Bobby hid his disappointment. "I'd rather have Mother ride with us," he said quickly. A lump came into Claudia's throat. Bobby had so much of David's sentiency, so much of David's sweetness. It was a lot to live up to. She wondered if she could. "Is Candy hurt badly?" Bobby continued in a whisper.

"Yes," Claudia said, "and she's very brave about it too."

They drove off. In a little while, Candy's head dropped against David's shoulder. He glanced down at her, and Claudia saw him smile. "Candy's asleep," Matthew whispered.

Claudia was too choked up to trust herself to answer. All her high resolutions suddenly went for nothing. It was agony to see Candy's head on David's shoulder. It was agony not to be sitting next to him. She had not known that she was capable of such ugliness of spirit. It had crept upon her like a sickness—first envy, then fear, and now this utter frustration and despair. She remembered how Edith Dexter had wanted to jump out of the window, and understood, at last, the black insanity of jealousy. She wanted to make David suffer by doing something dreadful to herself.

She looked at the sweet autumn countryside flying past, and tried to clear her brain of madness. But it came back upon her. How long would Candy have to stay at home? Men—the best of them—were susceptible to frailty, especially when a woman was smart enough to be strong about it. Candy was unconsciously setting this pattern for herself. Or was it unconscious? Was she really asleep, or had she already learned how to woo David by playing on his sympathy? She wondered how David could drive with Candy's head against his shoulder—he would never let the children so much as touch him when he drove. Perhaps he liked her head against his shoulder. Perhaps he had liked the soft feeling of her as he had carried her to the house. Why did Candy have to do everything that she, Claudia, had done? Fall down, wear a pink dress, look like twins in an old tweed suit and brown felt hat. It was all like some ironic prank, with David the unsuspecting victim.

"Are you crying?" Bobby asked in a frightened voice.

"Of course not," Claudia said.

"Your eyes are wet, and your mouth looks funny."

"It's the wind. And maybe I was just born with a funny mouth."

David looked around, cheating his gaze from the road for a fraction of an instant. If he could look at her long enough would he still call her a nice girl?

"What's the matter?" he asked.

"Nothing," she said.

She tried to think of other things. She thought of Jim Varney, and the job he'd offered her. It beckoned now like an open door. It offered escape, a refuge to her pride. "I'm crazy," she thought. "I'm behaving as if David were really in love with Candy." Sanity returned. She said to Bobby, "Look how red the leaves are in the sunset."

"I am," said Bobby obediently.

Candy wakened when the car drew up in front of Beekman House. She refused to believe that she had slept all the way home. "I never sleep in the daytime," she protested. "Neither do you—do you?"

"No," said Claudia.

"I don't know what got into me."

"Codeine," said David.

"Oh," said Candy. "Well anyway, I feel simply fine again, no pain or anything. I could go back to college, and be X-rayed up there."

Claudia's heart leapt ignominiouly, but David told Candy not to be a ninny. "I'll take the car around to the garage," he said to Claudia, "and see that she goes right to bed."

"But I don't want to," Candy objected. "I want to stay up and enjoy my illness."

"At least she's honest," Claudia injected, hoping that she sounded pleasant about it.

"If you're a good girl," David held out, "I'll come and say good night to you when I say good night to the children."

"Then I'll be good," Candy promised.

Katie and Mary had gone to church. Claudia helped Candy to undress before she took off her own hat and coat. "I bet I'm more than you bargained for when you got me along with the apartment," said Candy ruefully.

"Much more," said Claudia.

"Do you mind awfully? My being such a nuisance, I mean?"

"I'm jealous of you. I've always wanted a broken rib."

"Two," Candy bragged.

"I refuse to believe it until you're X-rayed."

"It would be awful, wouldn't it, if Dr. Barry was mistaken and I wasn't even cracked?—Not the wool bed jacket, please, the yellow silk. It's pretty isn't it? It was Mother's. She said it was too gay for her—Ouch!"

"Hurt?"

"Just when I raise my arm."

"Then better not put on any bed jacket. It's time to go to sleep anyway."

"But David said he was coming in."

"He isn't back from the garage. There was a knock in the motor he wanted to attend to. I wouldn't wait up for him if I were you."

The children tiptoed to the door and said good night. Already Candy was a stranger to them, separated from their hardy world by the mystery of illness. They tiptoed out.

"And David hasn't come back yet?" Candy asked a little wistfully.

"Not yet," said Claudia. "You'll see him in the morning."

"These beastly pills will probably make me sleep until noon."

"Supposing? You saw him all day, didn't you?"

Candy laughed. "So I did, what am I making all the fuss about?" She lifted her lips. "Good night, and thanks for everything."

"Good night," said Claudia.

She started to put the light out. "Leave it up," said Candy. "I want to read until I doze off." A thought occurred to her. "Look, you won't write Mother about this, will you? Please don't. Being so far away, she'd think it was a lot worse than it is."

"We won't tell her until you're up and around, and back at college," Claudia agreed. "Which," she added, "I hope will be soon."

"I don't," Candy giggled.

"I'll bet you don't," thought Claudia grimly. She went out and closed the door. She tiptoed into the children's room. They were asleep, worn out with excitement and fresh air. When David came home, she said, "Don't go in, you'll only wake them up."

"Is Candy asleep too?"

Claudia wished she were a big enough person to say, "No, go on in, she's waiting for you." She tried to say it. She felt herself standing there, with her mouth open, stammering in conflict. Then she said, "Candy's settled for the night. She's taken her medicine. It's silly to disturb her."

"I guess it is," said David. "I couldn't find what that damn knock in the car came from," he mentioned in annoyance.

"And did you finally?"

"They're checking it."

He began to take his things out of his pocket—Hartley's big

black cigar that he hadn't smoked, keys, wallet, and a notebook and pen. He laid them on his chest of drawers, all ready to go into another suit in the morning. "Katie can send this one to be sponged and pressed," he said.

"All right," said Claudia. She walked to the window. A tugboat chugged past, emitting a mournful bellow. "I hate that sound," Claudia cried out passionately.

"I love it," said David. "I thought you did too."

"It's all right when you're happy."

He came up behind her. "What's wrong, dear, aren't you happy?"

She couldn't tell him. She was too deeply ashamed of the unloveliness within her. He put his arms around her. Then the bell rang. She was glad. She could get away from him, she wouldn't have to face the knowing in his eyes.

"Telegram, Mrs. Naughton."

"Thank you." The war was over. Telegrams no longer filled her with terror.

"Telegram," she said to David. "It's for you."

He took it casually. "I'm expecting word from Pittsburgh on some glass–" He glanced at it. "It's a cable," he said, and tore it open.

She saw his face turn white. Foreboding churned inside of her. "David, what is it?"

"It's from Jerry."

"Elizabeth?"

He couldn't speak. She took the cable from his hands. The words swam before her eyes. "Elizabeth died suddenly of heart attack. Letter follows."

A voice in Claudia other than her own, said, "I think Elizabeth knew."

"I think so too," said David.

After a long moment, he said, "Candy."

"Oh David, must she know tonight?"

He nodded. "She'd never forgive us if we kept it from her. Besides, the sedative will help to dull the blow. You'd better go to her, Claudia."

"No," said Claudia. "You go to her. It's you she'll want."

She watched him go. Minutes passed. There was no sound from behind the closed door of the room across the hall. She felt her soul writhe in labor, as it tried to emerge full-born.

Ten

Bobby marched into Claudia's room and said, "I want to be called Robert."

Claudia dropped the tape measure, with which she had been measuring herself, and eyed him coldly. "My life is sufficiently complicated at this point," she informed him, "without the additional strain of rechristening elderly children."

"But I don't like the name of Bobby."

"You should have thought of that some years back."

"You call Matthew 'Matthew'," he persisted doggedly.

"Well, I'll call you Matthew too, if you like."

He whimpered in frustration. "Why aren't there any tangerines in the house?" he came back at her.

"Sorry to disappoint you, but I bought some this morning," she said.

He returned in a few moments, with his hands full of peel.

"I suppose you couldn't do that in the kitchen?"

"I'm not spilling. Do you want a piece?"

"No thanks."

"Why not, they're good."

"I'm not eating between meals any more. In fact, I'm not going to eat at all if I get one speck fatter."

"I like you to be fat," he remarked in deep satisfaction.

"I know," she said, "it adds to your security, but it happens to add to my waistline."

He must have glimpsed a little of what she meant. "Is Aunt Elizabeth really dead?" he asked soberly.

"Yes, dear."

"Candy told me she wanted to die, too."

"That's very foolish of Candy. And a little naughty, too."

"Why?"

"Because we have to go on living and take grief as it comes."

"But Aunt Elizabeth was Candy's mother."

Claudia noted his tense expression out of the corner of her eye, and decided that this was an opportune moment to tackle the umbilical cord. "It's natural for people to lose their mothers," she pointed out. "It's like when a flower loses its petals."

"No, that's how babies are born," Bobby interrupted sagely.

"No, that's with the bee in it," said Claudia. "Anyway, don't worry, I won't die until you're an old man."

He wanted it down in black and white. "How do you know? Did the doctor say so?"

"I don't have to go to a doctor."

"What did Aunt Elizabeth die of? Was she sick?"

He had her there. Elizabeth hadn't been ill. As far as they had been able to learn from Jerry's letter, Elizabeth had never been better, until one morning she complained of a strange sense of discomfort, and by the time the doctor came she was gone. It sounded like the same sort of thing that had happened to Jane.

"Was Aunt Elizabeth sick?" Bobby repeated.

She hesitated. She didn't want him to get the idea that perfectly healthy people made a practice of popping off out of a clear sky. "I don't know what Aunt Elizabeth died of," she evaded. "We'll hear more about it when Uncle Jerry gets back."

"When is he coming?"

"Sometime soon. He's trying to get passage."

"On a ship?"

"No, an aeroplane."

"I wish I could go in an aeroplane. I wish we could go some place like China, or California like Uncle Roger—do we always have to live in New York?"

"We'll be going home to the farm in the spring."

"This apartment doesn't belong to us, does it?"

"It belonged to Aunt Elizabeth. Now it belongs to Candy."

"Candy told me she wanted us to stay here forever and ever."

"That's sweet of Candy. Where is she, by the way?"

"Bertha's washing Matthew's hair, so she's going to wash Candy's too, because Candy can't lift her arms on account of her ribs. How long will her ribs be broken?"

"She'll be all right in another week or two."

"And then is she going back to college?"

"I hope so."

He fell silent.

"What's the matter," said Claudia, "can't you think up any more questions to ask?"

"Uncle Jerry is Candy's step-father, isn't he?"

"Yes."

"I don't think she likes having a step-father."

"Did she say so?"

"No. But you can tell when people like people."

"I suppose you can," said Claudia.

"Candy likes Daddy a lot," Bobby commented.

Claudia could feel her heart pound. How easy it would be to say, "How do you know?"

"You'd better do your lessons," she told him shortly.

He met Matthew coming in. Matthew smelled the tangerine. "I want one," he said promptly, and departed kitchenwards.

Claudia closed the door after them. For a brief span, following the news of Elizabeth's death, she had achieved heights of understanding and generosity. She had prayed with all her being that Candy's tortured heart might find acceptance and peace with David's help. But it wasn't easy to live in the rarefied atmosphere of self-sacrifice. She could feel herself backsliding until now Bobby's innocent remark revived all the old doubts and jealousies.

She rolled up the tape measure. "If you're so afraid of losing your husband," she told herself contemptuously, "get busy and do something about it." With grim resolution she picked up the telephone and called Helen Drew to find out the name of her masseuse.

Helen said, "I knew you'd come to it sooner or later, darling. Her name is Mrs. Haussmann and it's simply fantastic, what she can do; the fat just drips off. And wait a minute, take this number, too, it's a woman who gives the most divine colonics."

"No thank you," said Claudia.

"My dear, you don't *know* how much you need them until you find out," Helen assured her. "And be sure you keep up your facials *religiously* while you're losing weight."

"I can't keep up what I've never begun," said Claudia.

"You mean you don't have facials?" Helen demanded incredulously.

"No," said Claudia.

"My God," said Helen. "It's a mystery to me how you manage to hold that attractive husband of yours, pet. But your luck won't last forever, you'd better get busy."

"I'd better," thought Claudia, although it occurred to her that in spite of Helen's diligent campaign against the ravages of age, she hadn't made such a good job of keeping her own husbands.

Nevertheless, she lost no time in getting in touch with Mrs. Haussmann. Fortunately Mrs. Haussmann was home, listening to the radio, which she finally had to turn off. "Now again, please. I could not hear you."

Claudia began from the beginning. Mrs. Haussmann was quite independent, considering the kind of voice she had. She said she was much too busy to take on new cases, but only because Mrs. Naughton was a friend of Miss Drew's, she would set aside from six-to-seven on Thursday.

"Six-to-seven isn't very convenient," Claudia said.

"It is the only time I can give you," said Mrs. Haussmann firmly. "And I wouldn't have that hour free, but it so happens I have a client who is going now to Florida for the winter. Later I cannot even give you six-to-seven."

What a lot of fat women with five dollars to spend there must be in the world, thought Claudia. She took the six-to-seven, and rang off. It was cutting things pretty close, though, for David was sure to come home while Mrs. Haussmann was still there, and he was equally sure not to approve of her. Willy-nilly, he was going to lump massage into a class with red toenails, and child-study and all the other things he didn't like.

A knock sounded at the door. It was Bertha. She was dressed to leave, in her black coat and hat which always looked black whether it was or not. "I go now," she said. "And tomorrow I don't see you, I take Fritz to the doctor."

"Yes, I know. How is Fritz these days?"

Bertha's round face, which in spite of no facials, had changed so little during the years, drooped with sorrow. "Fritz is getting old," she admitted. "I am afraid he will never be again like he was."

"Will any of us?" said Claudia.

"No," said Bertha. "Time goes on but it does not go back." She shook her head. "Miss Candy, poor child, is learning that now. So lost she is. What she would do without you and Mr. David, I do not know. She told me tonight when I was washing her hair that Mr. David is like an angel from Heaven to her."

Claudia felt her lips grow tight.

"He knows so well what it is like," Bertha continued, "on account of the way you were when your mother died."

"I kept my grief to myself, Bertha."

"Perhaps too much," said Berth wisely. "Later you paid for it."

Bertha was right. She had paid for it later, but those nightmare days of illness no longer seemed real. It was hard to remember that she had ever been on the brink of what the doctors had called a nervous breakdown. "But it wasn't just one thing that landed me in a mess," she protested. "It was losing the baby too, and the war, and everything else."

"That is true," Bertha acknowledged. "You have been through plenty, but everything a person goes through should make them only more strong. That is the difference between you and Miss Candy. She is a child and you are a woman."

Claudia turned her head away to hide the tears that welled up in her eyes. What a blessed relief it would have been to sob her fears and confusion against Bertha's broad shoulder. Bertha stood, hesitant, sensing her unhappiness. "Miss Claudia," she said softly, "you lie down and rest a little before Mr. David comes home. Come, I will take the spread off. You are tired. You look tired."

"I don't know from what," said Claudia. "I worked twelve hours a day on the farm without feeling it, and here I hardly lift a finger, and my legs feel like lead half the time."

"It is not work that makes the tiredness," said Bertha.

Claudia thought, "How much does Bertha guess?" She lay

against the pillows and closed her eyes. It would be nice never to open them again, never to have to face the uncertainty of one's self. "I will see that the children and Miss Candy do not disturb you," said Bertha, and tiptoed out.

In a little while, the door opened cautiously, and a slice of light cut into the room. David bent over her, full of apprehension to find her lying down. His concern offered a temptation she could scarcely resist. She had only to admit illness, and for the moment at least, she would own him completely, she would become the substance and Candy the shadow. During the black months of her neurosis, when she had needed escape from reality, she had claimed illness with her unconscious mind; now she would be doing it deliberately, in full awareness. No. Something in her, more vital and more honest than her subterranean self, answered for her. "I'm all right, Bertha felt tired, so she made me take a rest."

He looked relieved. "That sounds like Bertha. Where's Candy. Where're the children?"

She noticed that he put Candy first. "Bertha must have muzzled them. I'm surprised they didn't hear you come in." She added, carefully, "Candy's usually counting the minutes and watching the door for an hour before you get here."

"These days are tough for her," said David. "She'll pull out of it, though, she's not as much of a child as I thought she was."

Claudia gripped her hands beneath the light quilt that covered her. "I told you that quite some time ago," she said levelly.

"I know you did," said David. She could feel his thoughts go back to Eastbrook, where only a few months ago, Candy had romped across the lawn with Matthew, her overalls rolled up and her hair in pigtails. Yes, there was a great change in Candy, but it had begun to take place long before Elizabeth's death. She wondered if now would not be a good time to say,

"David, can't you see that Candy's fallen in love with you? Or do you see it, and have you fallen in love with her? I don't blame you if you have, she's everything I used to be and can never be again, because women don't get younger, they get older, and when they do try to hold youth, things get mixed up, like with Edith and Phil, and that isn't good either."

He continued to stand, looking down at her. "You have a funny look on your face," he said. "I bet you're feeling things in your bones again."

"I am."

He moved to the door and closed it carefully. Then he came back and sat on the bed beside her.

"Claudia," he said, "this is going to be a shock, but I can't put off talking to you about it. We've got a big decision ahead of us, and we'll have to face it."

Her heart hammered the breath out of her. This wasn't clowning, the way he had clowned about Helen Drew a few short weeks ago. He was serious now, all the way through him. She braced herself against the moment when he would make a reality of her fear by putting it into words.

"Do you remember," he continued, "when Nancy Riddle came over the Sunday we drove up to the farm, and you thought she was trying to get Edward away from us?"

Nancy Riddle! It was so different from what she expected that she could hear her voice climb in hysterical relief. "Don't tell me she's managed to succeed, I can't bear it!"

"Wait," said David, "until you hear the rest of it. She not only wants Edward, she wants the farm, too."

Claudia sat up with a bounce. "But what for? She has a wonderful place of her own three miles away, it doesn't make sense."

"It makes sense," said David. "Surprising sense for Nancy. She wants to go into Angus cattle, and she hasn't got the land to pasture black stock. Also, building is difficult now. So she wants our place as an auxiliary farm."

"What a nerve!—And how about the house, what's she want to use that for—chickens?"

"No," said David, "her superintendent will live in it. He has a wife and six children."

"I hope," said Claudia, cold with outrage, "that you told her a thing or two."

"I didn't speak to Nancy, it was her lawyer who called. I told him we'd talk it over and let him know."

Claudia stared at him, searching his eyes for the telltale twinkle that would assure her that he thought Nancy's offer was as preposterous as she did. But his face remained grave. "It's an idea we shouldn't dismiss too quickly," he said. "In the first place, it isn't easy to sell a place lock, stock and barrel, and in the second place, you know how hard it is to keep things up with one man."

"And you still don't think we could possibly afford to get someone to help Edward?"

"Even if we could," said David, "it's a responsibility to run a farm at long distance."

"Responsibilities are good," Claudia argued dully.

"Not when they saddle you," he said. "Then it's smart to know when to get out from under."

"I didn't know you felt that way."

"Don't get me wrong," he said. "The point is, that I'm not sure what will turn up for us. Architects, the kind of an architect I've always wanted to be, can be commissioned to go anywhere. The world's changing, it's getting smaller. Maybe we'll land in Bridgeport, maybe we'll land in China."

"Bobby wants to go to China."

"Maybe he'd compromise on Iceland. They want a big broadcasting station in Iceland."

"I'm sure he'd like Iceland quite as well," said Claudia, politely.

"Look here," said David, "I can see how you feel about it, and we'll tell Nancy to jump in the lake. Settled."

"No, it isn't settled. I'd only want to keep the farm if it means as much to you as it does to me. And apparently it doesn't."

"It does," he insisted. "It always has, and it always will. But things sometimes outgrow their purpose."

"Even wives," said Claudia.

"Yes," said David, "sometimes even wives, I suppose. But certainly houses, and places. There comes a time when people grow out of the need of being tied to physical things. Having possessed them, you can possess them always. Without having them."

"I can't handle all that philosophy at the moment," said Claudia, "give it to me slowly." Her world was crumbling. She hadn't realized how much she had been counting on getting back to the farm. It was a way of holding life to what it had been. It was a way, she suddenly realized, of holding David, for David always forgot everything else when he was looking at his cows, or counting his chickens or walking across his beloved meadows. Only now David didn't want to be tied down to the farm. He had said so in plain language. He was cutting a cord, as surely as she had tried to release Bobby less than an hour ago in this very room. She felt stunned, and bruised.

"How soon do we have to decide?"

"Immediately. That's the trouble. Nancy's new shipment of cattle comes in from Maryland this week. She'll take the Cootz farm if she doesn't get ours."

"The Cootz farm can't be mentioned in the same breath."

"Nancy knows that. That's why she is willing to pay the difference for ours. Incidentally, she's offered forty-two thousand, which nets us quite a handsome profit. I talked to Hartley about it, and he's all for it. He says we'll never get another chance like this."

"All right, David, if you want to, go ahead," she agreed a little wearily.

"But it isn't that I want to," he tried to explain. "It's simply that it seems a wise move at this time."

"Except where would we live? We have to have a place to live."

"I thought of that, and luckily we can stay here as long as we need to. Candy dreads being alone, and until she gets her bearings I'd like to stick around, anyway, even if we didn't sell the farm. Elizabeth would want us to."

"I see," said Claudia. He had started out talking about Nancy, and now he was back again to Candy. He was going around in a circle without knowing it.

The children burst in. "You're home!" Bobby cried accusingly.

Matthew said, "Is Mother sick?"

"No," said Claudia, "your mother was never better." She threw the quilt back, and got to her feet. "Boys, how would you like it if we sold the farm?"

Bobby blinked. "And never go back?"

"And never go back."

"Where would we live?" he demanded.

"Like mother, like son," said David. "We'd stay here for the time being."

"I like to stay here," said Matthew.

"So do I," said Bobby.

Children were strangely fickle in a loyal sort of way, Claudia reflected. Bobby had wept when he left Eastbrook, he would probably weep when he left New York. "I suppose they carry their homes with them," she thought. David had achieved that kind of liberation, too. She felt alone in her

dependence on the past. Already Matthew was racing into Candy's room to tell her the news. A moment later they appeared on the threshold, hand in hand.

"Matthew's making it up," Candy cried. "It isn't true, is it? –Hello David!"

"Hello! We haven't decided yet."

"Yes we have," said Claudia.

Candy's listless eyes took on a glow of interest. "I think it's wonderful!"

"Why?" asked David curiously. "I thought you loved the farm almost as much as we did."

"I do," said Candy. "I did. But what's the use of having two places in Eastbrook? You can come and live in ours."

Claudia forced a smile. "Thanks. It's nice to know we'll have somewhere to go in case we find ourselves on the street."

"We won't find ourselves on the street," said David. "There's a lot of living in store for all of us."

"I wish I could believe that," said Candy.

He ruffled the soft halo of her hair. "Has your Uncle David ever lied to you?"

Candy smiled faintly. "No, but my Uncle David isn't God. He can't work miracles."

It was hard not to read innuendoes into what they were saying. Claudia was glad when Mary announced dinner. She ate little, but David only noticed that Candy ate a lot. She wasn't picking at her food like a bird, for a change. "I guess I'm glad you're selling the farm," she confessed. "It sort of makes this your home, and that makes me feel a lot better, selfish pig that I am."

Claudia rose abruptly. David held out his hand. "Where are you going?"

She could scarcely talk for the pounding on her pulses.

"Candy's hair looks so lovely, I think I'll wash mine and go to bed," she managed lightly. She left them alone.

David came in while her head was plunged into the basin. "It'll be a long evening for the youngster if we both turn in," he said. "I'm going to teach her how to play chess."

"Do," said Claudia. "She's a lot smarter than I am."

It was close to midnight when he crept in beside her. She made believe she was asleep, but her brain was feverishly awake, planning a new life, self-sufficient and independent of the past.

Jim Varney minced no words when she walked into his office the next morning. "Baby," he said, "you look like hell."

"I've had the grippe," Claudia lied. "How's your play doing on the road?"

"It's a smash," said Jim. "We open here on the twenty-sixth —by the way, Maggie's play opened in Philadelphia last night. Rave notices." He waved a theatrical newspaper. "I was just reading them. The upholsterer's daughter has turned out to be a find, it seems. I have to hand it to Maggie, she knows how to spot them." He eyed her shrewdly. "Does it make you feel bad, baby, because you lost your big chance? Is that why you've got circles under your eyes?"

Claudia shook her head. "I haven't had time to think of a career. Elizabeth Van Doren died, you know."

"So I heard. Too bad. When's Jerry coming back?"

"We're expecting him any day."

"What'd he do, marry her for her money?"

"He did not!" Claudia denied with asperity.

"All right, don't bite my head off. Jerry wasn't the marrying kind, that's all I meant. What about the daughter? Where is she now?"

"With us," said Claudia.

"Oh," said Jim.

"Jim, I'd like to have that job you said you'd give me."

Jim picked up a pencil and drew a house with smoke coming out of it on a piece of scrap paper.

"Stop it!" said Claudia.

He put the pencil down obediently.

"I didn't mean to stop drawing. I meant to stop looking so smug. I remember perfectly well that I told you a few weeks ago that I didn't want a job, the theatre wasn't my world—"

Jim's eyebrows climbed his forehead in a way that reminded her of David. "I seem to remember something of the sort too," he said, "so you can't blame me for putting two and two together, can you? Look, honey, it happens to the best husbands—in fact, the better the husband, the harder the fall. And she's a right pretty kid—if you happen to like pretty kids, which I don't. Nothing cockeyed with my sex. I don't like 'em old, and I don't like 'em young. I like 'em—" He grinned at her engagingly. "Just your age."

Claudia could feel her face burn with mortification. Was she wearing her heart on her sleeve for everyone to see? "If you'd give me a chance to finish," she said, in the most nonchalant voice she could command, "I was going to explain that things had changed since I saw you at Julia's party."

Jim continued to grin. "So I gather."

"We had a wonderful offer for the farm," she went on calmly, "so we decided to sell it."

Jim's suspicions turned to envy. "You're damn lucky," he said gloomily. "I have a farm—costs me five thousand a year to run it, and I never get a chance to go near the place." He looked up at her hopefully. "How'd you like to buy it? A hundred acres, a tennis court, and a couple of St. Bernards thrown in for good measure."

"We already have a Great Dane, thank you," said Claudia. "We're holding our breaths to see how he's going to like the apartment, and how the apartment is going to like him." She told him about Shakespeare, too, hoping to take his mind off David and Candy, but he was like a bird dog, not to be diverted. "I still don't see," he said, "what selling the farm has to do with your wanting a job. It doesn't add up."

"Yes, it does," she maintained casually. "While we lived in Eastbrook, I didn't want to be in New York away from my huband and children, naturally. But now that we're going to live in New York—" she shrugged, "there's nothing to stop me."

"Except finding the job," Jim supplemented. "You think jobs are so easy to get?"

"No," said Claudia, "I don't. You said I should come to you, though, so I did." She picked up the sable scarf that Julia had given her, and started to her feet. "I'm sorry I bothered you, I know how busy you are."

Jim leaned across the desk and pushed her back. "Did I say I was busy, did I say I couldn't come through with a job for you?—What are you doing tonight?"

"David and I are going out for dinner," she said. It was another lie. She and David hadn't gone out together since Julia's party. They'd been home with Candy every night.

"Chuck it," said Jim. "Come to Baltimore with me. I'm leaving on the four o'clock train. There's a bit part in my show that I'm going to recast before we open in New York. The girl that's playing it isn't right for it. Watch a couple of performances with me, and if you want it, it's yours."

She was overwhelmed. "It sounds wonderful! Jim, do you mean it?"

"Sure I mean it. But don't fool yourself that it's any great shakes of a part because it isn't. It's no more than ten sides, and pays a hundred bucks a week."

"It sounds wonderful anyway," she said. More wonderful than he knew, because it would mean that she would have a life of her own, David could go his way, and she could go her's. It might be the saving of their marriage, because it would be the means of unloosing them from each other.

"So," Jim drawled, "I take it we leave for Baltimore at four."

"Not this afternoon, I can't."

"Let David go out for dinner with Candy."

"It's not that. Bertha's off, I have the children."

"Oh, God. Thursday. Maid's day out. Curse of the great middle-class."

Thursday. Mrs. Haussman. "I thought it was Wednesday today," she exclaimed. "I forgot all about it, I have an appointment from six-to-seven."

"Okay," said Jim wryly. "Run along, and next time don't take up a busy director's time—not that I thought you were in earnest."

"But I was, I am!" she insisted. "You mean you were just joking about the part?"

"I wasn't joking. You are." He got up and came over to her. "And if you're not—listen; it's eleven-thirty. I'll give you until two-thirty to get squared around. Call me back and let me know if you're coming with me." His hand rested for a moment on her shoulder. "And don't be a damn fool."

"Which way?"

He gave his one-sided, attractive grin. "That's up to you to decide." He bent and touched her lips with his.

It was a light kiss, but its lightness was heavy with meaning. Five years ago, when Phil had liked her, that kind of a kiss would have meant nothing to her. Now it filled her with disturbing sensations. She left him quickly, and stood on the sidewalk, confused and uncertain. There was no reason why she should read anything into Jim's offer, she argued with herself, no reason at all why she shouldn't accept the job, and let the future take care of itself. The immediate thing was to make the decision, and she was sure that David would not stand in her way. Hadn't he wanted her to go into Miss Brewster's play? And that was before Candy had grown out of pigtails, too. She smiled grimly. "There's one person," she thought, "who will welcome my going to Baltimore this afternoon."

She glanced at her watch. Jim had said he would give her until two-thirty. She had no time to waste in speculation. She took a cab to David's office. Perhaps they could have lunch together like old times.

John Payne was working over blueprints when she got there. He scrambled into his coat, blushing hotly, and pulled out a chair for her. "Don't," she said. "You make me feel like the Boss's wife."

"The Boss," said John, "has just left."

She was bitterly disappointed. "But won't he be back, it's not lunch time yet?"

"Lunch doesn't mean anything to him these days," said John. "He went over to the site, he'll be tied up with contractors all afternoon."

"Can I reach him by telephone?"

"I'm afraid not. But he usually calls the office."

"Well I only hope he does. Tell him to phone me right away, will you John? It's frightfully important." She rose. "I'll go straight home and wait for the call."

He took her to the elevator, eager to talk. "David's doing a superb job on this project," he said, full of hero-worship.

"I knew he would," said Claudia. She smiled at him. He was so like David had been ten years ago. (Funny how everyone kept reminding her of parts of David.) "I've been wanting to ask you for dinner," she said. "But everything's been so upset since Mrs. Van Doren's death."

"I know," said John. "I started to come over a couple of

times and didn't. I thought Candy would rather not have people barging in."

"You're not people," said Claudia. "Why don't you run up tonight with David? I mightn't be there," she added, "so it would be company for both of them."

"I'll be working late, could I come tomorrow instead?"

"Yes, of course."

"And please be there."

He was looking at her with open admiration—a sweet and boyish admiration, healing to her spirit. Two men, within an hour, had found her desirable. It could have been that the kiss that Jim had laid upon her lips had left its lingering spell, for she felt more alive, more filled with confidence than she had for weeks.

When she got home, she found Candy going over old snapshots of Elizabeth. Candy's face was pale and heavy with weeping. She turned her face away to hide her tear-stained eyes. Pity took the place of fear in Claudia's heart. "Look," she said, "don't mind me, just go on and cry. I know what it's like. For weeks after Mamma died, the least little thing—a pair of old shoes, her handwriting on a letter—would tear me to pieces."

Candy nodded mutely and then broke down completely. "The days are so long," she sobbed. "When I tell myself she's never coming back, I won't ever seen her again—I can't face it. And it keeps getting harder every day—"

"And then suddenly, one day," said Claudia, "it'll begin to get easier."

"Never!" Candy cried.

"Yes," said Claudia. "It will. It has to."

"Why?"

"Because it's meant to be that way, I suppose. That is, if you're even passably normal and healthy—which you are. Now cry it out, and we'll have a bite of lunch."

Candy mopped her eyes and gulped. "You're so wonderful to me."

"Oh yes, I'm a wonderful person," said Claudia, dryly.

At lunch, she told Candy about her visit to Jim Varney. In spite of her grief, Candy was properly impressed. "And he wants you to go this afternoon? Oh, how exciting! What does David say?"

Claudia glanced at her watch. "I haven't told him yet. And if he doesn't telephone soon, I'll be in a fix. I have to let Jim know at two-thirty so he can get someone else if I don't go."

"He won't stand in your way, I don't think. David, I mean. But he's not going to like your going," said Candy.

"What makes you say that? He wanted me to go in Miss Brewster's play."

"That was different."

"How was it different?"

"It was such a big chance for you. A star part, and all—and even so, you didn't take it."

"No," said Claudia slowly, "I didn't take it. I didn't want to."

"And now, when a little tiny part comes up, you're interested. I mean—it seems funny."

"Little things lead to big things."

"I suppose so," said Candy. "But I wish—I mean, I know how wonderful it'll be and everything, but—" she faltered. "It's none of my business," she finished in a burst, "but I wish you'd think about it twice before you do it."

"I expected you to be pleased about my leaving," said Claudia bluntly.

"Why?"

It was Claudia's turn to falter as she met Candy's unclouded gaze. "I just thought perhaps you'd enjoy having David—and the children—to yourself. I mean you seem to like looking after people."

"I do. And I'm mad about David and the children. But the way I feel now, I guess I want to be looked after myself," Candy admitted tremulously. "It's been so wonderful being all together, and I've gotten to depend on you so, I'm going to miss you frightfully."

Claudia knew that Candy wasn't pretending. Whatever attachment she had for David, there was nothing devious about it. "Candy, you're a sweet person," she said simply, "and I ought to be ashamed of myself."

"Why?" Candy asked again.

"Because," said Claudia.

"If I was really sweet, I'd want you to go," said Candy. "But life's so short not to be with the people you love. I've learned that much the last few weeks."

"You've learned a lot," said Claudia. "I learned it too. And I forgot." She looked at Candy, with new eyes. Yes, Candy was learning—one step up and one step back—like a gigantic obstacle race—but may be that was the way one had to learn in life. "I went up a few notches, but I slipped back and lost my way," thought Claudia. It was strange that it was Candy who had pointed out the path again.

The telephone bell rang. Candy dropped her fork. "I bet that's David!"

"I bet so too," said Claudia.

"What's up?" he said at once.

"Nothing," said Claudia.

"But I just phoned the office, and John said you wanted to talk to me about something very important."

"It's nothing that can't wait. I'll tell you tonight."

His voice sounded in a hurry, but curiosity got the better of him: "What's the matter, have you changed your mind about selling the farm?"

"Oh no. Have you?"

"Not unless you have. Come on, what did you want to tell

me, darling, don't be coy, I've got half a dozen contractors waiting."

"I'm not coy, it was nothing really. I wanted to have lunch with you, that's all."

"You're a brazen hussy, don't you know I'm married?"

"What's a little thing like marriage got to do with two people liking each other?" Her heart rejoiced. It was getting to be like one of their old telephone conversations. "I'd better ring off," she said, "before I really do go coy."

"I'd appreciate it," said David. "Oh, and by the way, I won't be home for dinner."

"That's good," said Claudia, thinking of Mrs. Haussmann. "Maybe you'll drop in and see me later in the evening."

"I'll try and spend the night with you," said David, "if I can get away from my wife."

Candy was waiting anxiously. "Did you tell him? Are you going? What did he say?"

"He didn't say anything," said Claudia. "Because I didn't tell him. I've decided not to go." She glanced at her watch. "It's a quarter to two, I'd better call Jim."

She called Jim. He said, "You're not as much of a damn fool as I thought you were."

It was the last thing she expected him to say. No wonder she liked him, he was just like David.

"I almost was," she admitted humbly.

"Was what?"

"A damn fool."

"It would have been rather nice," said Jim, "but you'd have deserved to have your tail kicked. Good-bye."

"Good-bye," said Claudia.

"That was awfully quick," Candy commented, a little disappointed. "Wasn't he angry?"

"No," said Claudia. "There are lots of women ready to take small parts. How about going to the zoo again this afternoon? I haven't been yet, and the children simply adore it."

"I simply adore it too," said Candy.

They had a lovely time. They spent an hour at the monkey house, and spoiled all their appetites with ice-cream sodas.

Mrs. Haussman was waiting when they got home. "Who is she?" Bobby whispered.

"Nobody," Claudia whispered back, which really didn't hold water, as Mrs. Haussman was quite mammoth and had already taken command of the premises as if she belonged there.

"Little boys out of the bedroom," she ordained.

"Run along," said Claudia. "Mrs. Haussman is just a friend."

"What kind of a friend?" Bobby pursued distrustfully, watching Mrs. Haussman strip the bed and remake it for her purposes.

"Just a friend," Claudia repeated. "Do your lessons. I'll see you later. And keep Matthew out."

Reluctantly, Bobby departed full of unsatisfied curiosity.

"So," said Mrs. Haussman, "he is gone." She tied a white band around her head in a businesslike way. "Off with the clothes, and lie down, please."

Claudia obeyed, feeling odd about it. Mrs. Haussman laid a firm hand upon her. "Relax, please."

"I can't, if you pinch me," Claudia cried indignantly.

"The upper arm is always sensitive in the beginning," Mrs. Haussman explained. "After the eighth or ninth massage, you will not feel what I am doing."

"I don't believe it," said Claudia. She groaned. "You must have nails in your fingers."

Mrs. Haussman paused to extend her hands. "You see how soft my fingers are? What nice cushions they have? Because it hurts, shows only that you need these massages very badly. You see this?" Between her thumb and first finger, Mrs. Haussman picked up some of Claudia's flesh and regarded it as she would regard an inferior remnant of dress goods. "That is all no good," she affirmed.

"Sorry, but it's the best I've got," said Claudia.

"You will come to love these massages," Mrs. Haussman prophesied, kneading busily. "Miss Drew goes to sleep when I am massaging her."

"Miss Drew is crazy," said Claudia, but her respect of Helen went up. She gritted her teeth. What Helen could stand, she could stand. But would it do any good? Mrs. Haussman was working like a dog, and her arms were huge just the same. Maybe the only thing was to go on one of those dreadful diets of nothing worth while eating. "Ouch," she whimpered.

"If you do not relax, I can not accomplish," Mrs. Haussman reminded her sternly. She paused to wipe the sweat from her brow with her plump elbow, and Claudia suddenly realized why she wore the white band above her eyes. "I am going light," she said. "Until you are used to it, I am going very light."

"I'm glad you told me," Claudia murmured.

"You will have a nice body," Mrs. Haussman assured her kindly, "when you have had maybe a dozen massages. It is only that you are a little too much around the waistline."

"That's what I told you," Claudia moaned. "It's my worst place, so why don't you just skip to there and leave my legs alone?"

In answer, Mrs. Haussman took Claudia's foot and whirled it up and down and around and about. "This is for the circulation. Relax please. And twice a week you should have some steam baths. It is very important while I am breaking up the fat tissue, to see that it is all properly carried away, so if you will also please have—"

"Yes, I know," Claudia interrupted. "Colonics. But I won't."

"And no sweets," Mrs. Haussman went on firmly. "That is the most important thing of all, no starches and no sweets."

"Is an ice-cream soda sweets?" Claudia queried innocently.

Mrs. Haussman looked horrified. "An ice-cream soda is pure poison," she declared. "Hundreds of calories. Surely you are joking, you don't take ice-cream sodas!"

"Yes I was joking," Claudia shamelessly agreed.

"The best thing when you are hungry is a cup of tea without sugar or milk. A little lemon if you want it."

"What fun," said Claudia.

"And now the stomach," Mrs. Haussman finally said, with an air of leaving the best for the last.

"Hey!" said Claudia, writhing.

To her surprise, Mrs. Haussman's hands dropped obediently to her side. It was like having a toothache suddenly stop. She closed her eyes with the sheer pleasure of it. After a moment she opened them again, and found Mrs. Haussman looking down at her accusingly. For a moment, Claudia thought she had discovered the ice-cream soda. "What's the matter?" she asked sheepishly.

"You should have told me you are having a baby, Mrs. Naughton."

"I'm not."

"You are sure you are not?"

"Of course I'm sure I'm not. What gave you that idea?"

"It is more than an idea," Mrs. Haussman stated in a sepulchral voice. "It is my business to know what I feel. If you say you are not pregnant, then I would surely advise you to see your doctor."

"For what? If I was I would, but since I'm not, why should I?"

"It is not up to me to say why should you," said Mrs. Haussman portentously. "Your waistline does not get big from nothing, and I will only tell you that it is better you should see what it is before you have more massages—oh, I am sure it is not anything very serious," she hastened to add. "It does not always mean an operation."

"Oh," said Claudia. She knew a swift relief that she was not getting fat from age, but every silver lining had its cloud, and this particular cloud seemed to be a tumor, if she could read Mrs. Haussman's insinuation correctly. She knew all about tumors, because Julia had had one some years ago and had almost died. As it was, she had ended up by losing most of her best organs, and hadn't been the same since. But such things only happened to other people and not to herself. Besides, she had promised Bobby that she'd live until he was an old man. "I'm too healthy to go to a doctor," she had told him only yesterday.

"Don't be silly," she said to Mrs. Haussman.

Mrs. Haussman was not used to being called silly. "Come," she said with dignity, "I will do your neck."

"My neck's all right," Claudia grumbled. She could see no reason to waste money on a perfectly good neck. "You could do a little more on my hips," she suggested.

"I am keeping away from your middle," Mrs. Haussman stated with finality, "until you see your doctor."

"I'll go tomorrow," said Claudia, "but I know it's foolish."

David came home a little after ten. "Well," he greeted her, "Nancy's lawyer called today. He's mailing a down payment on the farm."

"That's fine," said Claudia. She had no intention of upsetting him with Mrs. Haussman's nonsense, but at the same time, she couldn't put it out of her mind. She thought,

"Maybe that down payment will come in handy to pay my hospital bill."

"What are you thinking of?" David asked. "You look worried."

"I'm not, it's just that life's a little complicated at the moment."

"It looks quite simple from where I'm standing," said David blandly.

"That's because I don't tell you everything."

"What don't you tell me?"

"For one thing, Bobby would like to be called Robert from here on out."

"I'll Robert him," said David.

She went to see Dr. Rowland the next day. He was as busy as ever, and looked just the same as always, except that he was getting a little old around the chin, and a little thick around the waist. "So men get that way too," Claudia discovered with satisfaction.

"It's quite some time since you've paid me a visit," he said. "How have you been? Sit down and tell me about yourself."

She told him about Mrs. Haussman. Dr. Rowland pooh-poohed Mrs. Haussman. "But as long as you're here," he said, "We might as well look you over."

He looked her over. There was no pooh-poohing about him now. "Discontinue all massage immediately," he said.

Claudia's heart beat in her ears. "An operation?"

"No," said Dr. Rowland. "A baby. Roughly speaking, I should say you're well in your third month."

"Well in my third month," Claudia echoed incredulously. "Do you mean to say I'm pregnant, I'm going to have a baby?"

"It's a usual combination of events," Dr. Rowland remarked, being quite humorous about it.

She couldn't believe it. "How could it be that I'm so far along without knowing it? It doesn't seem possible!"

"Nature plays strange tricks sometimes," said Dr. Rowland. "Especially after a miscarriage. Take it easy, we don't want any trouble like last time, and drop in again in a couple of weeks."

She left the office in a daze, unable to make head or tail of the situation. She stood on the corner of Madison Avenue, counting backwards, out loud. The night they'd gone to the movies—that wasn't three and a half months ago, though, and during the summer, David had been in no mood to add to his responsibilities.

"Keep back, lady, do you want to get run over?"

"No, officer, I certainly don't. Could you tell me where the nearest drugstore is around here?"

"One block down," he said. "And watch your traffic lights, lady."

"I will," she promised.

For a wonder, the booth was empty, and David's number wasn't busy. She caught him in, too, but he said he was just leaving. She was enormously vexed. It was no fun telling a man who was on his way somewhere else that she had been having a baby behind his back for over three months. She swallowed her pride. "I could meet you for lunch?" she suggested. "The lunch we didn't have yesterday."

"Sorry, darling, I can't. I'm late for a meeting as it is. Anyway, you'd better get home as fast as you can."

Fear chilled her blood. "Is anything wrong with the children?"

"They're all right. It's Jerry. He just got back. It seems when he phoned the house, Candy was out, and Katie asked him for dinner tonight. I think the youngster's pretty upset at the prospect."

"I think the youngster's being pretty dramatic about it if you ask me," Claudia commented impatiently.

"It's hard for her," he maintained. "A little like a delayed funeral."

"I suppose it is," she granted. "John was coming for dinner, perhaps you better tell him not to."

"No," said David, "let him come. It might be a good idea if he took Candy out after dinner."

It occurred to her, as she rang off, that David was a lot more interested in Candy than in his own child. Jealousy flared anew. Jealousy was like a nasty fire that you thought had died down. No sooner did you put it out in one place than it started up in another.

Candy met her at the door, tense and white-faced. "Jerry's come back."

"Yes," said Claudia shortly, "I know." She walked to the bedroom and hung away her hat and coat. Candy followed her. "I don't want to see him," she said.

"You must," said Claudia. "You can't run away from anything. I've tried to run away from things too, but something decent in me wouldn't let me."

"But I don't believe he loved my mother!" Candy rebelled passionately. "He wasn't good enough to love her!"

"I wasn't good enough to love David either when I first married him," said Claudia. "I was young, and silly and ignorant. But I've tried every day that I've lived with him to make myself into a better person. It's hard going. But I've tried. I'm still trying. I'm trying this minute. And you'll have to try. Because at this minute you're not worthy of Elizabeth, any more than I'm worthy of David."

Candy turned away, too engrossed in her own problem to analyze Claudia's allusion to herself. "I'll try," she said. "But I wish it was over. He's going to bring back so many memories."

"Memories can't hurt you," said Claudia. "Not when they're lovely memories like yours."

Toward evening Jerry came. David was right. It was a hard home-coming. There had been a quality of unreality about Elizabeth's death, but now Jerry brought the truth of it in his haggard face. Claudia was shocked at the change in him, she had not realized the vastness of his sorrow. Even Candy, looking at him, felt compassion. She gave him her hand, and he bent and kissed her. "Don't dislike me," he said. "Elizabeth wanted us to be friends. I think she felt that if you could share her with me, your grief would be shared too. Only she didn't want us to grieve. I'm sure of that."

"Do you think she knew?" Candy asked in a muffled voice.

"Yes," said Jerry, "looking back on everything, I do."

"But she was never ill!" cried Candy. "When did she begin to complain?"

"She didn't," said Jerry. "We'd had a lovely day. We'd just come back from a walk around the embankment. She was laughing when suddenly she reached for a chair—" He stopped, unable to go on.

"I know," said Candy softly. "It happened that way with Jane."

He looked at her gratefully. "I was afraid you'd think it was my fault," he said, quite simply. "I was afraid, too, for a time. But I don't think that happiness could kill anyone."

"I don't either," said Candy.

At the table, they talked of other things, like people coming home from the cemetery; as if the worst were over, and the bugaboo of death had been laid away in all its sombre accoutrements.

"What happened to Maggie Brewster's play?" Jerry asked.

"It opened out of town," said Claudia. "Jim Varney told me it was a great success."

"I don't see how Claudia can be so calm about it," said Candy. "I should think she'd be heartbroken."

"No," said Claudia. "This way, I can always feel I might have done it better than the girl who's playing it."

"I can't be that philosophical," said Candy.

"That's because you're young," said David.

Claudia thought, "I wish I could be young again. For David's sake." She knew she couldn't be. Life had taught her acceptance, and acceptance was maturity.

It was late when Jerry left. Candy hadn't come home yet. David paced the bedroom, restlessly. "I wonder where John took her. It's high time they were back."

Claudia wanted desperately to tell him about the baby. It was the first chance that she had had to be alone with him, but his preoccupation with Candy sealed her lips. She could not bring him back to her that way.

The key sounded in the latch as they were getting undressed. David stood at the door. "Is that you, Candy?" he called.

"Yes! May I come in?"

Claudia flung a robe across her shoulders as Candy hurried in. Candy's hair was blown and her cheeks were flushed. "I'm terribly sorry to keep you both up, I wanted to phone, but John thought maybe you'd be asleep."

"Where did you go?" Claudia asked. "We were worried about you."

"Only for a ride in John's car," said Candy. "But when we found ourselves on the parkway, John said we might as well go on to Greenwich and see his mother and father. So we did. They're so nice. John was born when his mother was forty-two, so she's almost like his grandmother. We had homemade cookies and hot chocolate. Poor thing, what she must have gone through. I didn't realize John had been a parachute jumper in the war. He went in behind the German lines and got a medal. He never told me; I worship that sort of modesty." Candy paused for breath. "What time did Jerry leave?"

"Just a little while ago," said Claudia.

"He's changed," said Candy. "I can begin to see why Mother loved him."

"That's good," said David.

"John liked him, too. He thinks I ought to have lunch with him tomorrow."

"Lunch with John?" Claudia queried.

"No, lunch with Jerry."

"It would be a nice idea," said David. "Your mother would like it."

"I think so too." On the threshold, Candy turned. "And I think Mother would like me to go back to college."

"I'm sure of it," said David.

"John said he'll drive me up on Sunday." She smiled suddenly. "I bet you two will be mighty glad to get rid of me." She blew them a kiss. "Good night." She vanished for an instant, only to return.

"Is it wrong for me to be happy like this?" she asked, a little wistfully.

"It's wrong for you not to be," said David.

"That's what John told me," said Candy.

For a long moment after her door closed, neither David nor Claudia spoke. Then David heaved a sigh. "Now I know how it feels to have a daughter," he said.

"Is that the way you feel toward Candy?" Claudia asked.

"How else?" he answered.

It was all the answer she wanted. She kicked off her mules, and tossed her robe away. He caught hold of her arm and turned her to him. "What in the name of Heaven are those black and blue spots?"

"Nothing," she said hastily.

"You fell down," he accused her. "You're as bad as Candy."

"I did not fall down. I got those black and blue marks from Mrs. Haussman."

"Who," David demanded, "is Mrs. Haussman?"

"She massages."

"You?"

"Yes."

He scowled savagely. "What for!"

"Because my waistline was twenty-eight."

"I like it twenty-eight!" he shouted. "I don't want you looking like a bluefish any longer, it's time you grew up and got yourself a shape!"

She knew then that she could tell him. He didn't want her to be young, like Candy, he wasn't in love with the girl that he had married, he loved the woman into which their marriage was molding her. It was the last, lingering shred of youngness that had made her judge him otherwise.

She waited until he had put the light out. "David—" she said softly.

"What, dear?"

"That daughter you were talking about has been on her way for quite a while."

He switched the light on, and leaned on his elbow to stare down at her. "How do you know?"

"Mrs. Haussman told me."

"Oh so Mrs. Haussman told you." His disgust was rich.

"I went to Dr. Rowland today. He told me too."

He put the light out again. They lay for a long while in each other's arms. Then David said, "I'm sorry we sold the farm, darling. I wouldn't have done it if I had known. Now we have no place of our own."